TARZAN, LORD OF THE JUNGLE

Edgar Rice Burroughs

BALLANTINE BOOKS • NEW YORK
An Intext Publisher

Edgar Rice Burroughs, Inc. Authorized Edition published
by Ballantine Books, Inc.

SBN 345-03009-5-095

First Printing: September, 1963
Second Printing: December, 1963
Third Printing: October, 1969
Fourth Printing: December, 1972

First Canadian Printing: January, 1964

Printed in the United States of America

Cover Painting: Robert Abbett

BALLANTINE BOOKS, INC.
101 Fifth Avenue, New York, New York 10003

CONTENTS

1

Tantor the Elephant

IS great bulk swaying to and fro as he threw his weight first upon one side and then upon the other. Tantor the elephant lolled in the shade of the father of forests. Almost omnipotent, he, in the realm of his people. Dango, Sheeta, even Numa the mighty were as naught to the pachyderm. For a hundred years he had come and gone up and down the land that had trembled to the comings and the goings of his forebears for countless ages.

In peace he had lived with Dango the hyena, Sheeta the leopard and Numa the lion. Man alone had made war upon him. Man, who holds the unique distinction among created things of making war on all living creatures, even to his own kind. Man, the ruthless; man, the pitiless; man, the most hated living organism that Nature has evolved.

Always during the long hundred years of his life, Tantor had known man. There had been black men, always. Big black warriors with spears and arrows, little black warriors, swart Arabs with crude muskets and white men with powerful express rifles and elephant guns. The white men had been the last to come and were the worst. Yet Tantor did not hate men—not even white men. Hate, vengeance, envy, avarice, lust are a few of the delightful emotions reserved exclusively for Nature's noblest work—the *lower* animals do not know them. Neither do they know fear as man knows it, but rather a certain bold caution that sends the antelope and the zebra, watchful and wary, to the water hole with the lion.

Tantor shared this caution with his fellows and avoided men —especially white men; and so had there been other eyes there that day to see, their possessor might almost have questioned their veracity, or attributed their error to the halflight of the forest as they scanned the figure sprawling prone upon the rough back of the elephant, half dozing in the heat to the swaying of the great body; for, despite the sunbronzed hide, the figure was quite evidently that of a white man. But there were no other eyes to see and Tantor drowsed in the heat of midday and Tarzan, Lord of the Jungle, dozed upon the back of his mighty friend. A sultry air current moved sluggishly from the north, bringing to the keen nostrils of the ape-man no disquieting perception. Peace lay upon the jungle and the two beasts were content.

In the forest Fahd and Motlog, of the tribe el-Harb, hunted north from the menzil of Shiek Ibn Jad of the Beny Salem fendy el-Guad. With them were black slaves. They advanced warily and in silence upon the fresh spoor of el-fil the elephant, the thoughts of the swart 'Aarab dwelling upon ivory, those of the black slaves upon fresh meat. The 'abd Fejjuan, black Galla slave, sleek, ebon warrior, eater of raw meat, famed hunter, led the others.

Fejjuan, as his comrades, thought of fresh meat, but also he thought of el-Habash, the land from which he had been stolen as a boy. He thought of coming again to the lonely Galla hut of his parents. Perhaps el-Habash was not far off now. For months Ibn Jad had been traveling south and now he had come east for a long distance. El-Habash must be near. When he was sure of that his days of slavery would be over and Ibn Jad would have lost his best Galla slave.

Two marches to the north, in the southern extremity of Abyssinia, stood the round dwelling of the father of Fejjuan, almost on the roughly mapped route that Ibn Jad had planned nearly a year since when he had undertaken this mad adventure upon the advice of a learned Sahar, a magician of repute. But of either the exact location of his father's house or the exact plans of Ibn Jad, Fejjuan was equally ignorant. He but dreamed, and his dreams were flavored with raw meat.

The leaves of the forest drowsed in the heat above the heads of the hunters. Beneath the drowsing leaves of other trees a stone's throw ahead of them Tarzan and Tantor slept, their perceptive faculties momentarily dulled by the soothing influence of fancied security and the somnolence that is a corollary of equatorial midday.

Fejjuan, the Galla slave, halted in his tracks, stopping those behind him by the silent mandate of an upraised hand. Directly before him, seen dimly between the boles and through the foliage, swayed the giant bulk of el-fil. Fejjuan motioned to Fahd, who moved stealthily to the side of the black. The Galla slave pointed through the foliage toward a patch of gray hide. Fahd raised el-Lazzary, his ancient matchlock, to his shoulder. There was a flash of flame, a burst of smoke, a roar and el-fil, unhit, was bolting through the forest.

As Tantor surged forward at the sound of the report Tarzan started to spring to an upright position, and at the same instant the pachyderm passed beneath a low hanging limb which struck the ape-man's head, sweeping him to the ground, where he lay stunned and unconscious.

Terrified, Tantor thought only of escape as he ran north through the forest, leaving in his wake felled trees, trampled or uptorn bushes. Perhaps he did not know that his friend lay helpless and injured, at the mercy of the common enemy, man. Tantor never thought of Tarzan as one of the Tarmangani, for the white man was synonymous with discomfort, pain, annoyance, whereas Tarzan of the Apes meant to him restful companionship, peace, happiness. Of all the jungle beasts, except his own kind, he fraternized with Tarzan only.

"Billah! Thou missed," exclaimed Fejjuan.

"Gluck!" ejaculated Fahd. "Sheytan guided the bullet. But let us see—perhaps el-fil is hit."

"Nay, thou missed."

The two men pushed forward, followed by their fellows, looking for the hoped-for carmine spoor. Fahd suddenly stopped.

"Wellah! What have we here?" he cried. "I fired at el-fil and killed a Nasrany."

The others crowded about. "It is indeed a Christian dog, and naked, too," said Motlog.

"Or some wild man of the forest," suggested another. "Where didst thy bullet strike him, Fahd?"

They stooped and rolled Tarzan over. "There is no mark of bullet upon him."

"Is he dead? Perhaps he, too, hunted el-fil and was slain by the great beast."

"He is not dead," announced Fejjuan, who had kneeled and placed an ear above the ape-man's heart. "He lives and from the mark upon his head I think but temporarily out of his wits from a blow. See, he lies in the path that el-fil made when he ran away—he was struck down in the brute's flight."

"I will finish him," said Fahd, drawing his khusa.

"By Ullah, no! Put back thy knife, Fahd," said Motlog. "Let the sheykh say if he shall be killed. Thou art always too eager for blood."

"It is but a Nasrany," insisted Fahd. "Think thou to carry him back to the menzil?"

"He moves," said Fejjuan. 'Presently he will be able to walk there without help. But perhaps he will not come with us, and look, he hath the size and muscles of a gaint. Wellah! What a man!"

'Bind him," commanded Fahd. So with thongs of camel hide they made the ape-man's two wrists secure together across his belly, nor was the work completed any too soon. They had scarce done when Tarzan opened his eyes and looked them slowly over. He shook his head, like some great lion, and presently his senses cleared. He recognized the 'Aarab instantly for what they were.

"Why are my wrists bound?" he asked them in their own tongue. "Remove the thongs!"

Fahd laughed. "Thinkest thou, Nasrany, that thou art some great sheykh that thou canst order about the Beduw as they were dogs?"

"I am Tarzan," replied the ape-man, as one might say, "I am the sheykh of sheykhs."

"Tarzan!" exclaimed Motlog. He drew Fahd aside. "Of all men," he said, lowering his voice, "that it should be our ill fortune to offend this one! In every village that we have entered in the past two weeks we have heard his name. 'Wait,' they have said, 'until Tarzan, Lord of the Jungle, returns. He will slay you when he learns that you have taken slaves in his country'."

"When I drew my khusa thou shouldst not have stopped my hand, Motlog," complained Fahd; "but it is not too late yet." He placed his hand upon the hilt of his knife.

"Billah, nay!" cried Motlog. "We have taken slaves in this country. They are with us now and some of them will escape. Suppose they carry word to the fendy of this great sheykh that we have slain him? Not one of us will live to return to Beled el-Guad."

"Let us then take him before Ibn Jad that the responsibility may be his," said Fahd.

"Wellah, you speak wisely," replied Motlog. "What the sheykh doeth with this man in the sheykh's business. Come!"

As they returned to where Tarzan stood he eyed them questioningly.

"What have you decided to do with me?" he demanded. "If you are wise you will cut these bonds and lead me to your sheykh. I wish a word with him."

"We are only poor men," said Motlog. "It is not for us to say what shall be done, and so we shall take you to our sheykh who will decide."

The Shiek Ibn Jad of the fendy el-Guad squatted in the open men's compartment of his beyt es-sh'ar, and beside him in the mukaad of his house of hair sat Tollog, his brother, and a young Beduin, Zeyd, who, doubtless, found less attraction

in the company of the shiek than in the proximity of the
sheik's hareem whose quarters were separated from the mukaad only by a breast high curtain suspended between the
waist poles of the beyt, affording thus an occasional glimpse
of Ateja, the daughter of Ibn Jad. That it also afforded an
occasional glimpse of Hirfa, his wife, raised not the tempera-
ture of Zeyd an iota.

As the men talked the two women were busy within their
apartment at their housewifely duties. In a great brazen jidda
Hirfa was placing mutton to be boiled for the next meal while
Ateja fashioned sandals from an old bag of camel leather
impregnated with the juice of the dates that it had borne
upon many a rahla, and meanwhile they missed naught of the
conversation that passed in the mukaad.

"We have come a long way without mishap from our own
beled," Ibn Jad was remarking, "and the way has been longer
because I wished not to pass through el-Habash lest we be
set upon or followed by the people of that country. Now may
we turn north again and enter el-Habash close to the spot
where the magician foretold we should find the treasure city of
Nimmr."

"And thinkest thou to find this fabled city easily, once we
are within the boundaries of el-Habash?" asked Tollog, his
brother.

"Wellah, yes. It is known to the people of this far south
Habash. Fejjuan, himself an Habashy, though he has never
been there, heard of it as a boy. We shall take prisoners
among them and, by the grace of Ullah, we shall find the
means to loose their tongues and have the truth from them."

"By Ullah, I hope it does not prove like the treasure that
lies upon the great rock el-Howwara in the plain of Medain
Salih," said Zeyd. "An afrit guards it where it lay sealed in a
stone tower and they say that should it be removed disaster
would befall mankind; for men would turn upon their friends,
and even upon their brothers, the sons of their fathers and
mothers, and the kings of the world would give battle, one
against another."

"Yea," testified Tollog, "I had it from one of the fendy
Hazim that a wise Moghreby came by there in his travels
and consulting the cabalistic signs in his book of magic discovered that indeed the treasure lay there."

"But none dared take it up," said Zeyd.

"Billah!" exclaimed Ibn Jad. "There be no afrit guarding
the treasures of Nimmr. Naught but flesh and blood Habush

that may be laid low with ball and powder. The treasure is ours for the taking."

"Ullah grant that it may be as easily found as the treasure of Geryeh," said Zeyd, "which lays a journey north of Tebuk in the ancient ruins of a walled city. There, each Friday, the pieces of money roll out of the ground and run about over the desert until sunset."

"'Once we are come to Nimmr there will be no difficulty finding the treasure," Ibn Jad assured them. "The difficulty will lie in getting out of el-Habash with the treasure and the woman; and if she is as beautiful as the sahar said, the men of Nimmr may protect her even more savagely than they would the treasure."

"Often do magicians lie," said Tollog.

"Who comes?" exclaimed Ibn Jad, looking toward the jungle that hemmed the menzil upon all sides.

"Billah! it is Fahd and Motlog returning from the hunt," said Tollog. "Ullah grant that they bring ivory and meat."

"They return too soon," said Zeyd.

"But they do not come empty handed," and Ibn Jad pointed toward the naked giant that accompanied the returning hunters.

The group surrounding Tarzan approached the sheik's beyt and halted.

Wrapped in his soiled calico thob, his head kerchief drawn across the lower part of his face, Ibn Jad exposed but two villainous eyes to the intent scrutiny of the ape-man which simultaneously included the pock-marked, shifty-eyed visage of Tollog, the shiek's brother, and the not ill-favored countenance of the youthful Zeyd.

"Who is sheykh here?" demanded Tarzan in tones of authority that belied the camel leather thongs about his wrists.

Ibn Jad permitted his thorrib to fall from before his face. "Wellah, I am sheykh," he said, "and by what name art thou known, Nasrany?"

"They call me Tarzan of the Apes, Moslem."

"Tarzan of the Apes," mused Ibn Jad. "I have heard the name."

"Doubtless. It is not unknown to 'Aarab slave raiders. Why, then, came you to my country, knowing I do not permit my people to be taken into slavery?"

"We do not come for slaves," Ibn Jad assured him. "We do but trade in peace for ivory."

"Thou liest in thy beard, Moslem," returned Tarzan, quietly. "I recognize both Manyuema and Galla slaves in thy menzil, and I know that they are not here of their own choosing. Then, too, was I not present when your henchmen fired a shot at el-fil? Is that peaceful trading for ivory? No! it is poaching, and that Tarzan of the Apes does not permit in his country. You are raiders and poachers."

"By Ullah! we are honest men," cried Ibn Jad. "Fahd and Motlog did but hunt for meat. If they shot el-fil it must be that they mistook him for another beast."

"Enough!" cried Tarzan. "Remove the thongs that bind me and prepare to return north from whence thou came. Thou shalt have an escort and bearers to the Soudan. There will I arrange for."

"We have come a long way and wish only to trade in peace," insisted Ibn Jad. "We shall pay our bearers for their labor and take no slaves, nor shall we again fire upon el-fil. Let us go our way and when we return we will pay you well for permission to pass through your country."

Tarzan shook his head. "No! you shall go at once. Come, cut these bonds!"

Ibn Jad's eyes narrowed. "We have offered thee peace and profits, Nasrany," he said, "but if thou wouldst have war let it be war. Thou art in our power and remember that dead enemies are harmless. Think it over." And to Fahd: "Take him away and bind his feet."

"Be careful, Moslem," warned Tarzan, "the arms of the ape-man are long—they may reach out even in death and their fingers encircle your throat."

"Thou shalt have until dark to decide, Nasrany, and thou mayest know that Ibn Jad will not turn back until he hath that for which he came."

They took Tarzan then and at a distance from the beyt of Ibn Jad they pushed him into a small hejra; but once within this tent it required three men to throw him to the ground and bind his ankles, even though his wrists were already bound.

In the beyt of the sheik the Beduins sipped their coffee, sickish with clove, cinnamon and other spice, the while they discussed the ill fortune that had befallen them; for, regardless of his bravado, Ibn Jad knew full well that only speed and most propitious circumstances could now place the seal of success upon his venture.

"But for Motlog," said Fahd, "we would now have no cause for worry concerning the Nasrany, for I had my knife ready to slit the dog's throat when Motlog interfered."

"And had word of his slaying spread broadcast over his

country before another sunset and all his people at our heels," countered Motlog.

"Wellah," said Tollog, the sheik's brother. "I wish Fahd had done the thing he wished. After all how much better off are we if we permit the Nasrany to live? Should we free him we know that he will gather his people and drive us from the country. If we keep him prisoner and an escaped slave carries word of it to his people will they not be upon us even more surely than as though we had slain him?"

"Tollog, thou speakest words of wisdom," said Ibn Jad, nodding appreciatively.

"But wait," said Tollog, "I have within me, unspoken, words of even greater worth." He leaned forward motioning the others closer and lowered his voice. "Should this one whom they call Tarzan escape during the night, or should we set him free, there would be no bad word for an escaped slave to bear to his people."

"Billah!" exclaimed Fahd disgustedly. "There would be no need for an escaped slave to bring word to his people—the Nasrany himself would do that and lead them upon us in person. Bah! the brains of Tollog are as camel's dung."

"Thou hast not heard all that I would say, brother," continued Tollog, ignoring Fahd. "It would only *seem* to the slaves that this man had escaped, for in the morning he would be gone and we would make great lamentation over the matter, or we would say: 'Wellah, it is true that Ibn Jad made peace with the stranger, who departed into the jungle, blessing him'."

"I do not follow thee, brother," said Ibn Jad.

"The Nasrany lies bound in yonder hejra. The night will be dark. A slim knife between his ribs were enough. There be faithful Habush among us who will do our bidding, nor speak of the matter after. They can prepare a trench from the bottom of which a dead Tarzan may not reach out to harm us."

"By Ullah, it is plain that thou art of sheykhly blood, Tollog," exclaimed Ibn Jad. "The wisdom of thy words proclaims it. Thou shalt attend to the whole matter. Then will it be done secretly and well. The blessings of Ullah be upon thee!" and Ibn Jad arose and entered the quarters of his hareem.

2

Comrades of the Wild

DARKNESS fell upon the menzil of Ibn Jad the sheik. Beneath the small flitting tent where his captors had left him, Tarzan still struggled with the bonds that secured his wrists, but the tough camel leather withstood even the might of his giant thews. At times he lay listening to the night noises of the jungle, many of them noises that no other human ear could have heard, and always he interpreted each correctly. He knew when Numa passed and Sheeta the leopard; and then from afar and so faintly that it was but the shadow of a whisper, there came down the wind the trumpeting of a bull elephant.

Without the beyt of Ibn Jad Ateja, the sheik's daughter, loitered, and with her was Zeyd. They stood very close to one another and the man held the maiden's hands in his.

"Tell me, Ateja," he said, "that you love no other than Zeyd."

"How many times must I tell you that?" whispered the girl.

"And you do not love Fahd?" insisted the man.

"Billah, no!" she ejaculated.

"Yet your father gives the impression that one day you will be Fahd's."

"My father wishes me to be of the hareem of Fahd, but I mistrust the man, and I could not belong to one whom I neither loved nor trusted."

"I, too, mistrust Fahd," said Zeyd. "Listen Ateja! I doubt his loyalty to thy father, and not his alone, but another whose name I durst not even whisper. Upon occasions I have seen them muttering together when they thought that there were no others about."

The girl nodded her head. "I know. It is not necessary even to whisper the name to me—and I hate him even as I hate Fahd."

"But he is of thine own kin," the youth reminded her.

"What of that? Is he not also my father's brother? If that bond does not hold him loyal to Ibn Jad, who hath treated

15

him well, why should I pretend loyalty for him? Nay, I think him a traitor to my father, but Ibn Jad seems blind to the fact. We are a long way from our own country and if aught should befall the sheykh, Tollog, being next of blood, would assume the skeykhly duties and honors. I think he hath won Fahd's support by a promise to further his suit for me with Ibn Jad, for I have noticed that Tollog exerts himself to praise Fahd in the hearing of my father."

"And perhaps a division of the spoils of the ghrazzu upon the treasure city," suggested Zeyd.

"It is not unlikely," replied the girl, "and—Ullah! what was that?"

The Beduins seated about the coffee fire leaped to their feet. The black slaves, startled, peered out into the darkness from their rude shelters. Muskets were seized. Silence fell again upon the tense, listening menzil. The weird, uncanny cry that had unnerved them was not repeated.

"Billah!" ejaculated Ibn Jad. "It came from the midst of the menzil, and it was the voice of a beast, where there are only men and a few domestic animals."

Could it have been———?" The speaker stopped as though fearful that the thing he would suggest might indeed be true.

"But he is a man and that was the voice of a beast," insisted Ibn Jad. "It could not have been he."

"But he is a Nasrany," reminded Fahd. "Perhaps he has league with Sheytan."

"And the sound came from the direction where he lies bound in a hejra," observed another.

"Come!" said Ibn Jad. "Let us investigate."

With muskets ready the 'Aarab, lighting the way with paper lanterns, approached the hejra where Tarzan lay. Fearfully the foremost looked within.

"He is here," he reported.

Tarzan, who was sitting in the center of the tent, surveyed the 'Aarab somewhat contemptuously. Ibn Jad pressed forward.

"You heard a cry?" he demanded of the ape-man.

"Yes, I heard it. Camest thou, Sheykh Ibn Jad, to disturb my rest upon so trivial an errand, or camest thou to release me?"

"What manner of cry was it? What did it signify?" asked Ibn Jad.

Tarzan of the Apes smiled grimly. "It was but the call of a beast to one of his kind," he replied. "Does the noble Beduwy tremble thus always when he hears the voices of the jungle people?"

"Gluck!" growled Ibn Jad, "the Beduw fear naught. We thought the sound came from this hejra and we hastened hither believing some jungle beast had crept within the menzil and attacked thee. Tomorrow it is the thought of Ibn Jad to release thee."

"Why not tonight?"

"My people fear thee. They would that when you are released you depart hence immediately."

"I shall. I have no desire to remain in thy lice infested menzil."

"We could not send thee alone into the jungle at night where el-adrea is abroad hunting," protested the sheik.

Tarzan of the Apes smiled again, one of his rare smiles. "Tarzan is more secure in his teeming jungle than are the Beduwy in their desert," he replied. "The jungle night has no terrors for Tarzan."

"Tomorrow," snapped the shiek and then, motioning to his followers, he departed.

Tarzan watched their paper lanterns bobbing across the camp to the sheik's beyt and then he stretched himself at full length and pressed an ear to the ground.

When the inhabitants of the 'Aarab menzil heard the cry of the beast shatter the quiet of the new night it aroused within their breasts a certain vague unrest, but otherwise it was meaningless to them. Yet there was one far off in the jungle who caught the call faintly and understood—a huge beast, the great, gray dreadnaught of the jungle, Tantor the elephant. Again he raised his trunk aloft and trumpeted loudly. His little eyes gleamed redly wicked as, a moment later, he swung off through the forest at a rapid trot.

Slowly silence fell upon the menzil of Sheik Ibn Jad as the 'Aarab and their slaves sought their sleeping mats. Only the sheik and his brother sat smoking in the sheik's beyt—smoking and whispering in low tones.

"Do not let the slaves see you slay the Nasrany, Tollog," cautioned Ibn Jad. "Attend to that yourself first in secrecy and in silence, then quietly arouse two of the slaves. Fejjuan would be as good as another, as he has been among us since childhood and is loyal. He will do well for one."

"Abbas is loyal, too, and strong," suggested Tollog.

"Yea, let him be the second," agreed Ibn Jad. "But it is well that they do not know how the Nasrany came to die. Tell them that you heard a noise in the direction of his hejra and that when you had come to learn the nature of it you found him thus dead."

"You may trust to my discretion, brother," Tollog assured.

"And warn them to secrecy," continued the sheik. "No man but we four must ever know of the death of the Nasrany, nor of his place of burial. In the morning we shall tell the others that he escaped during the night. Leave his cut bonds within the hejra as proof. You understand?"

"By Ullah, fully."

"Good! Now go. The people sleep." The sheik rose and Tollog, also. The former entered the apartment of his hareem and the latter moved silently through the darkness of the night in the direction of the hejra where his victim lay.

Through the jungle came Tantor the elephant and from his path fled gentle beasts and fierce. Even Numa the lion slunk growling to one side as the mighty pachyderm passed.

Into the darkness of the hejra crept Tollog, the sheik's brother; but Tarzan, lying with an ear to the ground, had heard him approaching from the moment that he had left the beyt of Ibn Jad. Tarzan heard other sounds as well and, as he interpreted these others, he interpreted the stealthy approach of Tollog and was convinced when the footsteps turned into the tent where he lay—convinced of the purpose of his visitor. For what purpose but the taking of his life would a Beduin visit Tarzan at this hour of the night?

As Tollog, groping in the dark, entered the tent Tarzan sat erect and again there smote upon the ears of the Beduin the horrid cry that had disturbed the menzil earlier in the evening, but this time it arose in the very hejra in which Tollog stood.

The Beduin halted, aghast. "Ullah!" he cried, stepping back. "What beast is there? Nasrany! Art thou being attacked?"

Others in the camp were awakened, but none ventured forth to investigate. Tarzan smiled and remained silent.

"Nasrany!" repeated Tollog, but there was no reply.

Cautiously, his knife ready in his hand, the Beduin backed from the hejra. He listened but heard no sound from within. Running quickly to his own beyt he made a light in a paper lantern and hastened back to the hejra, and this time he carried his musket and it was at full cock. Peering within, the lantern held above his head, Tollog saw the ape-man sitting upon the ground looking at him. There was no wild beast! Then the Beduin understood.

"Billah! It wast thou, Nasrany, who made the fearful cries."

"Beduwy, thou comest to kill the Nasrany, eh?" demanded Tarzan.

From the jungle came the roar of a lion and the trumpeting of a bull elephant, but the boma was high and sharp with thorns and there were guards and beast fire, so Tollog gave no thought to these familiar noises of the night. He did not answer Tarzan's question but laid aside his musket and drew his khusa, which after all was answer enough.

In the dim light of the paper lantern Tarzan watched these preparations. He saw the cruel expression upon the malevolent face. He saw the man approaching slowly, the knife ready in his hand.

The man was almost upon him now, his eyes glittering in the faint light. To the ears of the ape-man came the sound of a commotion at the far edge of the menzil, followed by an Arab oath. Then Tollog launched a blow at Tarzan's breast. The prisoner swung his bound wrists upward and struck the Beduin's knife arm away, and simultaneously he struggled to his knees.

With an oath, Tollog struck again, and again Tarzan fended the blow, and this time he followed swiftly with a mighty sweep of his arms that struck the Beduin upon the side of the head and sent him sprawling across the hejra; but Tollog was instantly up and at him again, this time with the ferocity of a maddened bull, yet at the same time with far greater cunning, for instead of attempting a direct frontal attack Tollog leaped quickly around Tarzan to strike him from behind.

In his effort to turn upon his knees that he might face his antagonist the ape-man lost his balance, his feet being bound together, and fell prone at Tollog's mercy. A vicious smile bared the yellow teeth of the Beduin.

"Die, Nasrany!" he cried, and then: "Billah! What was that?" as, of a sudden, the entire tent was snatched from above his head and hurled off into the night. He turned quickly and a shriek of terror burst from his lips as he saw, red-eyed and angry, the giant form of el-fil towering above him; and in that very instant a supple trunk encircled his body and Tollog, the sheik's brother, was raised high aloft and hurled off into the darkness as the tent had been.

For an instant Tantor stood looking about, angrily, defiantly, then he reached down and lifted Tarzan from the ground, raised him high above his head, wheeled about and trotted rapidly across the menzil toward the jungle. A frightened sentry fired once and fled. The other sentry lay crushed and dead where Tantor had hurled him when he entered the camp. An instant later Tarzan and Tantor were swallowed by the jungle and the darkness.

The menzil of Sheik Ibn Jad was in an uproar. Armed men hastened hither and thither seeking the cause of the disturbance, looking for an attacking enemy. Some came to the spot where had stood the hejra where the Nasrany had been confined, but Hejra and Nasrany both had disappeared. Nearby, the beyt of one of Ibn Jad's cronies lay flattened. Beneath it were screaming women and a cursing man. On top of it was Tollog, the sheik's brother, his mouth filled with vile Beduin invective, whereas it should have contained only praises of Allah and thanksgiving, for Tollog was indeed a most fortunate man. Had he alighted elsewhere than upon the top of a sturdily pegged beyt he had doubtless been killed or badly injured when Tantor hurled him thus rudely aside.

Ibn Jad, searching for information, arrived just as Tollog was extricating himself from the folds of the tent.

"Billah!" cried the sheik. "What has come to pass? What, O brother, art thou doing upon the beyt of Abd el-Aziz?"

A slave came running to the sheik. "The Nasrany is gone and he hath taken the hejra with him," he cried.

Ibn Jad turned to Tollog. "Canst thou not explain, brother?" he demanded. "Is the Nasrany truly departed?"

"The Nasrany is indeed gone," replied Tollog. "He is in league with Sheytan, who came in the guise of el-fil and carried the Nasrany into the jungle, after throwing me upon the top of the beyt of Abd el-Aziz whom I still hear squealing and cursing beneath as though it had been he who was attacked rather than I."

Ibn Jad shook his head. Of course he knew that Tollog was a liar—that he always had known—yet he could not understand how his brother had come to be upon the top of the beyt of Abed el-Aziz.

"What did the sentries see?" demanded the sheik. "Where were they?"

"They were at their post," spoke up Motlog. "I was just there. One of them is dead, the other fired upon the intruder as it escaped."

"And what said he of it?" demanded Ibn Jad.

"Wellah, he said that el-fil came and entered the menzil, killing Yemeny and rushing to the hejra where the Nasrany lay bound, ripping it aside, throwing Tollog high into the air. Then he seized the prisoner and bore him off into the jungle, and as he passed him Hasan fired."

"And missed," guessed Ibn Jad.

For several moments the sheik stood in thought, then he turned slowly toward his own beyt. "Tomorrow, early, is the rahla," he said; and the word spread quickly that early upon the morrow they would break camp.

Far into the forest Tantor bore Tarzan until they had come to a small clearing well carpeted with grass, and here the elephant deposited his burden gently upon the ground and stood guard above.

"In the morning," said Tarzan, "when Kudu the Sun hunts again through the heavens and there is light by which to see, we shall discover what may be done about removing these bonds, Tantor; but for now let us sleep."

Numa the lion, Dango the hyena, Sheeta the leopard passed near that night, and the scent of the helpless man-thing was strong in their nostrils, but when they saw who stood guard above Tarzan and heard the mutterings of the big bull, they passed on about their business while Tarzan of the Apes slept.

With the coming of dawn all was quickly astir in the menzil of Ibn Jad. Scarce was the meagre breakfast eaten ere the beyt of the sheik was taken down by his women, and at this signal the other houses of hair came tumbling to the ground, and within the hour the 'Aarab were winding northward toward el-Habash.

The Beduins and their women were mounted upon the desert ponies that had survived the long journey from the north, while the slaves that they had brought with them from their own country marched afoot at the front and rear of the column in the capacity of askari, and these were armed with muskets. Their bearers were the natives that they had impressed into their service along the way. These carried the impedimenta of the camp and herded the goats and sheep along the trail.

Zeyd rode beside Ateja, the daughter of the sheik, and more often were his eyes upon her profile than upon the trail ahead. Fahd, who rode near Ibn Jad, cast an occasional angry glance in the direction of the two. Tollog, the sheik's brother, saw and grinned.

"Zeyd is a bolder suitor than thou, Fahd," he whispered to the young man.

"He has whispered lies into her ears and she will have none of me," complained Fahd.

"If the sheykh favored thy suit though," suggested Tollog.

"But he does not," snapped Fahd. "A word from you might aid. You promised it."

"Wellah, yes, but my brother is an over-indulgent sire," explained Tollog. "He doth not mislike you, Fahd, but rather he would have his bint happy, and so leaves the selection of her mate to her."

"What is there to do, then?" demanded Fahd.

"If I were sheykh, now," suggested Tollog, "but alas I am not."

"If you were sheykh, what then?"

"My niece would go to the man of my own choosing."

"But you are not sheykh," Fahd reminded him.

Tollog leaned close and whispered in Fahd's ear. "A suitor as bold as Zeyd would find the way to make me sheykh."

Fahd made no reply but only rode on in silence, his head bowed and his brows contracted in thought.

3

The Apes of Toyat

THREE days crawled slowly out of the east and followed one another across the steaming jungle and over the edge of the world beyond. For three days the 'Aarab moved slowly northward toward el-Habash. For three days Tarzan of the Apes lay in the little clearing, bound and helpless, while Tantor the elephant stood guard above him. Once each day the great bull brought the ape-man food and water.

The camel leather thongs held securely and no outside aid appeared to release Tarzan from the ever increasing discomfort and danger of his predicament. He had called to Manu the monkey to come and gnaw the strands apart, but Manu, ever irresponsible, had only promised and forgotten. And so the ape-man lay uncomplaining, as is the way of beasts patiently waiting for release, knowing that it might come in the habiliment of death.

Upon the morning of the fourth day Tantor gave evidences of restlessness. His brief foragings had exhausted the nearby supply of food for himself and his charge. He wanted to move on and take Tarzan with him; but the ape-man was now convinced that to be carried farther into the elephant country would lessen his chances for succor, for he felt that the only one of the jungle people who could release him was Mangani the great ape. Tarzan knew that already he was practically at the outer limits of the Mangani country, yet there was a remote chance that a band of the great anthropoids might pass this way and discover him, while, should Tantor carry him farther north even this meager likelihood of release would be lost forever.

Tantor wanted to be gone. He nudged Tarzan with his trunk and rolled him over. He raised him from the ground.

"Put me down, Tantor," said the ape-man, and the pachyderm obeyed, but he turned and walked away. Tarzan watched him cross the clearing to the trees upon the far side. There Tantor hesitated, stopped, turned. He looked back at Tarzan and trumpeted. He dug up the earth with a great tusk and appeared angry.

"Go and feed," said Tarzan, "and then return. Tomorrow the Mangani may come."

Tantor trumpeted again and, wheeling about, disappeared in the jungle. For a long time the ape-man lay listening to the retreating footfalls of his old friend.

"He is gone," he mused. "I cannot blame him. Perhaps it is as well. What matter whether it be today, tomorrow, or the day after?"

The morning passed. The noonday silence lay upon the jungle. Only the insects were abroad. They annoyed Tarzan as they did the other jungle beasts, but to the poison of their stings he was immune through a lifetime of inoculation.

Suddenly there came a great scampering through the trees. Little Manu and his brothers, his sisters and his cousins came trooping madly through the middle terrace, squealing, chattering and scolding.

"Manu!" called Tarzan. "What comes?"

"The Mangani! The Mangani!" shrieked the monkeys.

"Go and fetch them, Manu!" commanded the ape-man.

"We are afraid."

"Go and call to them from the upper terraces," urged Tarzan. "They cannot reach you there. Tell them that one of their people lies helpless here. Tell them to come and release me."

"We are afraid."

"They cannot reach you in the upper terraces. Go! They will be your friends then."

"They cannot climb to the upper terraces," said an old monkey. "I will go."

The others, halted in their flight, turned and watched the gray-beard as he scampered quickly off amongst the loftiest branches of the great trees, and Tarzan waited.

Presently he heard the deep gutturals of his own people, the great apes, the Mangani. Perhaps there would be those among them who knew him. Perhaps, again, the band may have come from afar and have no knowledge of him, though that he doubted. In them, however, was his only hope. He lay there, listening, waiting. He heard Manu screaming and chattering as he scampered about high above the Mangani, then, of a sudden, silence fell upon the jungle. There was only the sound of insects, buzzing, humming.

The ape-man lay looking in the direction from which had come the sounds of the approaching anthropoids. He knew what was transpiring behind that dense wall of foliage. He knew that presently a pair of fierce eyes would be examining him, surveying the clearing, searching for an enemy, warily probing for a trick or a trap. He knew that the first sight of him might arouse distrust, fear, rage; for what reason had they to love or trust the cruel and merciless Tarmangani?

There lay great danger in the possibility that, seeing him, they might quietly withdraw without showing themselves. That, then, would be the end, for there were no others than the Mangani to whom he might look for rescue. With this in mind he spoke.

"I am a friend," he called to them. "The Tarmangani caught me and bound my wrists and ankles. I cannot move. I cannot defend myself. I cannot get food nor water. Come and remove my bonds."

From just behind the screen of foliage a voice replied, "You are a Tarmangani."

"I am Tarzan of the Apes," replied the ape-man.

"Yes," screamed Manu, "he is Tarzan of the Apes. The Tarmangani and the Gomangani bound him and Tantor brought him here. Four times has Kudu hunted across the sky while Tarzan of the Apes lay bound."

"I know Tarzan," said another voice from behind the foliage and presently the leaves parted and a huge, shaggy ape lumbered into the clearing. Swinging along with knuckles to the ground the brute came close to Tarzan.

"M'walat!" exclaimed the ape-man.

"It is Tarzan of the Apes," said the great ape, but the others did not understand.

"What?" they demanded.

"Whose band is this?" asked Tarzan.

"Toyat is king," replied M'walat.

"Then do not tell them it is really I," whispered Tarzan, "until you have cut these bonds. Toyat hates me. He will kill me if I am defenseless."

"Yes," agreed M'walat.

"Here," said Tarzan, raising his bound wrists. "Bite these bonds in two."

"You are Tarzan of the Apes, the friend of M'walat. M'walat will do as you ask," replied the ape.

Of course, in the meager language of the apes, their conversation did not sound at all like a conversation between men, but was rather a mixture of growls and grunts and gestures which, however, served every purpose that could have been served by the most formal and correct of civilized speech since it carried its messages clearly to the minds of both the Mangani and the Tarmangani, the Great Ape and the Great White Ape.

As the other members of the band pressed forward into the clearing, seeing that M'walat was not harmed, the latter stooped and with powerful teeth severed the camel leather thongs that secured the wrists of the ape-man, and similarly he freed his ankles.

As Tarzan came to his feet the balance of the fierce and shaggy band swung into the clearing. In the lead was Toyat, king ape, and at his heels eight more full grown males with perhaps six or seven females and a number of young. The young and the shes hung back, but the bulls pressed forward to where Tarzan stood with M'walat at his side.

The king ape growled menacingly. "Tarmangani!" he cried. Wheeling in a circle he leaped into the air and came down on all fours; he struck the ground savagely with his clenched fists; he growled and foamed, and leaped again and again. Toyat was working himself to a pitch of rage that would nerve him to attack the Tarmangani, and by these maneuvers he hoped also to arouse the savage fighting spirit of his fellows.

"It is Tarzan of the Apes, friend of the Mangani," said M'walat.

"It is a Tarmangani, enemy of the Mangani," cried Toyat. "They come with great thunder sticks and kill us. They make our shes and our balus dead with a loud noise. Kill the Tarmangani."

"It is Tarzan of the Apes," growled Gayat. "When I was a little balu he saved me from Numa. Tarzan of the Apes is the friend of the Mangani."

"Kill the Tarmangani!" shrieked Toyat, leaping high into the air.

Several of the other bulls were now circling and leaping into the air as Gayat placed himself at Tarzan's side. The ape-man knew them well. He knew that sooner or later one of them would have excited himself to such a pitch of maniacal frenzy that he would leap suddenly upon him. M'walat and Gayat would attack in his defense; several more bulls would launch themselves into the battle and there would ensue a free for all fight from which not all of them would emerge alive, and none without more or less serious injuries; but Tarzan of the Apes did not wish to battle with his friends.

"Stop!" he commanded raising his opened palm to attract attention. "I am Tarzan of the Apes, mighty hunter, mighty fighter; long did I range with the tribe of Kerchak; when Kerchak died I became king ape; many of you know me; all know that I am first a Mangani; that I am friend to all Mangani. Toyat would have you kill me because Toyat hates

Tarzan of the Apes. He hates him not because he is a Tarmangani but because Tarzan once kept Toyat from becoming king. That was many rains ago when some of you were still balus. If Toyat has been a good king Tarzan is glad, but now he is not acting like a good king for he is trying to turn you against your best friend.

"You, Zutho!" he exclaimed, suddenly pointing a finger at a huge bull. "You leap and growl and foam at the mouth. You would sink your fangs into the flesh of Tarzan. Have you forgotten, Zutho, the time that you were sick and the other members of the tribe left you to die? Have you forgotten who brought you food and water? Have you forgotten who it was that kept Sabor the lioness and Sheeta the panther and Dango the hyena from you during those long nights?"

As Tarzan spoke, his tone one of quiet authority, the apes gradually paused to listen to his words. It was a long speech for the jungle folk. The great apes nor the little monkeys long concentrated upon one idea. Already, before he had finished, one of the bulls was overturning a rotted log in search of succulent insects. Zutho was wrinkling his brows in unaccustomed recollection. Presently he spoke.

"Zutho remembers," he said. "He is the friend of Tarzan," and ranged himself beside M'walat. With this the other bulls, except Toyat, appeared to lose interest in the proceedings and either wandered off in search of food or squatted down in the grass.

Toyat still fumed, but as he saw his cause deserted he prosecuted his war dance at a safer distance from Tarzan and his defenders, and it was not long before he, too, was attracted by the more profitable business of bug hunting.

And so Tarzan ranged again with the great apes. And as he loafed lazily through the forest with the shaggy brutes he thought of his foster mother, Kala, the great she-ape, the only mother he had ever known; he recalled with a thrill of pride her savage defense of him against all their natural enemies of the jungle and against the hate and jealousy of old Tublat, her mate, and against the enmity of Kerchak, the terrible old king ape.

As it had been but yesterday since he had seen him, Tarzan's memory projected again upon the screen of recollection the huge bulk and the ferocious features of old Kerchak. What a magnificent beast he had been! To the childish mind of the ape-boy Kerchak had been the personification of savage ferocity and authority, and even today he recalled him with almost a sensation of awe. That he had overthrown and slain this gigantic ruler still seemed to Tarzan almost incredible.

He fought again his battles with Terkoz and with Bolgani the gorilla. He thought of Teeka, whom he had loved, and of Thaka and Tana, and of the little black boy, Tibo, whom he had endeavored to adopt; and so he dreamed through lazy daylight hours while Ibn Jad crept slowly northward toward the leopard city of Nimmr and in another part of the jungle events were transpiring that were to entangle Tarzan in the meshes of a great adventure.

A BLACK porter caught his foot in an entangling creeper and stumbled, throwing his load to the ground. Of such trivialities are crises born. This one altered the entire life of James Hunter Blake, young, rich, American, hunting big game for the first time in Africa with his friend Wilbur Stimbol who, having spent three weeks in the jungle two years before, was naturally the leader of the expedition and an infallible authority on all matters pertaining to big game, African jungle, safari, food, weather and Negroes. The further fact that Stimbol was twenty-five years Blade's senior naturally but augmented his claims to omniscience.

These factors did not in themselves constitute the basis for the growing differences between the two men, for Blake was a phlegmatically inclined young man of twenty-five who was rather amused at Stimbol's egotism than otherwise. The first rift had occurred at railhead when, through Stimbol's domineering manner and ill temper, the entire purpose of the expedition had been abandoned by necessity, and what was to have been a quasi scientific motion picture camera study of wild African life had resolved itself into an ordinary big game hunt.

At railhead, while preparations were going on to secure equipment and a safari, Stimbol had so offended and insulted the cameraman that he had left them flat and returned to the coast. Blake was disappointed, but he made up his mind to go on through and get what pictures he could with a still camera. He was not a man who enjoyed killing for the mere sport of taking life, and as originally planned there was to have been no shooting of game except for food and half a dozen trophies that Stimbol particularly wished to add to his collection.

There had since been one or two altercations relative to Stimbol's treatment of the black porters, but these matters, Blake was hopeful, had been ironed out and Stimbol had promised to leave the handling of the safari to Blake and refrain from any further abuse of the men.

They had come into the interior even farther than they had planned, had had the poorest of luck in the matter of game and were about to turn back toward railhead. It seemed now to Blake that after all they were going to pull through without further difficulty and that he and Stimbol would return to America together, to all intent and purpose still friends; but just then a black porter caught his foot in an entangling creeper and stumbled, throwing his load to the ground.

Directly in front of the porter Stimbol and Blake were walking side by side and, as though guided by a malevolent power, the load crashed into Stimbol, hurling him to the ground. Stimbol and the porter scrambled to their feet amidst the laughter of the Negroes who had witnessed the accident. The porter was grinning. Stimbol was flushed with anger.

"You damned clumsy swine!" he cried, and before Blake could interfere or the porter protect himself the angry white man stepped quickly over the fallen load and struck the black a terrific blow in the face that felled him; and as he lay there, Stimbol kicked him in the side. But only once! Before he could repeat the outrage Blake seized him by the shoulder, wheeled him about and struck him precisely as he had struck the black.

Stimbol fell, rolled over on his side and reached for the automatic that hung at his hip, but quick as he was Blake was quicker. "Cut that!" said Blake, crisply, covering Stimbol with a .45. Stimbol's hand dropped from the grip of his gun. "Get up!" ordered Blake, and when the other had risen: "Now listen to me, Stimbol—this is the end. You and I are through. Tomorrow morning we split the safari and equipment, and whichever way you go with your half I'll go in the opposite direction."

Blake had returned his gun to its holster as he spoke, the black had risen and was nursing a bloody nose, the other blacks were looking sullenly. Blake motioned to the porter to pick up his load and presently the safari was again on the move—a sullen safari without laughter or song.

Blake made camp at the first available ground shortly before noon in order that the division of equipment, food and men could be made during the afternoon and the two safaris thus be enabled to make an early start the following morning.

Stimbol, sullen, would give no assistance, but, taking a couple of the askari, the armed natives who act as soldiers for the safari, started out from camp to hunt. He had proceeded scarcely a mile along a mould padded game trail which gave forth no sound in answer to their falling footsteps, when one of the natives in the lead held up his hand in warning as he halted in his tracks.

Stimbol advanced cautiously and the black pointed toward the left, through the foliage. Dimly, Stimbol saw a black mass moving slowly away from them.

"What is it?" he whispered.

"Gorilla," replied the black.

Stimbol raised his rifle and fired at the retreating figure. The black was not surprised that he missed.

"Hell!" ejaculated the white. "Come on, get after him! I've got to have him. Gad! what a trophy he'll make."

The jungle was rather more open than usual and again and again they came within sight of the retreating gorilla. Each time Stimbol fired and each time he missed. Secretly the blacks were amused and pleased. They did not like Stimbol.

At a distance Tarzan of the Apes, hunting with the tribe of Toyat, heard the first shot and immediately took to the trees and was racing in the direction of the sound. He felt sure that the weapon had not been discharged by the Beduins, for he well knew and could differentiate between the reports of their muskets and those made by modern weapons.

Perhaps, he thought, there may be among them such a rifle, because such was not impossible, but more likely it meant white men, and in Tarzan's country it was his business to know what strangers were there and why. Seldom they came even now, though once they had never come. It was those days that Tarzan regretted, for when the white man comes peace and happiness depart.

Racing through the trees, swinging from limb to limb, Tarzan of the Apes unerringly followed the direction of the sound of the succeeding shots; and as he approached more closely the scene of the pursuit of Bolgani the gorilla, he heard the crashing of underbrush and the voices of men.

Bolgani, fleeing with greater haste than caution, his mind and attention occupied by thoughts of escape from the hated Tarmangani and the terrifying thunder stick that roared each time the Tarmangani came within sight of him, abandoned his accustomed wariness and hurried through the jungle forgetful of what few other enemies might beset his path; and so it was that he failed to see Histah the snake draped in sinuous loops along an overhanging branch of a nearby patriarch of the forest.

The huge python, naturally short tempered and irritable, had been disturbed and annoyed by the crashing sounds of pursuit and escape and the roaring voice of the rifle. Ordinarily he would have permitted a full grown bull gorilla to pass unmolested, but in his present state of mind he might have attacked even Tantor himself.

His beady eyes glaring fixedly, he watched the approach of the shaggy Bolgani, and as the gorilla passed beneath the limb to which he clung Histah launched himself upon his prey.

As the great coils, powerful, relentless, silent, encircled Bolgani, he sought to tear the hideous folds from him. Great is the strength of Bolgani, but even greater is that of Histah the snake. A single hideous, almost human scream burst from the lips of Bolgani with the first realization of the disaster that had befallen him, and then he was on the ground tearing futilely at the steadily tightening bands of living steel that would crush the life from him, crush until his bones gave to the tremendous pressure, until only broken pulp remained within a sausage like thing that would slip between the distended jaws of the serpent.

It was upon this sight that Stimbol and Tarzan came simultaneously—Stimbol stumbling awkwardly through the underbrush, Tarzan of the Apes, demi-god of the forest, swinging gracefully through the foliage of the middle terraces.

They arrived simultaneously but Tarzan was the only one of the party whose presence was unsuspected by the others, for, as always, he had moved silently and with the utmost wariness because of the unknown nature of the conditions he might discover.

As he looked down upon the scene below his quick eye and his knowledge of the jungle revealed at a glance the full story of the tragedy that had overtaken Bolgani, and then he saw Stimbol raise his rifle, intent upon bagging two royal specimens with a single shot.

In the heart of Tarzan was no great love for Bolgani the gorilla. Since childhood the shaggy, giant man-beast had been the natural foe of the ape-man. His first mortal combat had been with Bolgani. For years he had feared him, or rather avoided him through caution, for of fear Tarzan was ignorant; and since he had emerged from childhood he had continued to avoid Bolgani for the simple reason that his own people, the great apes, avoided him.

But now when he saw the huge brute beset by two of the natural enemies of both the Mangani and the Bolgani, there

flared within his breast a sudden loyalty that burned away the
personal prejudices of a lifetime.

He was directly above Stimbol, and with such celerity do
the mind and muscles of the ape-man coordinate that even as
the American raised his weapon to his shoulder Tarzan had
dropped upon his back, felling him to the earth; and before
Stimbol could discover what had happened to him, long before
he could stumble, cursing, to his feet, Tarzan, who had been
unarmed, had snatched the hunter's knife from its scabbard
and leaped full upon the writhing, struggling mass of python
and gorilla. Stimbol came to his feet ready to kill but what he
saw before him temporarily drove the desire for vengeance
from his mind.

Naked but for a loin cloth, bronzed, black-haired, a giant
white man battled with the dread python; and as Stimbol
watched he shuddered as he became aware that the low,
beast-like growls he heard came not alone from the savage
lips of the gorilla but from the throat of the god-like man-
thing that fought for him.

Steel fingers encircled the python just back of its head,
while those of the free hand drove Stimbol's hunting knife
again and again into the coiling, writhing body of the serpent.
With the projection of a new and more menacing enemy into
the battle, Histah was forced partially to release his hold
upon Bolgani with, at first, the intention of including Tarzan
in the same embrace that he might crush them both at once;
but soon he discovered that the hairless man-thing constituted
a distinct menace to his life that would necessitate his un-
divided attention, and so he quickly uncoiled from about
Bolgani and in a frenzy of rage and pain that whipped his
great length into a lashing fury of destruction he sought to
encircle the ape-man; but wheresoever his coils approached,
the keen knife bit deep into tortured flesh.

Bolgani, the spark of life all but crushed from him, lay
gasping upon the ground, unable to come to the aid of his
preserver, while Stimbol, goggle-eyed with awe and terror,
kept at a safe distance, momentarily forgetful both of his lust
for trophies and his bent for revenge.

Thus was Tarzan pitted, single-handed, against one of the
mightiest of Nature's creations in a duel to the death, the result of which seemed to the watching American already a
foregone conclusion, for what man born of woman could
hope, unaided, to escape from the embrace of the deadly coils
of a python?

Already Histah had encircled the torso and one leg of the

ape-man, but his powers of constriction, lessened by the frightful wounds he had received, had as yet been unable to crush his adversary into helplessness, and Tarzan was now concentrating his attention and the heavy blade of the hunting knife upon a single portion of the weakening body in an attempt to cut Histah in two.

Man and serpent were red with blood; and crimson were the grasses and the brush for yards in all directions as, with a final effort, Histah closed his giant coils spasmodically about his victim at the instant that Tarzan with a mighty upward heavy lunge cut through the vertebrae of the great snake.

Lashing and writhing, the nether portion, headless, flopped aside while the ape-man, still fighting with what remained, exerting his superhuman strength to its ultimate utmost, slowly forced the coils from about his body and cast the dying Histah from him. Then, without a glance at Stimbol, he turned to Bolgani.

"You are hurt to death?" he asked in the language of the great apes.

"No," replied the gorilla. "I am Bolgani! I kill, Tarmangani!"

"I am Tarzan of the Apes," said the ape-man. "I saved you from Histah."

"You did not come to kill Bolgani?" inquired the gorilla.

"No. Let us be friends."

Bolgani frowned in an effort to concentrate upon this remarkable problem. Presently he spoke. "We will be friends," he said. "The Tarmangani behind you will kill us both with his thunder stick. Let us kill him first." Painfully he staggered to his feet.

"No," remonstrated Tarzan. "I will send the Tarmangani away."

"You? He will not go."

"I am Tarzan, Lord of the Jungle," replied the ape-man. "The word of Tarzan is law in the jungle."

Stimbol, who had been watching, was under the impression that the man and the beast were growling at one another and that a new duel impended. Had he guessed the truth and suspicioned that they considered him a common enemy he would have felt far less at ease. Now, his rifle regained, he started toward Tarzan just as the latter turned to address him.

"Stand to one side, young fellow," said Stimbol, "while I finish that gorilla. After the experience you just had with the snake, I doubt if you want that fellow to jump you, too." The American was none too sure of what the attitude of the white giant might be, for all too fresh in his mind was the startling and disconcerting manner of the wild man's introduction; but he felt safe because he held a rifle, while the other was unarmed, and he guessed that the giant might be only too glad to be saved from the attentions of the gorilla, which, from Stimbol's imagined knowledge of such beasts, appeared to him to be quite evidently threatening.

Tarzan halted directly between Bolgani and the hunter and eyed the latter appraisingly for a moment. "Lower your rifle," he said, presently. "You are not going to shoot the gorilla."

"The hell I'm not!" ejaculated Stimbol. "What do you suppose I've been chasing him through the jungle for?"

"Under a misapprehension," replied Tarzan.

"What misapprehension?" demanded Stimbol.

"That you were going to shoot him. You are not."

"Say, young man, do you know who I am?" demanded Stimbol.

"I am not interested," replied Tarzan coldly.

"Well you'd better be. I'm Wilbur Stimbol of Stimbol & Company, brokers, New York!" That was a name to conjure with—in New York. Even in Paris and London it had opened many a door, bent many a knee. Seldom had it failed the purpose of this purse-arrogant man.

"What are you doing in my country?" demanded the ape-man, ignoring Stimbol's egotistical statement of his identity.

"Your country? Who the hell are you?"

Tarzan turned toward the two blacks who had been standing a little in the rear of Stimbol and to one side. "I am Tarzan of the Apes," he said to them in their own dialect. "What is this man doing in my country? How many are there in his party—how many white men?"

"Big Bwana," replied one of the men with sincere deference, "we knew that you were Tarzan of the Apes when we saw you swing from the trees and slay the great snake. There is no other in all the jungle who could do that. This white man is a bad master. There is one other white man with him. The other is kind. They came to hunt Simba the lion and other big game. They have had no luck. Tomorrow they turn back."

"Where is their camp?" demanded Tarzan.

The black who had spoken pointed. "It is not far," he said.

The ape-man turned to Stimbol. "Go back to your camp," he said. "I shall come there later this evening and talk with you and your companion. In the meantime hunt no more except for food in Tarzan's country."

There was something in the voice and manner of the stranger that had finally gone through Stimbol's thick sensibilities and impressed him with a species of awe—a thing he had scarcely ever experienced in the past except in the presence of wealth that was grossly superior to his own. He did not reply. He just stood and watched the bronzed giant turn to the gorilla. He heard them growl at one another for a moment and then, to his vast surprise, he saw them move off through the jungle together, shoulder to shoulder. As the foliage closed about them he removed his helmet and wiped the sweat from his forehead with a silken handkerchief as he stood staring at the green branches that had parted to receive this strangely assorted pair.

Finally he turned to his men with an oath. "A whole day wasted!" he complained. "Who is this fellow? You seemed to know him."

"He is Tarzan," replied one of the blacks.

"Tarzan? Never heard of him," snapped Stimbol.

"All who know the jungle, know Tarzan."

"Humph!" sneered Stimbol. "No lousy wild man is going to tell Wilbur Stimbol where he can hunt and where he can't."

"Master," said the black who had first spoken, "the word of Tarzan is the law of the jungle. Do not offend him."

"I'm not paying you damn fools for advice," snapped Stimbol. "If I say hunt, we hunt, and don't you forget it." But on their return to camp they saw no game, or at least Stimbol saw none. What the blacks saw was their own affair.

5

The Tarmangani

URING Stimbol's absence from camp Blake had been occupied in dividing the food and equipment into two equal parts which were arranged for Stimbol's inspection and approval; but the division of the porters and askari he had left until the other's return, and was writing in his diary when the hunting party entered the camp.

He could see at a glance that Stimbol was in bad humor, but as that was the older man's usual state of temper it caused Blake no particular anxiety, but rather gave him cause for added relief that on the morrow he would be rid of his ill-natured companion for good.

Blake was more concerned, however, by the sullen demeanor of the askari who had accompanied Stimbol for it meant to the younger man that his companion had found some new occasion for bullying, abusing or insulting them, and the difficulty of dividing the safari thus increased. Blake had felt from the moment that he had definitely reached the decision to separate from Stimbol that one of the greatest obstacles they would have to overcome to carry out the plan would be to find sufficient men willing to submit themselves to Stimbol's ideas of discipline, properly to transport his luggage and provisions and guard them and him.

As Stimbol passed and saw the two piles of equipment the frown upon his face deepened. "I see you've got the stuff laid out," he remarked, as he halted before Blake.

'Yes, I wanted you to look it over and see that it is satisfactorily divided before I have it packed."

"I don't want to be bothered with it," replied the other. "I know you wouldn't take any advantage of me on the division."

"Thanks," replied Blake.

"How about the porters?"

"That's not going to be so easy. You know you haven't treated them very well and there will not be many of them anxious to return with you."

"There's where you're dead wrong, Blake. The trouble

37

with you is that you don't know anything about natives. You're
too easy with 'em. They haven't any respect for you, and
the man they don't respect they don't like. They know that a
fellow who beats 'em is their master, and they know that a
master is going to look after them. They wouldn't want to
trust themselves on a long trek with you. You divided the
junk, now let me handle the men—that's more in my line—
and I'll see that you get a square deal and a good, safe bunch,
and I'll put the fear of God into 'em so they won't dare be
anything but loyal to you."

"Just how do you propose selecting the men?" asked Blake.

"Well, in the first place I'd like you to have those men who
may wish to accompany you—I'll grant there are a few—so
we'll just have 'em all up, explain that we are separating, and
I'll tell all those who wish to return with your safari to step
forward, then I'll choose some good men from what are left
and make up enough that way to complete your quota—
see? That's fair enough, isn't it?"

"It's quite fair," agreed Blake. He was hoping that the plan
would work out as easily as Stimbol appeared to believe that
it would, but he was far from believing and so he thought it
best to suggest an alternative that he was confident would
have to be resorted to in the end. "In the event that one of us
has difficulty in securing the requisite number of volunteers,"
he said, "I believe that we can enlist the necessary men by
offering a bonus to be paid upon safe arrival at railhead. If
I am short of men I shall be willing to do so."

"Not a bad idea if you're afraid you can't hold 'em together
after I leave you," said Stimbol. "It will be an added factor of
safety for you, too; but as for me my men will live up to their
original agreement or there'll be some mighty sick porters in
these parts. What say we have 'em up and find out just how
much of a job we've got on our hands?" He glanced about
until his eyes fell on a head man. "Here, you!" he called.
"Come here and make it snappy."

The black approached and stopped before the two white
men. "You called me, Bwana?" he asked.

"Gather up every one in camp," directed Stimbol. "Have
them up here in five minutes for a palaver—every last man-
jack of them."

"Yes, Bwana."

As the head man withdrew Stimbol turned to Blake. "Any
stranger in camp today?" he asked.

"No, why?"

"Ran across a wild man while I was hunting," replied Stimbol. "He ordered me out of the jungle. What do you know about that?" and Stimbol laughed.

"A wild man?"

"Yes. Some crazy nut I suppose. The askari seemed to know about him."

"Who is he?"

"Calls himself Tarzan."

Blake elevated his brows. "Ah!" he exclaimed. "You have met Tarzan of the Apes and he has ordered you out of the jungle?"

"You've heard of him?"

"Certainly, and if he ever orders me out of his jungle, I'll go."

"*You* would, but not Wilbur Stimbol."

"Why did he order you out?" asked Blake.

"He just ordered me out, that's all. Wouldn't let me shoot a gorilla I'd been stalking. The fellow saved the gorilla from a python, killed the python, ordered me out of the jungle, said he'd visit us in camp later and walked away with the gorilla like they were old pals. I never saw anything like it, but it doesn't make any difference to me who or what he thinks he is, I know who and what I am and it's going to take more than a half-wit to scare me out of this country till I'm good and ready to go."

"So you think Tarzan of the Apes is a half-wit?"

"I think anyone's a half-wit who'd run about this jungle naked and unarmed."

"You'll find he's not a half-wit, Stimbol; and unless you want to get in more trouble than you ever imagined existed, you'll do just as Tarzan of the Apes tells you to do."

"What do you know about him? Have you ever seen him?"

"No," replied Blake. "But I have heard a lot about him from our men. He's as much a part of this locality as the jungle, or the lions. Very few, if any, of our men have seen him, but he has the same hold upon their imaginations and superstitions as any of their demons, and they are even more fearful of incurring his displeasure. If they think Tarzan has it in for us we're out of luck."

"Well, all I've got to say is that if this monkey-man knows when he's well off he'll not come butting into the affairs of Wilbur Stimbol."

"And he's coming to visit us, is he?" said Blake. "Well, I certainly want to see him. I've heard of little else since we struck his country."

"It's funny I never heard of him," said Stimbol.

"You never talk with the men," Blake reminded him.

"Gad, it seems as though I'm doing nothing but talk to them," grumbled Stimbol.

"I said, talk *with* them."

"I don't chum with porters," sneered Stimbol.

Blake grinned.

"Here are the men," said Stimbol. He turned toward the waiting porters and askari and cleared his throat. "Mr. Blake and I are going to separate," he announced. "Everything has been divided. I am going to hunt a little farther to the west, make a circle toward the south and return to the coast by a new route. I do not know what Mr. Blake's plans are, but he is going to get half the porters and half the askari, and I want to tell you right now that there isn't going to be any funny business about it. Half of you are going with Mr. Blake whether you like it or not."

He paused, impressively, to let the full weight of his pronouncement sink home. "As usual," he continued, "I wish to keep everyone contented and happy, so I'm going to give you who may want to go with Mr. Blake an opportunity to do so. Now listen! The packs over on that side are Mr. Blake's; those on this side are mine. All those who are willing to accompany Mr. Blake go over on that side!"

There was a moment's hesitation upon the part of the men and then some of them moved quietly over among Blake's packs. Others followed as their understandings slowly grasped the meaning of Stimbol's words until all of the men stood upon Blake's side.

Stimbol turned to Blake with a laugh and a shake of his head. "Gad!" he exclaimed. "Did you ever see such a dumb bunch? No one could have explained the thing more simply than I and yet look at 'em! Not one of them understood me!"

"Are you quite sure of that, Stimbol?" inquired Blake.

Stimbol did not immediately grasp the insinuation. When he did he scowled. "Don't be a fool," he snapped. "Of course they misunderstood me." He turned angrily toward the men. "You thick-skulled, black idiots! Can't you understand anything?" he demanded. "I did not say that you all had to go with Mr. Blake—only those who wished to. Now the rest of you—those who wish to accompany me—get back over here on this side with my packs, and step lively!"

No one moved in the direction of Stimbol's packs. The man flushed.

"This is mutiny!" he stormed. "Whoever is at the bottom of this is going to suffer. Come here, you!" He motioned to a head man. "Who put you fellows up to this? Has Mr. Blake been telling you what to do?"

"Don't be a fool, Stimbol," said Blake. "No one has influenced the men and there is no mutiny. The plan was yours. The men have done just what you told them to. If it had not been for your insufferable egotism you would have known precisely what the outcome would be. These black men are human beings. In some respects they are extremely sensitive human beings, and in many ways they are like children. You strike them, you curse them, you insult them and they will fear you and hate you. You have done all these things to them and they do fear you and hate you. You have sowed and now you are reaping. I hope to God that it will teach you a lesson. There is just one way to get your men and that is to offer them a big bonus. Are you willing to do that?"

Stimbol, his self assurance momentarily shaken at last, wilted in the face of the realization that Blake was right. He looked about helplessly for a moment. The blacks, sullen-faced, stood there like dumb beasts, staring at him. In all those eyes there was no single friendly glance. He turned back to Blake. "See what you can do with them," he said.

Blake faced the men. "It will be necessary for half of you to accompany Mr. Stimbol back to the coast," he said. "He will pay double wages to all those who go with him, provided that you serve him loyally. Talk it over among yourselves and send word to us later by your head man. That is all. You may go."

The balance of the afternoon passed, the two white men keeping to their respective tents; the blacks gathered in groups, whispering. Blake and Stimbol no longer messed together, but after the evening meal each appeared with his pipe to await the report of the head men. After half an hour Blake sent his boy to summon them and presently they came and stood before the young man.

"Well, have the men decided who will accompany Mr. Stimbol?" he asked.

"No one will accompany the old bwana," replied their spokesman. "All will go with the young bwana."

"But Mr. Stimbol will pay them well," Blake reminded, "and half of you must go with him."

The black shook his head. "He could not make the pay big enough," he said. "No boy will go with him."

"You agreed to come out with us and return with us," said Blake. "You must fulfil your agreement."

"We agreed to come out with both of you and return with

both of you. There was nothing said about returning separately. We will live up to our agreement and the old bwana may return in safety with the young bwana." There was finality in the tone of the spokesman.

Blake thought for a moment before replying. "You may go," he said. "I will talk with you again in the morning."

The blacks had departed but a moment when the figure of a man appeared suddenly out of the darkness into the light of the camp fire.

"Who the—oh, it's you is it?" exclaimed Stimbol. "Here's the wild man, Blake."

The young American turned and surveyed the figure of the bronze giant who was standing just within the circle of the firelight. He noted the clean cut features, the quiet dignity, the majestic mien and smiled inwardly at recollection of Stimbol's description of this god-like creature—half-wit!

"So you are Tarzan of the Apes!" he said.

Tarzan inclined his head. "And you?" he asked.

"I am Jim Blake of New York," replied the American.

"Hunting of course?"

"With a camera."

"Your companion was using a rifle," Tarzan reminded him.

"I am not responsible for his acts. I cannot control them," replied Blake.

"Nor anyone else," snapped Stimbol.

Tarzan permitted his gaze to move to Stimbol for an instant, but ignored his boast.

"I overheard the conversation between you and the head men," he said, addressing Blake. "Some of your blacks had already told me something about your companion, and twice today I have had an opportunity to form an estimate of my own from personal observation, so I assume that you are separating because you cannot agree. Am I right?"

"Yes," acknowledged Blake.

"And after you separate—what are your plans?"

"I intend to push in a little farther west and then swing——" commenced Stimbol.

"I was speaking to Blake," interrupted Tarzan; "my plans concerning you are already made."

"Well, who the——"

"Silence!" admonished the ape-man. "Go ahead, Blake!"

"We have not had much luck so far," replied Blake, "principally because we never can agree on methods. The result is that I have scarcely a single decent wild animal study. I had planned to go north a way in search of lion pictures. I dislike going back without anything to show for the time and money I have put into the expedition, but now that the men have refused to accompany us separately there is nothing for it but to return to the coast by the shortest route."

"You two don't seem to be taking me into consideration at all," grumbled Stimbol. "I've got as much money and time in this trip as Blake. You forget that I'm here to hunt, and what's more I'm going to hunt and I'm not going straight back to the coast by a damned sight, monkey-man or no monkey-man."

Again Tarzan ignored Stimbol. "Get ready to move out about an hour after sunrise," he said to Blake. "There will be no trouble about dividing the safari. I shall be here to attend to that and give you your final instructions," and as he spoke he turned and disappeared in the darkness.

6

Ara the Lightning

BEFORE dawn the camp was astir and by the appointed hour the packs were made and all was in readiness. The porters loitered, awaiting the word that would start the safari upon its eastward journey toward the coast. Blake and Stimbol smoked in silence. The foliage of a nearby tree moved to the swaying of a branch and Tarzan of the Apes dropped lightly into the camp. Exclamations of surprise broke from the lips of the Negroes—surprise clearly tinged with terror. The ape-man turned toward them and addressed them in their own dialect.

"I am Tarzan of the Apes," he said, "Lord of the Jungle. You have brought white men into my country to kill my people. I am displeased. Those of you who wish to live to return to your villages and your families will listen well and do as Tarzan commands.

"You," he pointed at the chief head man, "shall accompany the younger white man whom I will permit to make pictures in my country where and when he will. Select half the men of the safari to accompany the young bwana."

"And you," he addressed another head man, "take those men that remain and escort the older bwana to railhead in the most direct route and without delay. He is not permitted to hunt and there will be no killing except for food or self-defense. Do not fail me. Remember always that Tarzan watches and Tarzan never forgets."

He turned then to the white men. "Blake," he said, "the arrangements are made. You may leave when you please, with your own safari, and go where you please. The question of hunting is left to your own discretion—you are the guest of Tarzan."

"And you," he addressed Stimbol, "will be taken directly out of the country by the shortest route. You will be permitted to carry firearms for use in self-defense. If you abuse this permission they will be taken away from you. Do not hunt, even for food—your head man will attend to that."

"Now just hold your horses," blustered Stimbol. "If you think I'm going to put up with any such high-handed interference with my rights as an American citizen you're very much mistaken. Why I could buy and sell you and your damned jungle forty times and not know that I'd spent a cent. For God's sake, Blake, tell this poor fool who I am before he gets himself into a lot of trouble."

Tarzan turned to the head man he had selected for Stimbol. "You may up-load and march," he said. "If this white man does not follow you, leave him behind. Take good care of him if he obeys me and deliver him safely at railhead. Obey his orders if they do not conflict with those that I have given you. Go!"

A moment later Stimbol's safari was preparing to depart and, at Tarzan's request, Blake's too was moving out of camp. Stimbol swore and threatened, but his men, sullenly ignoring him, filed off into the jungle toward the east. Tarzan had departed, swinging into the trees and disappearing among the foliage, and at last Stimbol stood alone in the deserted camp.

Thwarted, humiliated, almost frothing with rage he ran after his men, screaming commands and threats that were ignored. Later in the day, sullen and silent, he marched near the head of the long file of porters and askari, convinced at last that the power of the ape-man was greater than his; but in his heart burned resentment and in his mind rioted plans for vengeance—plans that he knew were futile.

Tarzan, wishing to assure himself that his instructions were being carried out, had swung far ahead and was waiting in the crotch of a tree that overhung the trail along which Stimbol must pass. In the distance he could hear the sounds that arose from the marching safari. Along the trail from the opposite direction something was approaching. The ape-man could not see it but he knew what it was. Above the tree tops black clouds rolled low, but no air stirred in the jungle.

Along the trail came a great, shaggy, black man-thing. Tarzan of the Apes hailed it as it came in sight of his arboreal perch.

"Bolgani!" he called in low tones.

The gorilla stopped. He stood erect upon his hind feet and looked about.

"I am Tarzan," said the ape-man.

Bolgani grunted. "I am Bolgani," he replied.

"The Tarmangani comes," warned Tarzan.

"I kill!" growled Bolgani.

"Let the Tarmangani pass," said Tarzan. "He and his people have many thunder sticks. I have sent this Tarmangani out of the jungle. Let him pass. Go a little way from the trail —the stupid Gomangani and the Tarmangani, who is stupider, will pass by without knowing that Tarzan and Bolgani are near."

From the darkening sky distant thunder boomed and the two beasts looked upward toward the broad field of Nature's powers, more savage and destructive than their own.

"Pand the thunder hunts in the sky," remarked the apeman.

"Hunts for Usha the wind," said Bolgani.

"Presently we shall hear Usha fleeing through the trees to escape." Tarzan viewed the lowering, black clouds. "Even Kudu the sun fears Pand, hiding his face when Pand hunts."

Ara the lightning shot through the sky. To the two beasts it was a bolt from Pand's bow and the great drops of rain that commenced to fall shortly after was Meeta, the blood of Usha the wind, pouring from many a wound.

The jungle bent to a great pressure but as yet there was no other noise than the rolling thunder. The trees whipped back and Usha tore through the forest. The darkness increased. The rain fell in great masses. Leaves and branches hurtled through the air, trees crashed amongst their fellows. With deafening roars the elements unleashed their pent anger. The beasts cowered beneath the one awe inspiring power that they acknowledged as supreme.

Tarzan crouched in the crotch of a great tree with his shoulders arched against the beating rain. Just off the trail Bolgani squatted in drenched and bedraggled misery. They waited. There was nothing else that they could do.

Above them the storm broke again with maniacal fury. The thunder crashed with deafening reverberation. There was a blinding flash of light and the branch upon which Tarzan squatted sagged and hurtled to the trail beneath.

Stunned, the ape-man lay where he had fallen, the great branch partially across his body.

As quickly as it had come, the storm departed. Kudu the sun burst through the clouds. Bolgani, dejected and still terrified, remained where he had squatted, motionless and silent. Bolgani had no desire to attract the attention of Pand the thunder.

Soaked with water, cold, furious, Stimbol slopped along the slippery, muddy trail. He did not know that his safari was some little distance behind him, for he had forged ahead during the storm while they had taken refuge beneath the trees.

At a turn in the trail he came suddenly upon a fallen branch that blocked the way. At first he did not see the body of the man lying beneath it, but when he did he recognized it instantly and a new hope sprang to life within his breast. With Tarzan dead he could be free to do as he pleased; but was the ape-man dead?

Stimbol ran forward and, kneeling, placed an ear to the breast of the prostrate figure. An expression of disappointment crossed his face—Tarzan was not dead. The expression upon Stimbol's face changed—a cunning look came into his eyes as he glanced back down the trail. His men were not in sight! He looked quickly about him. He was alone with the unconscious author of his humiliation!

He thought he was alone. He did not see the shaggy figure that had silently arisen as the sound of Stimbol's approach had come to its sensitive ears and was now peering at him through the foliage—peering at him and at the silent figure of the apeman.

Stimbol drew his hunting knife from its scabbard. He could clip its point into the wild man's heart and run back down the trail. His men would find him waiting for them. Later they would come upon the dead Tarzan, but they would not guess how he had met his end.

The ape-man moved—consciousness was returning. Stimbol realized that he must act quickly, and at the same instant a great hairy arm reached out through the foliage and a mighty hand closed upon his shoulder. With a screaming curse he turned to look into the hideous face of Bolgani. He tried to strike at the shaggy breast of his antagonist with his hunting knife, but the puny weapon was torn from his grasp and hurled into the bushes.

The great yellow fangs were bared against Stimbol's throat as Tarzan opened his eyes.

"Kreeg-ah!" cried the ape-man in warning.

Bolgani paused and looked at his fellow beast.

"Let him go," said Tarzan.

"The Tarmangani would have killed Tarzan," explained the gorilla. "Bolgani stopped him. Bolgani kill!" He growled horribly.

"No!" snapped Tarzan. "Free the Tarmangani!"

The gorilla released his grasp upon Stimbol just as the first of the hunter's men came in sight of them, and as Bolgani saw the blacks and how numerous they were his nervousness and irritability increased.

"Take to the jungle, Bolgani," said Tarzan. "Tarzan will take care of this Tarmangani and the Gomangani."

With a parting growl the gorilla merged with the foliage and the shadows of the jungle as Tarzan of the Apes faced Stimbol and his boys.

"You had a close call then, Stimbol," said the ape-man. "It is fortunate for you that you didn't succeed in killing me. I was here for two reasons. One was to see that you obeyed my instructions and the other to protect you from your men. I did not like the way they eyed you in camp this morning. It would not be a difficult thing to lose you in the jungle, you know, and that would put a period to you as surely as poison or a knife. I felt a certain responsibility for you because you are a white man, but you have just now released me from whatever obligation racial ties may have influenced me to acknowledge.

"I shall not kill you, Stimbol, as your deserve; but from now on you may reach the coast on your own, and you will doubtless discover that one cannot make too many friends in the jungle or afford a single unnecessary enemy." He wheeled upon Stimbol's black boys. "Tarzan of the Apes goes his way. You will not see him again, perhaps. Do your duty by this white man as long as he obeys the word of Tarzan, *but see that he does not hunt!*"

With this final admonition the ape-man swung into the lower branches and was gone.

When Stimbol, after repeatedly questioning his men, discovered that Tarzan had practically assured them that they would see no more of him, he regained much of his former assurance and egotistical bluster. Once more he was the leader of men, shouting at the blacks in a loud tone, cursing them, ridiculing them. He thought that it impressed them with his greatness. He believed that they were simple people whom he could deceive into thinking that he was not afraid of Tarzan, and by flaunting Tarzan's commands win their respect. Now that Tarzan had promised not to return Stimbol felt safer in ignoring his wishes, and so it befell that just before they reached a camping ground Stimbol came upon an antelope and without an instant's hesitation fired and killed it.

It was a sullen camp that Stimbol made that night. The men gathered in groups and whispered. "He has shot an antelope and Tarzan will be angry with us," said one.

"He will punish us," said a head man.

"The bwana is a bad man," said another. "I wish he was dead."

"We may not kill him. Tarzan has said that."

"If we leave him in the jungle he will die."

"Tarzan told us to do our duty."

"He said to do it as long as the bad bwana obeyed the commands of Tarzan."

"He has disobeyed them."

"Then we may leave him."

Stimbol, exhausted by the long march, slept like a log. When he awoke the sun was high. He shouted for his boy. There was no response. Again he shouted and louder, adding an oath. No one came. There was no sound in camp.

"The lazy swine," he grumbled. "They'll step a little livelier when I get out there."

He arose and dressed, but as he was dressing the silence of the camp came to impress him as something almost menacing, so that he hastened to be through and out of the tent. As he stepped into the open the truth was revealed at almost the first quick glance about. Not a human being was in sight and all but one of the packs containing provisions were gone. He had been deserted in the heart of Africa!

His first impulse was to seize his rifle and start after the blacks, but second thought impressed him with the danger of such procedure and convinced him that the last thing he should do would be to place himself again in the power of these men who had demonstrated that they felt no compunction in abandoning him to almost certain death. If they wanted to be rid of him they could easily find even a quicker means if he returned and forced himself upon them again.

There was but a single alternative and that was to find Blake and remain with him. He knew that Blake would not abandon him to death in the jungle.

The blacks had not left him without provisions, nor had they taken his rifle or ammunition, but the difficulty that now confronted Stimbol was largely in the matter of transportation for his food. There was plenty of it to last many days, but he knew that he could not carry it through the jungle together with his rifle and ammunition. To remain where the food was would be equally futile. Blake was returning to the coast by another route; the ape-man had said that he would not follow Stimbol's safari farther; it might be years, therefore, before another human being chanced along this little used game trail.

He knew that he and Blake were now separated by about

two marches and if he travelled light and Blake did not march too rapidly he might hope to overtake him inside a week. Perhaps Blake would find good camera hunting soon and make a permanent camp. In that case Stimbol would find him even more quickly.

He felt better when he had definitely decided upon a plan of action, and after a good breakfast he made up a small pack of provisions, enough to last him a week, filled his belts and pockets with ammunition and started off along the back trail.

It was easy going for the trail of the day before was plain and this was the third time that Stimbol had been over it, so he had no difficulty in reaching the camp at which he and Blake had parted company.

As he entered the little clearing early in the afternoon he determined to keep on and cover as much ground on Blake's trail as he could before dark, but for a few minutes he would rest. As he sat down with his back against the bole of a tree he did not notice a movement of the tops of a clump of jungle grasses a few yards distant, and if he had he would, doubtless, have attached no importance to the matter.

Finishing a cigarette Stimbol arose, rearranged his pack and started off in the direction Blake's men had taken early the preceding morning; but he had covered but a yard or two when he was brought to a sudden halt by an ominous growl that arose from a little clump of jungle grasses close in front of him. Almost simultaneously the fringing grasses parted and there appeared in the opening the head of a great black-maned lion.

With a scream of fear, Stimbol dropped his pack, threw aside his rifle and started on a run for the tree beneath which he had been sitting. The lion, itself somewhat surprised, stood for an instant watching him and then started in pursuit at an easy lope.

Stimbol, casting an affrighted glance rearward, was horrified —the lion seemed so close and the tree so far away. If distance lends enchantment to the view, proximity may also at times have its advantage. In this instance it served to accelerate the speed of the fleeing man to a most surprising degree, and though he was no longer young he clawed his way to the lower branches of the tree with speed, if not with grace, that would have done justice to a trained athlete.

Nor was he an instant too speedy. Numa's raking talons touched his boot and sent him swarming up among the higher branches, where he clung weak and panting looking down into the snarling visage of the carnivore.

For a moment Numa growled up at him and then, with a coughing grunt, turned away and strode majestically in the direction of the clump of grasses from which he had emerged. He stopped to sniff at the pack of provisions Stimbol had discarded and, evidently piqued by the man scent clinging to it, cuffed at it angrily. It rolled to one side and Numa stepped back, eyeing it warily, then, with a growl, he leaped upon it and commenced to maul the insensate thing, ripping and tearing until its contents were scattered about upon the ground. He bit into tins and boxes until scarcely an article remained intact, while Stimbol crouched in the tree and watched the destruction of his provisions, utterly helpless to interfere.

A dozen times he cursed himself for having thrown away his rifle and even more frequently he vowed vengeance. He consoled himself, however, with the realization that Blake could not be far away and that with Blake there were ample provisions which could be augmented by trading and hunting. When the lion left he would descend and follow Blake's trail.

Numa, tired of the contents of the pack, resumed his way toward the long grass, but again his attention was distracted— this time by the thunder stick of the Tarmangani. The lion smelled of the discarded rifle, pawed it and finally picked it up between his jaws. Stimbol looked on, horrified. What if the beast damaged the weapon? He would be left without means of defense or for obtaining food!

"Drop it!" shouted Stimbol. "Drop it!"

Numa, ignoring the ravings of the despised man-thing, strode into his lair, carrying the rifle with him.

That afternoon and night spelled an eternity of terror for Wilbur Stimbol. While daylight lasted the lion remained in the nearby patch of grass effectually deterring the unhappy man from continuing his search for Blake's camp, and after night fell no urge whatever could have induced Stimbol to descend to the paralyzing terrors of the jungle night even had he known that the lion had departed and no sounds had apprised him of the near presence of danger; but sounds did apprise him. From shortly after dark until nearly dawn a perfect bedlam of howls and growls and coughs and grunts and barks arose from directly beneath him as there had been held a convention of all the horrid beasts of the jungle at the foot of the tree that seemed at best an extremely insecure sanctuary.

When morning came the jungle lay silent and peaceful about him and only torn canvas and empty cans bore mute evidence to the feast of the hyenas that had passed into jungle history. Numa had departed leaving the remains of the kill upon which he had lain as the piece de resistance of the hyenian banquet for which Stimbol had furnished the hors d'oeuvres.

Stimbol, trembling, descended. Through the jungle, wild-eyed, startled by every sound, scurried a pitiful figure of broken, terror stricken old age. Few could have recognized in it Wilbur Stimbol of Stimbol & Company, brokers, New York.

7

The Cross

THE storm that had overtaken Stimbol's safari wrought even greater havoc with the plans of Jim Blake, altering in the instant of a single blinding flash of lightning the course of his entire life.

Accompanied by a single black, who carried his camera and an extra rifle, Blake had struck out from the direct route of his safari in search of lion pictures, there being every indication that the great carnivores might be found in abundance in the district through which they were passing.

It was his intention to parallel the route of his main body and rejoin it in camp in the afternoon. The boy who accompanied him was intelligent and resourceful, the direction and speed of the marching safari were mutually agreed upon and the responsibility for bringing Blake into camp safely was left entirely to the Negro. Having every confidence in the boy, Blake gave no heed to either time or direction, devoting all his energies to the fascinating occupation of searching for photographic studies.

Shortly after leaving the safari Blake and his companion encountered a herd of seven or eight lions which included a magnificent old male, an old lioness and five or six young, ranging from half to full grown.

At sight of Blake and his companion the lions took off leisurely through rather open forest and the men followed, awaiting patiently the happy coincidence of time, light and grouping that would give the white man such a picture as he desired.

In the mind of the black man was pictured the route of the safari and its relation to the meanderings of the quarry. He knew how far and in what directions he and his companion were being led from their destination. To have returned to the trail of the safari would have been a simple matter to him, but Blake, depending entirely upon the black, gave no heed either to time or direction.

For two hours they clung doggedly to the spoor, encouraged

by occasional glimpses of now one, now several members of
the regal group, but never was the opportunity afforded for a
successful shot. Then the sky became rapidly overcast by black
clouds and a few moments later the storm broke in all the
terrific fury that only an Equatorial storm can achieve, and
an instant later amidst the deafening roar of thunder and a
blinding flash of lightning utter disaster engulfed James Hunter
Blake.

How long he lay, stunned by the shock of the bolt that had
struck but a few feet from him, he did not know. When he
opened his eyes the storm had passed and the sun was shining
brightly through the leafy canopy of the forest. Still dazed,
uncomprehending the cause or extent of the catastrophe,
he raised himself slowly upon an elbow and looked about him.

One of the first sights that met his eyes aided materially in
the rapid recovery of his senses. Less than a hundred feet from
him stood a group of lions, seven of them, solemnly regarding
him. The characteristics of individual lions differ as greatly
from those of their fellows as do the characteristics of in-
dividuals of the human race and, even as a human being, a
lion may have his moods as well as his personal idiosyncrasies.

These lions that gravely inspected the man-thing had been
spared any considerable experience with the human species;
they had seen but few men; they had never been hunted; they
were well fed; Blake had done nothing greatly to upset their
easily irritated nervous systems. Fortunately for him they were
merely curious.

But Blake did not know all this. He knew only that seven
lions were standing within a hundred feet of him, that they
were not in a cage and that while he had pursued them to
obtain photographs, the thing that he most desired at the
moment was not his camera but his rifle.

Stealthily, that he might not annoy them, he looked about
him for the weapon. To his consternation it was nowhere in
sight, nor was his gun bearer with the extra rifle. Where could
the boy be? Doubtless, frightened by the lions, he had de-
camped. Twenty feet away was a most inviting tree. Blake
wondered if the lions would charge the moment that he rose
to his feet. He tried to remember all that he had heard about
lions and he did recall one fact that applies with almost
axiomatic verity to all dangerous animals—if you run from
them they will pursue you. To reach the tree it would be
necessary to walk almost directly toward the lions.

Blake was in a quandary, and then one of the younger

lions moved a few steps nearer! That settled the matter as far as Blake was concerned. for the closer the lions came the shorter his chance of gaining the tree ahead of them in the event that they elected to prevent.

In the midst of a tremendous forest, entirely surrounded by trees, Nature had chosen to strike him down almost in the center of a natural clearing. There was a good tree a hundred feet away and on the opposite side of the clearing from the lions. Blake stole a longing glance at it and then achieved some rapid mental calculations. If he ran for the farther tree the lions would have to cover two hundred feet while he was covering one hundred, while if he chose the nearer tree, they must come eighty feet while he was going twenty. There seemed, therefore, no doubt as to the greater desirability of the nearer tree which ruled favorite by odds of two to one. Against it, however, loomed the mental hazard that running straight into the face of seven lions involved.

Jim Blake was sincerely, genuinely and honestly scared; but unless the lions were psychoanalysts they would never have dreamed the truth as he started nonchalantly and slowly toward them—and the tree. The most difficult feat that he had ever accomplished lay in making his legs behave themselves. They wanted to run. So did his feet and his heart and his brain. Only his will held them in leash.

Those were tense moments for Jim Blake—the first half dozen steps he took with seven great lions watching his approach. He saw that they were becoming nervous. The lioness moved uneasily. The old male growled. A younger male, he who had started forward, lashed his sides with his tail, flattened his head, bared his fangs and stealthily approached.

Blake was almost at the tree when something happened—he never knew what the cause, but inexplicably the lioness turned and bounded away, voicing a low whine, and after her went the other six.

The man leaned against the bole of the tree and fanned himself with his helmet. "Whew!" he breathed, "I hope the next lion I see is in the Central Park Zoo."

But even lions were forgotten in the developments that the next few moments revealed after repeated shouts for the black boy had brought no response and Blake had determined that he must set out in search of him. Nor did he have far to go. On the back track, just inside the clearing, Blake found a few remnants of charred flesh and a blackened and half molten rifle barrel. Of the camera not a vestige remained. The bolt that had bowled Blake over must have squarely struck his gun bearer, killing him instantly, exploding all the ammunition, destroying the camera and ruining the rifle that he had carried. *far too much*

But what had become of the rifle that had been in Blake's hands? The man searched in all directions, but could not find it and was finally forced to the conclusion that its disappearance could be attributed only to one of those freakish tricks which severe electrical storms so often play upon helpless and futile humanity.

Frankly aware that he was lost and had not the faintest conception of the direction in which lay the proposed camp of his safari, Blake started blindly off on what he devoutly hoped would prove the right route. It was not. His safari was moving northeast. Blake headed north.

For two days he trudged on through dense forest, sleeping at night among the branches of trees. Once his fitful slumbers were disturbed by the swaying of a branch against which he was braced. As he awoke he felt it sag as to the weight of some large animal. He looked and saw two fiery eyes gleaming in the dark. Blake knew it to be a leopard as he drew his automatic and fired point blank. With a hideous scream the great cat sprang or fell to the ground. Blake never knew if he hit it. It did not return and there were no signs of it in the morning.

He found food and water in abundance, and upon the morning of the third day he emerged from the forest at the foot of a range of lofty mountains and for the first time in weeks reveled in an unobstructed view of the blue sky and saw the horizon again and all that lay between himself and it. He had not realized that he had been depressed by the darkness and the crowding pressure of the trees, but now he experienced all the spiritual buoyancy of a released convict long immured from freedom and the light of day. Rescue was no longer problematical, merely a matter of time. He wanted to sing and shout; but he conserved his energies and started toward the mountains. There had been no native villages in the forest and so, he reasoned, as there must be native villages in a well-watered country stocked with game, he would find them upon the mountain slopes.

Topping a rise he saw below him the mouth of a canyon in the bed of which ran a small stream. A village would be built on water.

If he followed the water he would come to the village. Quite easy! He descended to the stream where he was deeply gratified to find that a well-worn path paralleled it. Encouraged by the belief that he would soon encounter natives and believing that he would have no difficulty in enlisting their services in aiding him to relocate his safari, Blake followed the path upward into the canyon.

He had covered something like three miles without having discovered any sign of habitation when, at a turn in the path, he found himself at the foot of a great white cross of enormous proportions. Hewn from limestone, it stood directly in the center of the trail and towered above him fully sixty feet. Checked and weatherworn, it gave an impression of great antiquity, which was further borne out by the remains of an almost obliterated inscription upon the face of its massive base.

Blake examined the carved letters, but could not decipher their message. The characters appeared of early English origin, but he dismissed such a possibility as too ridiculous to entertain. He knew that he could not be far from the southern boundary of Abyssinia and that the Abyssinians are Christians. Thus he explained the presence of the cross; but he could not explain the suggestion of sinister menace that this lonely, ancient symbol of the crucifix held for him. Why was it? What was it?

Standing there, tongueless, hoary with age, it seemed to call upon him to stop, to venture not beyond it into the unknown; it warned him back, but not, seemingly, out of a spirit of kindliness and protection, but rather with arrogance and hate.

With a laugh Blake threw off the mood that had seized him and went on; but as he passed the great white monolith he crossed himself, though he was not a Catholic. He wondered what had impelled him to the unfamiliar act, but he could no more explain it than he could the strange and uncanny suggestion of power and personality that seemed to surround the crumbling cross.

Another turn in the path and the trail narrowed where it passed between two huge boulders that might have fallen from the cliff top towering far above. Cliffs closed in closely now in front and upon two sides. Apparently he was close to the canyon's head and yet there was no slightest indication of a village. Yet where did the trail lead? It had an end and a purpose. He would discover the former and, if possible, the latter.

Still under the depressing influence of the cross, Blake passed between the two boulders; and the instant that he had passed them a man stepped out behind him and another in front. They were Negroes, stalwart, fine-featured fellows, and in themselves nothing to arouse wonder or surprise. Blake had expected to meet Negroes in Africa; but not Negroes wearing elaborately decorated leathern jerkins upon the breasts of which red crosses were emblazoned, close fitting nether garments and sandals held by doeskin thongs, cross gartered half way to their knees; not Negroes wearing close fitting bassinets of leopard skin that fitted their heads closely and reached to below their ears; not Negroes armed with two handed broad swords and elaborately tipped pikes.

Blake was acutely aware of the pike tips as there was one pressing against his belly and another in the small of his back.

"Who be ye?" demanded the Negro that faced Blake.

Had the man addressed him in Greek Blake would have been no more surprised than he was by the incongruity of this archaic form of speech falling from the lips of a twentieth century central African black. He was too dumbfounded for an instant to reply.

"Doubtless the fellow be a Saracen, Paul!" said the black behind Blake, "and understands not what thou sayest—a spy, perchance."

"Nay, Peter Wiggs, as my name be Paul Bodkin he be no infidel—that I know of mine own good eyes."

"Whatsoe'er he be it is for ye to fetch him before the captain of the gate who will question him, Paul Bodkin."

"Natheless there be no hurt in questioning him first, an he will answer."

"Stop thy tongue and take him to the captain," said Peter. "I will abide here and guard the way until thou returnest."

Paul stepped aside and motioned for Blake to precede him. Then he fell in behind and the American did not need to glance back to know that the ornate tip of the pike was ever threateningly ready.

The way lay plain before him and Blake followed the trail toward the cliffs where there presently appeared the black mouth of a tunnel leading straight into the rocky escarpment. Leaning against the sides of a niche just within the entrance were several torches made of reeds or twigs bound tightly together and dipped in pitch. One of these Paul Bodkin selected, took some tinder from a metal box he carried in a pouch at his side, struck a spark to it with flint and steel; and having thus ignited the tinder and lighted the torch he pushed Blake on again with the tip of his pike and the two entered the tunnel, which the American found to be narrow and winding, well suited to defense. Its floor was worn smooth until the stones of which it was composed shone polished in the flaring of the torch. The sides and roof were black with the soot of countless thousands, perhaps, of torch-lighted passages along this strange way that led to—what?

Really Jerrout —

8

The Snake Strikes

UNVERSED in jungle craft, overwhelmed by the enormity of the catastrophe that had engulfed him, his reasoning faculties numbed by terror, Wilbur Stimbol slunk through the jungle, the fleeing quarry of every terror that imagination could conjure. Matted filth caked the tattered remnants of his clothing that scarce covered the filth of his emaciated body. His once graying hair had turned to white, matching the white stubble of a four days' beard.

He followed a broad and well marked trail along which men and horses, sheep and goats had passed within the week, and with the blindness and ignorance of the city dweller he thought that he was on the spoor of Blake's safari. Thus it came that he stumbled, exhausted, into the menzil of the slow moving Ibn Jad.

Fejjuan, the Galla slave, discovered him and took him at once to the sheik's beyt where Ibn Jad, with his brother, Tollog, and several others were squatting in the mukaad sipping coffee.

"By Ullah! What strange creature hast thou captured now, Fejjuan?" demanded the sheik.

"Perhaps a holy man," replied the black, "for he is very poor and without weapons and very dirty—yes, surely he must be a very holy man."

"Who art thou?" demanded Ibn Jad.

"I am lost and starving. Give me food," begged Stimbol. But neither understood the language of the other.

"Another Nasrany," said Fahd, contemptuously. "A Frenjy, perhaps."

"He looks more like one of el-Engleys," remarked Tollog.

"Perhaps he is from Fransa," suggested Ibn Jad. "Speak to him that vile tongue, Fahd, which thou didst come by among the soldiers in Algeria."

"Who are you, stranger?" demanded Fahd, in French.

"I am an American," replied Stimbol, relieved and delighted to have discovered a medium of communication with

60

the Arabs. "I have been lost in the jungle and I am starving."

"He is from the New World and he has been lost and is starving," translated Fahd.

Ibn Jad directed that food be brought, and as the stranger ate they carried on a conversation through Fahd. Stimbol explained that his men had deserted him and that he would pay well to be taken to the coast. The Beduin had no desire to be further hampered by the presence of a weak old man and was inclined to have Stimbol's throat slit as the easiest solution of the problem, but Fahd, who was impressed by the man's boastings of his great wealth, saw the possibilities of a large reward or ransom and prevailed upon the sheik to permit Stimbol to remain among them for a time at least, promising to take him into his own beyt and be responsible for him.

"Ibn Jad would have slain you, Nasrany," said Fahd to Stimbol later, "but Fahd saved you. Remember that when the time comes for distributing the reward and remember, too, that Ibn Jad will be as ready to kill you tomorrow as he was today and that always your life is in the hands of Fahd. What is it worth?"

"I will make you rich," replied Stimbol.

During the days that followed, Fahd and Stimbol became much better acquainted and with returning strength and a feeling of security Stimbol's old boastfulness returned. He succeed in impressing the young Beduin with his vast wealth and importance, and so lavish were his promises that Fahd soon commenced to see before him a life of luxury, ease and power; but with growing cupidity and ambition developed an increasing fear that someone might wrest his good fortune from him. Ibn Jad being the most logical and powerful competitor for the favors of the Nasrany, Fahd lost no opportunity to impress upon Stimbol that the sheik was still thirsting for his blood; though, as a matter of fact, Ibn Jad was so little concerned over the affairs of Wilbur Stimbol that he would have forgotten his presence entirely were he not occasionally reminded of it by seeing the man upon the march or about the camps.

One thing, however, that Fahd accomplished was to acquaint Stimbol with the fact that there was dissension and treachery in the ranks of the Beduins and this he determined to use to his own advantage should necessity demand.

And ever, though slowly, the 'Aarab drew closer to the fabled Leopard City of Nimmr, and as they marched Zeyd found opportunity to forward his suit for the hand of Ateja the daughter of Sheik Ibn Jad, while Tollog sought by insinuation to advance the claims of Fahd in the eyes of the Sheik. This he did always and only when Fahd might hear as, in reality, his only wish was to impress upon the young traitor the depth of the latter's obligation to him. When Tollog should become sheik he would not care who won the hand of Ateja.

But Fahd was not satisfied with the progress that was being made. Jealousy rode him to distraction until he could not look upon Zeyd without thoughts of murder seizing his mind; at last they obsessed him. He schemed continually to rid himself and the world of his more successful rival. He spied upon him and upon Ateja, and at last a plan unfolded itself with opportunity treading upon its heels.

Fahd had noticed that nightly Zeyd absented himself from the gatherings of the men in the mukaad of the sheik's tent and that when the simple household duties were performed Ateja slipped out into the night. Fahd followed and confirmed what was really too apparent to be dignified by the name of suspicion—Zeyd and Ateja met.

And then one night, Fahd was not at the meeting in the sheik's beyt. Instead he hid near the tent of Zeyd, and when the latter had left to keep his tryst Fahd crept in and seized the matchlock of his rival. It was already loaded and he had but to prime it with powder. Stealthily he crept by back ways through the camp to where Zeyd awaited his light of love and sneaked up behind him.

At a little distance, sitting in his mukaad with his friends beneath the light of paper lanterns, Ibn Jad the sheik was plainly visible to the two young men standing in the outer darkness. Ateja was still in the women's quarters.

Fahd, standing behind Zeyd, raised the ancient matchlock to his shoulder and aimed—very carefully he aimed, but not at Zeyd. No, for the cunning of Fahd was as the cunning of the fox. Had Zeyd been murdered naught could ever convince Ateja that Fahd was not the murderer. Fahd knew that, and he was equally sure that Ateja would have naught of the slayer of her lover.

Beyond Zeyd was Ibn Jad, but Fahd was not aiming at Ibn Jad either. At whom was he aiming? No one. Not yet was the time ripe to slay the sheik. First must they have their hands upon the treasure, the secret of which he alone was supposed to hold.

Fahd aimed at one of the am'dan of the sheik's tent. He aimed with great care and then he pulled the trigger. The prop splintered and broke a foot above the level of Ibn Jad's head, and simultaneously Fahd threw down the musket and leaped upon the startled Zeyd, at the same time crying loudly for help.

Startled by the shot and the cries, men ran from all directions and with them was the sheik. He found Zeyd being held tightly from behind by Fahd.

"What is the meaning of this?" demanded Ibn Jad.

"By Ullah, Ibn Jad, he would have slain thee!" cried Fahd. "I came upon him just in time, and as he fired I leaped upon his back, else he would have killed you."

"He lies!" cried Zeyd. "The shot came from behind me. If any fired upon Ibn Jad it was Fahd himself."

Ateja, wide-eyed, ran to her lover. "Thou didst not do it, Zeyd; tell me that thou didst not do it."

"As Allah is my God and Mohammed his prophet I did not do it," swore Zeyd.

"I would not have thought it of him," said Ibn Jad.

Cunning, Fahd did not mention the matchlock. Shrewdly he guessed that its evidence would be more potent if discovered by another than he, and that it would be discovered he was sure. Nor was he wrong. Tollog found it.

"Here," he exclaimed, "is the weapon."

"Let us examine it beneath the light," said Ibn Jad. "It should dispel our doubts more surely than any lying tongue."

As the party moved in the direction of the sheik's beyt Zeyd experienced the relief of one reprieved from death, for he knew that the testimony of the matchlock would exonerate him. It could not be his. He pressed the hand of Ateja, walking at his side.

Beneath the light of the paper lanterns in the mukaad Ibn Jad held the weapon beneath his gaze as, with craning necks, the others pressed about him. A single glance sufficed. With stern visage the sheik raised his eyes.

"It is Zeyd's," he said.

Ateja gasped and drew away from her lover.

"I did not do it! It is some trick," cried Zeyd.

"Take him away!" commanded Ibn Jad. "See that he is tightly bound."

Ateja rushed to her father and fell upon her knees. "Do not slay him!" she cried. "It could not have been he. I know it was not he."

"Silence, girl!" commanded the sheik sternly. "Go to thy quarters and remain there!"

They took Zeyd to his own beyt and bound him securely, and in the mukaad of the sheik the elders sat in judgment while from behind the curtains of the women's quarters, Ateja listened.

"At dawn, then, he shall be shot!" This was the sentence that Ateja heard passed upon her lover.

Behind his greasy thorrib Fahd smiled a crooked smile. In his black house of hair Zeyd struggled with the bonds that held him, for though he had not heard the sentence he was aware of what his fate would be. In the quarters of the hareem of the Sheik Ibn Jad the sheik's daughter lay sleepless and suffering. Her long lashes were wet with tears but her grief was silent. Wide eyed she waited, listening, and presently her patience was rewarded by the sounds of the deep, regular breathing of Ibn Jad and his wife, Hirfa. They slept.

Ateja stirred. Stealthily she raised the lower edge of the tent cloth beside which lay her sleeping mat and rolled quietly beneath it into the mukaad, now deserted. Groping, she found the matchlock of Zeyd where Ibn Jad had left it. She carried also a bundle wrapped in an old thorrib, the contents of which she had gathered earlier in the evening when Hirfa, occupied with her duties, had been temporarily absent from the women's quarters.

Ateja emerged from the tent of her father and crept cautiously along the single, irregular street formed by the pitched tents of the 'Aarab until she came to the beyt of Zeyd. For a moment she paused at the opening, listening, then she entered softly on sandalled feet.

But Zeyd, sleepless, struggling with his bonds, heard her. "Who comes?" he damanded.

"S-s-sh!" cautioned the girl. "It is I, Ateja." She crept to his side.

"Beloved!" he murmured.

Deftly the girl cut the bonds that held his wrists and ankles. "I have brought thee food and thy musket," she told him. "These and freedom I give thee—the rest thou must do thyself. Thy mare stands tethered with the others. Far is the beled el-Guad, beset with dangers is the way, but night and day will Ateja pray to Allah to guide thee safely. Haste, my loved one!"

Zeyd pressed her tightly to his breast, kissed her and was gone into the night.

THE FLOOR of the tunnel along which Paul Bodkin conducted Blake inclined ever upwards, and again and again it was broken by flights of steps which carried them always to higher levels. To Blake the way seemed interminable. Even the haunting mystery of the long tunnel failed to overcome the monotony of its unchanging walls that slipped silently into the torch's dim ken for a brief instant and as silently back into the Cimmerian oblivion behind to make place for more wall unvaryingly identical.

But, as there ever is to all things, there was an end to the tunnel. Blake first glimpsed it in a little patch of distant daylight ahead, and presently he stepped out into the sunlight and looked out across a wide valley that was tree-dotted and beautiful. He found himself standing upon a wide ledge, or shelf, some hundred feet above the base of the mountain through which the tunnel had been cut. There was a sheer drop before him, and to his right the ledge terminated abruptly at a distance of a hundred feet or less. Then he glanced to the left and his eyes went wide in astonishment.

Across the shelf stood a solid wall of masonry flanked at either side by great, round towers pierced by long, narrow embrasures. In the center of the wall was a lofty gateway which was closed by a massive and handsomely wrought portcullis behind which Blake saw two Negroes standing guard. They were clothed precisely as his captors, but held great battle-axes, the butts of which rested upon the ground.

"What ho, the gate!" shouted Paul Bodkin. "Open to the outer guard and a prisoner!"

Slowly the portcullis rose and Blake and his captor passed beneath. Directly inside the gateway and at the left, built into the hillside, was what was evidently a guardhouse. Before it loitered a score or so of soldiers, uniformed like Paul Bodkin, upon the breast of each the red cross. To a heavy wooden rail gaily caparisoned horses were tethered, their handsome trappings recalling to Blake's memory paintings he had seen of mounted knights of medieval England.

There was so much of unreality in the strangely garbed blacks, the massive barbican that guarded the way, the trappings of the horses, that Blake was no longer capable of surprise when one of the two doors in the guardhouse opened and there stepped out a handsome young man clad in a hauberk of chain mail over which was a light surcoat of rough stuff, dyed purple. Upon the youth's head fitted a leopard skin bassinet from the lower edge of which depended a casmail or gorget of chain mail that entirely surrounded and protected his throat and neck. He was armed only with a heavy sword and a dagger, but against the side of the guardhouse, near the doorway where he paused to look at Blake, leaned a long lance, and near it was a shield with a red cross emblazoned upon its boss.

"Od zounds!" exclaimed the young man. "What has thou there, varlet?"

"A prisoner, an' it pleases thee, noble lord," replied Paul Bodkin, deferentially.

"A Saracen, of a surety," stated the young man.

"Nay, an I may make so bold, Sir Richard," replied Paul —"but me thinks he be no Saracen."

"And why?"

"With mine own eyes I didst see him make the sign before the Cross."

"Fetch him hither, lout!"

Bodkin prodded Blake in the rear with his pike, but the American scarce noticed the offense so occupied was his mind by the light of truth that had so suddenly illuminated it. In the instant he had grasped the solution. He laughed inwardly at himself for his denseness. Now he understood everything—and these fellows thought they could put it over on him, did they? Well, they had come near to doing it, all right.

He stepped quickly toward the young man and halted, upon his lips a faintly sarcastic smile. The other eyed him with haughty arrogance.

"Whence comest thou," he asked, "and what doest thou in the Valley of the Sepulcher, varlet?"

Blake's smile faded—too much was too much. "Cut the comedy, young fellow," he drawled in his slow way. "Where's the director?"

"Director? Forsooth, I know not what thou meanest."

"Yes you don't!" snapped Blake, with fine sarcasm. "But

let me tell you right off the bat that no seven-fifty a day extra
can pull anything like that with me!"

"Od's blud, fellow! I ken not the meaning of all the words,
but I mislike thy tone. It savors o'er much of insult to fall
sweetly upon the ears of Richard Montmorency."

· "Be yourself," advised Blake. "If the director isn't handy
send for the assistant director, or the camera man—even the
continuity writer may have more sense than you seem to have."

"Be myself? And who thinkest thee I would be other than
Richard Montmorency, a noble knight of Nimmr."

Blake shook his head in despair, then he turned to the soldiers who were standing about listening to the conversation.
He thought some of them would be grinning at the joke that
was being played on him, but he saw only solemn, serious
faces.

"Look here," he said, addressing Paul Bodkin, "don't any of
you know where the director is?"

" 'Director'?" repeated Bodkin, shaking his head. "There
be none in Nimmr thus y-clept, nay, nor in all the Valley of
the Sepulcher that I wot."

"I'm sorry," said Blake, "the mistake is mine; but if there
is no director there must be a keeper. May I see him?"

"Ah, keeper!" cried Bodkin, his face lighting with under-
standing. "Sir Richard is the keeper."

"My gawd!" exclaimed Blake, turning to the young man. "I
beg your pardon, I thought that you were one of the inmates."

"Inmates? Indeed thou speakest a strange tongue and yet
withall it hath the flavor of England," replied the young man
gravely. "But yon varlet be right—I am indeed this day the
Keeper of the Gate."

Blake was commencing to doubt his own sanity, or at least
his judgment. Neither the young white man nor any of the
Negroes had any of their facial characteristics of mad men.
He looked up suddenly at the keeper of the gate.

"I am sorry," he said, flashing one of the frank smiles that
was famous amongst his acquaintants. "I have acted like a
boor, but I've been under considerable of a nervous strain
for a long time, and on top of that I've been lost in the jungle
for days without proper or sufficient food.

"I thought that you were trying to play some sort of a joke
on me and, well, I wasn't in any mood for jokes when I expected friendship and hospitality instead.

"Tell me, where am I? What country is this?"

"Thou art close upon the city of Nimmr," replied the
young man.

"I suppose this is something of a national holiday or something?" suggested Blake.

"I do not understand thee," replied the young man.

"Why, you're all in a pageant or something, aren't you?"

"Od's bodikins! the fellow speaks an outlandish tongue! Pageant?"

"Yes, those costumes."

"What be amiss with this apparel? True, 'tis not of any wondrous newness, but methinks it be at least more fair than thine. At least it well suffices the daily service of a knight."

"You don't mean that you dress like this every day?" demanded Blake.

"And why not? But enough of this. I have no wish to further bandy words with thee. Fetch him within, two of thee. And thou, Bodkin, return to the outer guard!" The young man turned and re-entered the building, while two of the soldiers seized Blake, none too gently, and hustled him within.

He found himself in a high-ceiled room with walls of cut stone and great, hand-hewn beams and rafters blackened with age. Upon the stone floor stood a table behind which, upon a bench, the young man seated himself while Blake was placed facing him with a guard on either hand.

"Thy name," demanded the young man.

"Blake."

"That be all—just Blake?"

"James Hunter Blake."

"What title bearest thou in thine own country?"

"I have no title."

"Ah, thou art not a gentleman, then?"

"I am called one."

"What is thy country?"

"America."

"America! There is no such country, fellow."

"And why not?"

"I never heard of it. What doest thou near the Valley of the Sepulcher? Didst not know 'tis forbidden?"

"I told you I was lost. I didn't know where I was. All I want is to get back to my safari or to the coast."

"That be impossible. We be surrounded by Saracens. For seven hundred and thirty-five years we have been invested by their armies. How come you through the enemies' lines? How passed you through his vast army?"

"There isn't any army."

"Givest thou the lie to Richard Montmorency, varlet? An' thou wert of gentle blood thou shouldst account to me that insult upon the field of honor. Methink'st thou beest some low-born spy sent hither by the Saracen sultan. 'Twould be well an thou confessed all to me, for if I take thee before the Prince he will wrest the truth from thee in ways that are far from pleasant. What say?"

"I have nothing to confess. Take me before the Prince, or whoever your boss is; perhaps he will at least give me food."

"Thou shalt have food here. Never shall it be said that Richard Montmorency turned a hungry man from his doorway Hey! Michel! Michel! Where is the lazy brat? Michel!"

A door opened from an inner apartment to admit a boy, sleepy eyed, digging a grimy fist into one eye. He was clothed in a short tunic, his legs encased in green tights. In his cap was a feather.

"Sleeping again, eh?" demanded Sir Richard. "Thou lazy knave! Fetch bread and meat for this poor wayfarer and be not until the morrow at it!"

Wide-eyed and rather stupidly, the boy stared at Blake. "A Saracen, master?" he asked.

"What boots it?" snapped Sir Richard. "Did not our Lord Jesus feed the multitude, nor ask if there were unbelievers among them? Haste, churl! The stranger be of great hunger."

The youth turned and shuffled from the room, wiping his nose upon his sleeve, and Sir Richard's attention came back to Blake.

"Thou are not ill-favored, fellow," he said. " 'Tis a pity that thou beest not of noble blood, for thy mien appearth not like that of one lowborn."

"I never considered myself lowborn," said Blake, with a grin.

"Thy father, now—was he not at least a sir knight?"

Blake was thinking quickly now. He was far from being able as yet to so much as hazard a guess that might explain his host's archaic costume and language, but he was sure that the man was in earnest, whether sane or not, and were he not sane it seemed doubly wise to humor him.

"Yes, indeed," he replied, "my father is a thirty second degree Mason and a Knight Templar."

"Sblud! I knew it," cried Sir Richard.

"And so am I," added Blake, when he realized the happy effect his statement had produced.

"Ah, I knew it! I knew it!" cried Sir Richard. "Thy bearing proclaimed thy noble blood; but why didst thou seek to deceive me? And so thou are one of the poor Knights of Christ and of the Temple of Solomon who guard the way of the pilgrims to

the Holy Land! This explaineth thy poor raiment and glorifies
it."

Blake was mystified by the allusion, as the picture always
suggested by a reference to Knights Templar was of waving
white plumes, gorgeous aprons and glittering swords. He did
not know that in the days of their origin they were clothed in
any old garments that the charity of others might bequeath
them.

At this moment Michel returned bearing a wooden trencher
containing cold mutton and several pieces of simnel bread and
carrying in one hand a flagon of wine. These he set upon the
table before Blake and going to a cupboard fetched two metal
goblets into which he decanted a portion of the contents of
the flagon.

Sir Richard arose and taking one of the goblets raised it before him on a level with his head.

"Hal, Sir James!" he cried, "and welcome to Nimmr and
the Valley of the Sepulcher!"

"Here's looking at you!" replied Blake.

"A quaint saying," remarked Sir Richard. "Methinks the
ways of England must be changed since the days of Richard
the Lion Hearted when my noble ancestor set forth upon the
great crusade in the company of his king. Here's looking at
you! Ods bodikins! I must not let that from my memory.
Here's looking at you! Just wait thou 'til some fair knight doth
drink my health——I shall lay him flat with that!

"But, stay! Here, Michel, fetch yon stool for Sir James, and
eat, sir knight. Thou must be passing hungry."

"I'll tell the world I am," replied Blake, feelingly, as he sat
down on the stool that Michel brought. There were no knives
or forks, but there were fingers and these Blake used to advantage while his host sat smiling happily at him from across the
rude table.

"Thou art better than a minstrel for pleasure," cried Sir
Richard. "I'll tell the world I am! Ho, ho! Thou wilt be a gift
from heaven in the castle of the prince. I'll tell the world I am!"

When Blake had satisfied his hunger, Sir Richard ordered
Michel to prepare horses. "We ride down to the castle, Sir
James," he explained. "No longer art thou my prisoner, but
my friend and guest. That I should have received thee so
scurvily shalt ever be to my discredit."

Mounted upon prancing chargers and followed at a respect-
ful distance by Michel, the two rode down the winding mountain road. Sir Richard now carried his shield and lance, a
pennon fluttering bravely in the wind from just below the tip

of the latter, the sun glancing from the metal of his hauberk, a smile upon his brave face as he chattered with his erstwhile prisoner. To Blake he seemed a gorgeous picture ridden from out the pages of a story book. Yet, belying his martial appearance, there was a childlike simplicity about the man that won Blake's liking from the first, for there was that about him that made it impossible for one to conceive him as the perpetrator of a dishonorable act.

His ready acceptance of Blake's statements about himself bespoke a credulity that seemed incompatible with the high intelligence reflected by his noble countenance, and the American preferred to attribute it to a combination of unsophistication and an innate integrity which could not conceive of perfidy in others.

As the road rounded the shoulder of a hill, Blake saw another barbican barring the way and, beyond, the towers and battlements of an ancient castle. At a command from Sir Richard the warders of the gate opened to them and the three rode through into the ballium. This space between the outer and inner walls appeared unkept and neglected. Several old trees flourished within it and beneath the shade of one of these, close to the outer gateway, lolled several men-at-arms, two of whom were engaged in a game that resembled draughts.

At the foot of the inner wall was a wide moat, the waters of which reflected the gray stones of the wall and the ancient vines that, growing upon its inner side, topped it to form a leaf coping that occasionally hung low upon the outer side.

Directly opposite the barbican was the great gateway in the inner wall and here a drawbridge spanned the moat and a heavy portcullis barred the way into the great court of the castle; but at a word from Sir Richard the gate lifted and, clattering across the drawbridge, they rode within.

Before Blake's astonished eyes loomed a mighty castle of rough hewn stone, while to the right and left, within the great court, spread broad gardens not illy kept, in which were gathered a company of men and women who might have just stepped from Arthur's court.

At sight of Sir Richard and his companion the nearer members of the company regarded Blake with interest and evident surprise. Several called greetings and questions to Sir Richard as the two men dismounted and turned their horses over to Michel.

"Ho, Richard!" cried one. "What bringest thou—a Saracen?"

"Nay," replied Richard. "A fair sir knight who would do his devoir to the prince. Where be he?"

"Yonder," and they pointed toward the far end of the court where a large company was assembled.

"Come, Sir James!" directed Richard, and led him down the courtyard, the knights and ladies following closely, asking questions, commenting with a frankness that brought a flush to Blake's face. The women openly praised his features and his carriage while the men, perhaps prompted by jealousy, made unflattering remarks about his soiled and torn apparel and its, to them, ridiculous cut; and indeed the contrast was great between their gorgeous dalmaticas of villosa or cyclas, their close fitting tights, their colored caps and Blake's drab shirt, whipcord breeches and cordovan boots, now soiled, torn and scratched.

The women were quite as richly dressed as the men, wearing clinging mantles of rich stuff, their hair and shoulders covered with dainty wimples of various colors and often elaborately embroidered.

None of these men, nor any of those in the assemblage they were approaching wore armor, but Blake had seen an armored knight at the outer gateway and another at the inner and he judged that only when engaged in military duties did they wear this heavy and uncomfortable dress.

When they reached the party at the end of the court Sir Richard elbowed his way among them to the center of the group where stood a tall man of imposing appearance, chatting with those about him. As Sir Richard and Blake halted before him the company fell silent.

"My lord prince," said Richard, bowing, "I bring thee Sir James, a worthy Knight Templar who hath come under the protection of God through the lines of the enemy to the gates of Nimmr."

The tall man eyed Blake searchingly and he had not the appearance of great credulity.

"Thou sayest that thou comest from the Temple of Solomon in the Kingdom of Jerusalem?" he demanded.

"Sir Richard must have misunderstood me," replied Blake.

"Then thou art no Knight Templar?"

"Yes, but I am not from Jerusalem."

"Perchance he is one of those doughty sir knights that guard the pilgrims' way to the Holy Land," suggested a young woman standing near the prince.

Blake glanced quickly at the speaker and as their eyes met,

hers fell, but not before he had seen that they were very beautiful eyes set in an equally beautiful, oval face.

"More like it haps he be a Saracen spy sent among us by
the sultan," snapped a dark man who stood beside the girl.

The latter raised her eyes to the prince. "He looketh not
like a Saracen, my father," she said.

"What knowest thou of the appearance of a Saracen, child?"
demanded the prince. "Hast seen so many?" The party laughed
and the girl pouted.

"Verily an' I hast seen full as many a Saracen as has Sir
Malud or thyself, my lord prince," she snapped, haughtily.
"Let Sir Malud describe a Saracen."

The dark young man flushed angrily. "At least," he said,
"my lord prince, I knowest an English knight when I seest one,
an' if here be an English knight then Sir Malud be a Saracen!"

"Enough," said the prince and then, turning to Blake:
"If thou art not from Jerusalem where art thou from?"

"New York," replied the American.

"Ha," whispered Sir Malud to the girl, "didst I not tell
you?"

"Tell me what—that he is from New York? Where is that?"
she demanded.

"Some stronghold of the infidel," asserted Malud.

"New York?" repeated the prince. "Be that in the Holy
Land?"

"It is sometimes called New Jerusalem," explained Blake.

"And thou comest to Nimmr through the lines of the enemy?
Tell me, sir knight, had they many men-at-arms? And how
were their forces disposed? Be they close upon the Valley of
the Sepulcher? Thinkest thou they plan an early attack? Come,
tell me all—thou canst be of great service."

"I have come for days through the forest and seen no living
man," said Blake. "No enemy surrounds you."

"What?" cried the prince.

"Didst I not tell thee?" demanded Malud. "He is an enemy
spy. He wouldst lead us into the belief that we are safe that
the forces of the sultan may find us off our guard and take
Nimmr and the Valley."

"Ods blud! Methinks thou beest right, Sur Malud," cried the
prince. "No enemy indeed! Why else then hast the knights of
Nimmr lain here seven and a half centuries if there be no
horde of infidels surrounding our stronghold?"

"Search me," said Blake.

"Eh, what?" demanded the prince.

"He hath a quaint manner of speech, my lord prince," explained Richard, "but I do not think him an enemy of England. Myself will vouch for him an' you will take him into your service, my lord prince."

"Wouldst enter my service, sir?" demanded the prince.

Blake glanced at Sir Malud and looked dubious—then his eyes wandered to those of the girl. "I'll tell the world I would!" he said.

This one is really too far out - this has not the restraint & level headedness of The Madman, which was a good adventure yarn. This is silly, and rather than bizarre, it's preposterous. I hope it's not his usual. enough

10

The Return of Ulala

NUMA was hungry. For three days and three nights he had hunted but always the prey had eluded him. Perhaps Numa was growing old. Not so keen were his scent and his vision, not so swift his charges, nor well timed the spring that heretofore had brought down the quarry. So quick the food of Numa that a fraction of a second, a hair's breadth, might mark the difference between a full belly and starvation.

Perhaps Numa was growing old, yet he still was a mighty engine of destruction, and now the pangs of hunger had increased his ferocity many-fold, stimulated his cunning, emboldened him to take great risks that his belly might be filled. It was a nervous, irascible, ferocious Numa that crouched beside the trail. His up-pricked ears, his intent and blazing eyes, his quivering nostrils, the gently moving tail-tip, evidenced his awareness of another presence.

Down the wind to the nostrils of Numa the lion came the man-scent. Four days ago, his belly full, Numa had doubtless slunk away at the first indication of the presence of man, but today is another day and another Numa.

Zeyd, three days upon the back track from the menzil of the sheik Ibn Jad, thought of Ateja, of far Guad, congratulated himself upon the good fortune that had thus far smiled upon his escape and flight. His mare moved slowly along the jungle trail, unurged, for the way was long; and just ahead a beast of prey waited in ambush.

But Numa's were not the only ears to hear, nor his nostrils the only nostrils to scent the coming of the man-thing—another beast crouched near, unknown to Numa.

Overanxious, fearful of being cheated of his meat, Numa made a false move. Down the trail came the mare. She must pass within a yard of Numa, but Numa could not wait. Before she was within the radius of his spring he charged, voicing a horrid roar. Terrified the mare reared and, rearing, tried to turn and bolt. Overbalanced, she toppled backward and fell, and in falling unhorsed Zeyd; but in the instant she was up and flying back along the trail, leaving her master in the path of the charging lion.

Horrified, the man saw the snarling face, the bared fangs almost upon him. Then he saw something else—something equally awe-inspiring—a naked giant who leaped from a swaying branch full upon the back of the great cat. He saw a bronzed arm encircle the neck of the beast of prey as the lion was borne to earth by the weight and impact of the man's body. He saw a heavy knife flashing in the air, striking home again and again as the frenzied lion threw itself about in futile effort to dislodge the thing upon its back. He heard the roars and the growls of el adrea, and mingled with them were growls and snarls that turned his blood cold, for he saw that they came from the lips of the man-beast.

Then Numa went limp and the giant arose and stood above the carcass. He placed one foot upon it and, raising his face toward the heavens, voiced a hideous scream that froze the marrow in the bones of the Beduin—a scream that few men have heard: the victory cry of the bull ape.

It was then that Zeyd recognized his saviour and shuddered again as he saw that it was Tarzan of the Apes. The ape-man looked down at him.

"Thou art from the menzil of Ibn Jad," he said.

"I am but a poor man," replied Zeyd. "I but followed where my sheykh led. Hold it not against Zeyd sheykh of the jungle, that he be in thy beled. Spare my poor life I pray thee and may Allah bless thee."

"I have no wish to harm thee, Beduwy," replied Tarzan. "What wrong hath been done in my country is the fault of Ibn Jad alone. Is he close by?"

"Wellah nay, he be many marches from here."

"Where art thy companions?" demanded the ape-man.

"I have none."

"Thou art alone?"

"Billah, yes."

Tarzan frowned. "Think well Beduwy before lying to Tarzan," he snapped.

"By Ullah, I speak the truth! I am alone."

"And why?"

"Fahd did plot against me to make it appear that I had tried to take the life of Ibn Jad, which, before Allah, is a lie that stinketh to heaven, and I was to be shot; but Ateja, the daughter of the sheykh, cut my bonds in the night and I escaped."

"What is thy name?"

"Zeyd."

"Whither goest thou—to thine own country?"

"Yes, to beled el-Guad, a Beny Salem fendy of el-Harb."

"Thou canst not, alone, survive the perils of the way," Tarzan warned him.

"Of that I be fearful, but death were certain had I not escaped the wrath of Ibn Jad."

For a moment Tarzan was silent in thought. "Great must be the love of Ateja, the daughter of the sheik, and great her belief in you," he said.

"Wellah, yes, great is our love and, too, she knew that I would not slay her father, whom she loves."

Tarzan nodded. "I believe thee and shall help thee. Thou canst not go on alone. I shall take thee to the nearest village and there the chief will furnish you with warriors who will take you to the next village, and thus from village to village you will be escorted to the Soudan."

"May Allah ever watch over and guard thee!" exclaimed Zeyd.

"Tell me," said Tarzan as the two moved along the jungle trail in the direction of the nearest village which lay two marches to the south of them, "tell me what Ibn Jad doth in this country. It is not true that he came for ivory alone. Am I not right?"

"Wellah yes, Sheykh Tarzan," admitted Zeyd. "Ibn Jad came for treasure, but not for ivory."

"What, then?"

"In el-Habash lies the treasure city of Nimmr," explained Zeyd. "This Ibn Jad was told by a learned sahar. So great is the wealth of Nimmr that a thousand camels could carry away not a tenth part of it. It consists of gold and jewels and—a woman."

"A woman?"

"Yes, a woman of such wondrous beauty that in the north she alone would bring a price that would make Ibn Jad rich beyond dreams. Surely thou must have heard of Nimmr."

"Sometimes the Gallas speak of it," said Tarzan, "but always I thought it of no more reality than the other places of their legends. And Ibn Jad undertook this long and dangerous journey on no more than the word of a magician?"

"What could be better than the word of a learned sahar?" demanded Zeyd.

Tarzan of the Apes shrugged.

During the two days that it took them to reach the village Tarzan learned of the white man who had come to the camp

of Ibn Jad, but from Zeyd's description of him he was not
positive whether it was Blake or Stimbol.

As Tarzan travelled south with Zeyd, Ibn Jad trekked
northward into el-Habash, and Fahd plotted with Tollog, and
Stimbol plotted with Fahd, while Fejjuan the Galla slave
waited patiently for the moment of his delivery from bondage,
and Ateja mourned for Zeyd.

"As a boy thou wert raised in this country, Fejjuan," she
said one day to the Galla slave. "Tell me, dost thou think Zeyd
could make his way alone to el-Guad?"

"Billah, nay," replied the black. "Doubtless he be dead by
now."

The girl stifled a sob.

"Fejjuan mourns with thee, Ateja," said the black, "for
Zeyd was a kindly man. Would that Allah had spared your
lover and taken him who was guilty."

"What do you mean?" asked Ateja. "Knowest thou, Fejjuan,
who fired the shot at Ibn Jad, my father? It was not Zeyd! Tell
me it was not Zeyd! But thy words tell me that, which I well
knew before. Zeyd could not have sought the life of my father!"

"Nor did he," replied Fejjuan.

"Tell me what you know of this thing."

"And you will not tell another who told you?" he asked.
"It would go hard with me if one I am thinking of knew that
I had seen what I did see."

"I swear by Allah that I wilt not betray you, Fejjuan," cried
the girl. "Tell me, what didst thou see?"

"I did not see who fired the shot at thy father, Ateja," replied the black, "but something else I saw before the shot was
fired."

"Yes, what was it?"

"I saw Fahd creep into the beyt of Zeyd and come out
again bearing Zeyd's matchlock. That I saw."

"I knew it! I knew it!" cried the girl.

"But Ibn Jad will not believe if you tell him."

"I know; but now that I am convinced perhaps I shall
find a way to have Fahd's blood for the blood of Zeyd," cried
the girl, bitterly.

For days Ibn Jad skirted the mountains behind which he
thought lay the fabled city of Nimmr as he searched for an
entrance which he hoped to find without having recourse to the
natives whose haunts he had sedulously avoided lest through
them opposition to his venture might develop.

The country was sparsely settled, which rendered it easy for the 'Aarab to avoid coming into close contact with the natives, though it was impossible that the Gallas were ignorant of their presence. If however the blacks were willing to leave them alone, Ibn Jad had no intention of molesting them unless he found that it would be impossible to carry his project to a successful issue without their assistance, in which event he was equally ready to approach them with false promises or ruthless cruelty, whichever seemed the more likely to better serve his purpose.

As the days passed Ibn Jad waxed increasingly impatient, for, search as he would, he could locate no pass across the mountains, nor any entrance to the fabled valley wherein lay the treasure city of Nimmr.

"Billah!" he exclaimed one day, "there be a City of Nimmr and there be an entrance to it, and, by Allah, I will find it! Summon the Habush, Tollog! From them or through them we shall have a clew in one way or another."

When Tollog had fetched the Galla slaves to the beyt of Ibn Jad, the old sheik questioned them but there was none who had definite knowledge of the trail leading to Nimmr.

"Then, by Allah," exclaimed Ibn Jad, "we shall have it from the native Habush!"

"They be mighty warriors, O brother," cried Tollog, "and we be far within their country. Should we anger them and they set upon us it might fare ill with us."

"We be Bedauwy," said Ibn Jad proudly, "and we be armed with muskets. What could their simple spears and arrows avail against us?"

"But they be many and we be few," insisted Tollog.

"We shall not fight unless we be driven to it," said Ibn Jad. "First we shall seek, by friendly overtures, to win their confidence and cajole the secret from them.

"Fejjuan!" he exclaimed, turning to the great black. "Thou are a Habashy. I have heard thee say that thou well rememberest the days of thy childhood in the hut of thy father and the story of Nimmr was no new story to you. Go, then, and seek out thy people. Make friends with them. Tell them that the great Sheykh Ibn Jad comes among them in friendliness and that he hath gifts for their chiefs. Tell them also that he would visit the city of Nimmr, and if they will lead him there he will reward them well."

"I but await thy commands," said Fejjuan, elated at this opportunity to do what he had long dreamed of doing. "When shall I set forth?"

"Prepare thyself tonight and when dawn comes depart," replied the sheik.

And so it was that Fejjuan, the Galla slave, set forth early the following morning from the menzil of Ibn Jad, sheik of the fendy el-Guad, to search for a village of his own people.

By noon he had come upon a well-worn trail leading toward the west, and this he followed boldly, guessing that he would best disarm suspicion thus than by attempting to approach a Galla village by stealth. Also he well knew that there was little likelihood that he could accomplish the latter in any event. Fejjuan was no fool. He knew that it might be difficult to convince the Gallas that he was of their blood, for there was against him not alone his 'Aarab garments and weapons but the fact that he would be able to speak the Galla tongue but lamely after all these years.

That he was a brave man was evidenced by the fact that he well knew the suspicious and warlike qualities of his people and their inborn hatred of the 'Aarab and yet gladly embraced this opportunity to go amongst them.

How close he had approached a village Fejjuan did not know. There were neither sounds nor odors to enlighten him when there suddenly appeared in the trail ahead of him three husky Galla warriors and behind him he heard others, though he did not turn.

Instantly Fejjuan raised his hands in sign of peace and at the same time he smiled.

"What are you doing in the Galla country?" demanded one of the warriors.

"I am seeking the house of my father," replied Fejjuan.

"The house of your father is not in the country of the Gallas, growled the warrior. "You are one of these who come to rob us of our sons and daughters."

"No," replied Fejjuan. "I am a Galla."

"If you were a Galla you would speak the language of the Gallas better. We understand you, but you do not speak as a Galla speaks."

"That is because I was stolen away when I was a child and have lived among the Bedauwy since, speaking only their tongue."

"What is your name?"

"The Bedauwy call me Fejjuan, but my Galla name was Ulala."

"Do you think he speaks the truth?" demanded one of the blacks of a companion. "When I was a child I had a brother whose name was Ulala."

"Where is he?" asked the other warrior.

"We do not know. Perhaps simba the lion devoured him. Perhaps the desert people took him. Who knows?"

"Perhaps he speaks the truth," said the second warrior. "Perhaps he is your brother. Ask him his father's name."

"What was your father's name?" demanded the first warrior.

"Naliny," replied Fejjuan.

At this reply the Galla warriors became excited and whispered among themselves for several seconds. Then the first warrior turned again to Fejjuan.

"Did you have a brother?" he demanded.

"Yes," replied Fejjuan.

"What was his name?"

"Tabo," answered Fejjuan without hesitation.

The warrior who had questioned him leaped into the air with a wild shout.

"It is Ulala!" he cried. "It is my brother. I am Tabo, Ulala. Do you not remember me?"

"Tabo!" cried Fejjuan. "No, I would not know you, for you were a little boy when I was stolen away and now you are a great warrior. Where are our father and mother? Are they alive? Are they well?"

"They are alive and well, Ulala," replied Tabo. "Today they are in the village of the chief, for there is a great council because of the presence of some desert people in our country. Came you with them?"

"Yes, I am a slave to the desert people," replied Fejjuan. "Is it far to the village of the chief? I would see my mother and my father and, too, I would talk with the chief about the desert people who have come to the country of the Gallas."

"Come, brother!" cried Tabo. "We are not far from the village of the chief. Ah, my brother, that I should see you again whom we thought to be dead all these years! Great will be the joy of our father and mother.

"But, tell me, have the desert people turned you against your own people? You have lived with them many years. Perhaps you have taken a wife among them. Are you sure that you do not love them better than you love those whom you have not seen for many years?"

"I do not love the Bedauwy," replied Fejjuan, "nor have I taken a wife among them. Always in my heart has been the hope of returning to the mountains of my own country, to the house of my father. I love my own people, Tabo. Never again shall I leave them."

"The desert people have been unkind to you—they have treated you with cruelty?" demanded Tabo.

"Nay, on the contrary they have treated me well," replied Fejjuan. "I do not hate them, but neither do I love them. They are not of my own blood. I am a slave among them."

As they talked the party moved along the trail toward the village while two of the warriors ran ahead to carry the glad tidings to the father and mother of the long missing Ulala. And so it was that when they came within sight of the village they were met by a great crowd of laughing, shouting Gallas, and in the forerank were the father and mother of Fejjuan, their eyes blinded by the tears of love and joy that welled at sight of this long gone child.

After the greetings were over, and every man, woman and child in the company must crowd close and touch the returned wanderer, Tabo conducted Fejjuan into the village and the presence of the chief.

Batando was an old man. He had been chief when Ulala was stolen away. He was inclined to be skeptical, fearing a ruse of the desert people, and he asked many questions of Fejjuan concerning matters that he might hold in his memory from the days of his childhood. He asked him about the house of his father and the names of his playmates and other intimate things that an impostor might not know, and when he had done he arose and took Fejjuan in his arms and rubbed his cheek against the cheek of the prodigal.

"You are indeed Ulala," he cried. "Welcome back to the land of your people. Tell me now what the desert people do here. Have they come for slaves?"

"The desert people will always take slaves when they can get them, but Ibn Jad has not come first for slaves, but for treasure."

"Ai! what treasure?" demanded Batando.

"He has heard of the treasure city of Nimmr," replied Fejjuan. "It is a way into the valley where lies Nimmr that he seeks. For this he sent me to find Gallas who would lead him to Nimmr. He will make gifts and he promises rich rewards when he shall have wrested the treasure from Nimmr."

"Are these true words?" asked Batando.

"There is no truth in the beards of the desert dwellers," replied Fejjuan.

"And if he does not find the treasure of Nimmr perhaps he will try to find treasure and slaves in the Galla country to repay the expense of the long journey he has undertaken from the desert country?" asked Batando.

"Batando speaks out of the great wisdom of many years," replied Fejjuan.

"What does he know of Nimmr?" asked the old chief.

"Naught other than what an old medicine man of the 'Aarab told him," replied Fejjuan. "He said to Ibn Jad that great treasure lay hoarded in the City of Nimmr and that there was a beautiful woman who would bring a great price in the far north."

"Nothing more he told him?" demanded Batando. "Did he not tell him of the difficulties of entering the forbidden valley?"

"Nay."

"Then we can guide him to the entrance to the valley," said Batando, smiling slyly.

A S TARZAN and Zeyd journeyed toward the village in
which the ape-man purposed to enlist an escort for the
Arab upon the first stage of his return journey toward
his desert home, the Beduin had time to meditate much
upon many matters, and having come to trust and respect his
savage guide he at last unbosomed himself to Tarzan.

"Great Sheykh of the Jungle," he said one day, "by thy
kindness thou hast won the undying loyalty of Zeyd who begs
that thou wilt grant him one more favor."

"And what is that?" asked the ape-man.

"Ateja, whom I love, remains here in the savage country in
constant danger so long as Fahd be near her. I dare not now
return to the menzil of Ibn Jad even could I find it, but later,
when the heat of Ibn Jad's anger will have had time to cool,
then I might come again among them and convince him of
my innocence, and be near Ateja and protect her from Fahd."

"What, then, would you do?" demanded Tarzan.

"I would remain in the village to which you are taking me
until Ibn Jad returns this way toward el-Guad. It is the only
chance that I have to see Ateja again in this life, as I could
not cross the Soudan alone and on foot should you compel me
to leave your country now."

"You are right," replied the ape-man. "You shall remain
here six months. If Ibn Jad has not returned in that time I
shall leave word that you be sent to my home. From there I
can find a way to return you in safety to your own country."

"May the blessings of Allah be upon thee!" cried Zeyd.

And when they came at last to the village Tarzan received
the promise of the chief to keep Zeyd until Ibn Jad returned.

After he had left the village again the ape-man headed
north, for he was concerned over the report that Zeyd had
given him of the presence of a European prisoner among the
'Aarab. That Stimbol, whom he had sent eastward toward the
coast, should be so far north and west as Zeyd had reported
appeared inconceivable, and so it seemed more probable that

the prisoner was young Blake, for whom Tarzan had conceived a liking. Of course the prisoner might not be either Stimbol or Blake, but who ever he was Tarzan could not readily brook the idea of a white man being permitted to remain a prisoner of the Beduins.

But Tarzan was in no hurry, for Zeyd had told him that the prisoner was to be held for ransom. He would have a look about for Blake's camp first and then follow up the spoor of the Arabs. His progress, therefore, was leisurely. On the second day he met the apes of Toyat and for two days he hunted with them, renewing his acquaintance with Gayat and Zutho, listening to the gossip of the tribe, often playing with the balus.

Leaving them, he loafed on through the jungle, stopping once for half a day to bait Numa where he lay upon a fresh kill, until the earth trembled to the thunderous roars of the maddened king of beasts as the ape-man taunted and annoyed him.

Sloughed was the thin veneer of civilization that was Lord Greystoke; back to the primitive, back to the savage beast the ape-man reverted as naturally, as simply, as one changes from one suit to another. It was only in his beloved jungle, surrounded by its savage denizens, that Tarzan of the Apes was truly Tarzan, for always in the presence of civilized men there was a certain restraint that was the outcome of that inherent suspicion that creatures of the wild ever feel for man.

Tired of throwing ripe fruit at Numa, Tarzan swung away through the middle terraces of the forest, lay up for the night far away and in the morning, scenting Bara the deer, made a kill and fed. Lazy, he slept again, until the breaking of twigs and the rustle of down tramped grasses awoke him.

He sniffed the air with sensitive nostrils and listened with ears that could hear an ant walk, and then he smiled. Tantor was coming.

For half a day he lolled on the huge back, listening to Manu the Monkey chattering and scolding among the trees. Then he moved on again.

A day or two later he came upon a large band of monkeys. They seemed much excited and at sight of him they all commenced to jabber and chatter.

"Greetings, Manu!" cried the ape-man. "I am Tarzan, Tarzan of the Apes. What happens in the jungle?"

"Gomangani! Gomangani!" cried one.

"Strange Gomangani!" cried another.

"Gomangani with thunder sticks!" chattered a third.

"Where?" asked the ape-man.

"There! There!" they shouted in chorus, pointing toward the northeast.

"Many sleeps away?" asked Tarzan.

"Close! Close!" the monkeys answered.

"There is one Tarmangani with them?"

"No, only Gomangani. With their thunder sticks they kill little Manu and eat him. Bad Gomangani!"

"Tarzan will talk with them," said the ape-man.

"They will kill Tarzan with their thunder sticks and eat him," prophesied a graybeard.

The ape-man laughed and swung off through the trees in the direction Manu had indicated. He had not gone far when the scent spoor of blacks came faintly to his nostrils and this spoor he followed until presently he could hear their voices in the distance.

Silently, warily Tarzan came through the trees, noiseless as the shadows that kept him company, until he stood upon a swaying limb directly above a camp of Negroes.

Instantly Tarzan recognized the safari of the young American, Blake, and a second later he dropped to the ground before the astonished eyes of the blacks. Some of them would have run, but others recognized him.

"It is Big Bwana!" they cried. "It is Tarzan of the Apes!"

"Where is your head man?" demanded Tarzan.

A stalwart Negro approached him. "I am head man," he said.

"Where is your master?"

"He is gone, many days," replied the black.

"Where?"

"We do not know. He hunted with a single askar. There was a great storm. Neither of them ever returned. We searched the jungle for them, but could not find them. We waited in camp where they were to have joined us. They did not come. We did not know what to do. We would not desert the young Bwana, who was kind to us; but we feared that he was dead. We have not provisions to last more than another moon. We decided to return home and tell our story to the friends of the young Bwana."

"You have done well," said Tarzan. "Have you seen a company of the desert people in the jungle?"

"We have not seen them," replied the head man, "but while we were searching for the young Bwana we saw where desert people had camped. It was a fresh camp."

"Where?"

The black pointed. "It was on the trail to the north Galla country in Abyssinia and when they broke camp they went north."

"You may return to your village," said Tarzan, "but first take those things which are the young Bwana's to his friends to keep for him and send a runner to the home of Tarzan with this message: Send one hundred Waziri to Tarzan in the north Galla country. From the water hole of the smooth, round rocks follow the trail of the desert people."

"Yes, Big Bwana, it will be done," said the head man.

"Repeat my message."

The black boy did as he was bidden.

"Good!" said Tarzan. "I go. Kill not Manu the monkey if you can find other food, for Manu is the cousin of Tarzan and of you."

"We understand, Big Bwana."

In the castle of Prince Gobred in the City of Nimmr James Hunter Blake was being schooled in the duties of a Knight of Nimmr. Sir Richard had taken him under his protection and made himself responsible for his training and his conduct.

Prince Gobred, quick to realize Blake's utter ignorance of even the simplest observances of knighthood, was frankly skeptical, and Sir Malud was almost openly antagonistic, but the loyal Sir Richard was a well beloved knight and so he had his way. Perhaps, too, the influence of the Princess Guinalda was not without its effect upon her sire, for first among the treasurers of the Prince of Nimmr ranked his daughter Guinalda; and Guinalda's curiosity and interest had been excited by the romance of the coming of this fair stranger knight to the buried and forgotten city of Nimmr.

Sir Richard had clothed Blake from his own wardrobe until a weaver, a cutter of cloth, a seamstress and an armorer could fashion one for him. Nor did it take long. A week found Sir James clothed, armored and horsed as befitted a Knight of Nimmr, and when he spoke to Sir Richard of payment for all this he found that money was almost unknown among them. There were, Sir Richard told him, a few pieces of coin that their ancestors had brought here seven hundred and thirty five years before, but payment was made by service.

The knights served the prince and he kept them. They protected the laborers and the artisans and in return received what they required from them. The slaves received their food and clothing from the prince or from whichever knight they served. Jewels and precious metals often changed hands in return for goods or service, but each transaction was a matter of barter as there were no standards of value.

They cared little for wealth. The knights valued most highly their honor and their courage upon which there could be no price. The artisan found his reward in the high perfection of his handicraft and in the honors that it brought him.

The valley provided food in plenty for all; the slaves tilled the ground; the freedmen were the artisans, the men-at-arms, the herders of cattle; the knights defended Nimmr against its enemies, competed in tourneys and hunted wild game in the valley and its surrounding mountains.

As the days passed Blake found himself rapidly acquiring a certain proficiency in knightly arts under the wise tutorage of Sir Richard. The use of sword and buckler he found most difficult, notwithstanding the fact that he had been proficient with the foils in his college days, for the knights of Nimmr knew naught of the defensive use of their two edged weapons and seldom used the point for other purpose than the *coup-de-grace*. For them the sword was almost wholly a cutting weapon, the buckler their sole defense; but as Blake practiced with this weapon it dawned upon him that his knowledge of fencing might be put to advantage should the necessity arise, to the end that his awkwardness with the buckler should be outweighed by his nicer defensive handling of his sword and his offensive improved by the judicious use of the point, against which they had developed little or no defense.

The lance he found less difficult, its value being so largely dependent upon the horsemanship of him who wielded it, and that Blake was a splendid horseman was evidenced by his polo rating as an eight goal man.

The ballium, or outer court, which lay between the inner and outer walls of the castle and entirely surrounded it, was, upon the north or valley side, given over entirely to knightly practice and training. Here the ballium was very wide, and against the inner wall was built a wooden grand stand that could be quickly removed in the event of an attack upon the castle.

Jousts and tilts were held here weekly, while the great tourneys that occurred less often were given upon a field outside the castle wall upon the floor of the valley.

Daily many knights and ladies came to watch the practice and training that filled the ballium with life and action and color during the morning hours. Good-natured banter flew back and forth, wagers were laid, and woe betide the contender who was unhorsed during these practice bouts, for the thing that a knight dreaded even more than he dreaded death was ridicule.

In the formal jousts that were held weekly greater decorum was observed by the audience, but during the daily practice their raillery verged upon brutality.

It was before such an audience as this that Blake received his training, and because he was a novelty the audiences were larger than usual, and because the friends of Sir Malud and the friends of Sir Richard had tacitly acknowledged him as an issue both the applause and the ridicule were loud and boisterous.

Even the Prince came often and Guinalda always was there. It was soon apparent that Prince Gobred leaned slightly to the side of Sir Malud, with the natural result that Malud's party immediately acquired numerous recruits.

The training of the lads who were squires to the knights and who would one day be admitted to the charmed circle of knighthood occupied the earlier hours of the morning. This was followed by practice tilts between knights, during which Sir Richard or one of his friends undertook the training of Blake at the far side of the ballium, and it was during this practice that the American's outstanding horsemanship became apparent, even Gobred being led to applause.

" 'Od's bodikins," he exclaimed, "the man be a part of his charger!"

" 'Twas but chance that saved him from a fall," said Malud.

"Mayhap," agreed Gobred, "but at that me likes the looks of him within a saddle."

"He doeth not too ill with his lance," admitted Malud. "But, 'od's blud! didst ever see a more awkward lout with a buckler? Methinks he hath had more use for a trencher." This sally elicited roars of laughter in which the Princess Guinalda did not join, a fact which Malud, whose eyes were often upon her, was quick to note. "Thou still believest this churl to be a knight, Princess Guinalda?" he demanded.

"Have I said aught?" she asked.

"Thou didst not laugh," he reminded her.

"He is a stranger knight, far from his own country and it seemeth not a knightly nor a gentle thing to ridicule him," she replied. "Therefore I did not laugh, for I was not amused."

Later that day as Blake joined the others in the great court, he ran directly into Malud's party, nor was it at all an accident, as he never made any effort to avoid Malud or his friends and was, seemingly, oblivious to their thinly veiled taunts and insinuations. Malud himself attributed this to the density and ignorance of a yokel, which he insisted Blake to be, but there were others who rather admired Blake for his attitude, seeing in it a studied affront that Malud was too dense to perceive.

Most of the inmates of the grim castle of Nimmr were inclined pleasantly toward the newcomer. He had brought with him an air of freshness and newness that was rather a relief from the hoary atmosphere that had surrounded Nimmr for nearly seven and a half centuries. He had brought them new words and new expressions and new views, which many of them were joyously adopting, and had it not been for the unreasoning antagonism of the influential Sir Malud, Blake had been accepted with open arms.

Sir Richard was far more popular then Malud, but lacked the latter's wealth in horses, arms and retainers and consequently had less influence with Prince Gobred. However there were many independent souls who either followed Sir Richard because they were fond of him or arrived at their own decisions without reference to the dictates of policy, and many of these were staunch friends to Blake.

Not all of those who surrounded Malud this afternoon were antagonistic to the American, but the majority of them laughed when Malud laughed and frowned when he frowned, for in the courts of kings and princes flourished the first order of "yes men."

Blake was greeted by many a smile and nod as he advanced and bowed low before the Princess Guinalda who was one of the company and, being of princely blood, entitled to his first devoirs.

"Thou didst well this morning, Sir James," said the princess, kindly. "It pleases me greatly to see thee ride."

"Methinketh 'twould be a rarer treat to see him serve a side of venison," sneered Malud.

This provoked so much laughter that Malud was encouraged to seek further applause.

"Odzooks!" he cried, "arm him with a trencher and carving knife and he would be at home."

"Speaking of serving," said Blake, "and Sir Malud's mind seems to be more occupied with that than with more knightly things, does any of you know what is necessary quickly to serve fresh pig?"

"Nay, fair sir knight," said Guinalda, "we know not. Prithee tell us.

"Yes, tell us," roared Malud, "thou, indeed, shouldst know."

"You said a mouthful, old scout, I do know!"

"And what be necessary that you may quickly serve fresh pig?" demanded Malud, looking about him and winking.

"A trencher, a carving knife and you, Sir Malud," replied Blake.

It was several seconds before the thrust penetrated their simple minds and it was the Princess Guinalda who first broke into merry laughter and soon all were roaring, while some explained the quip to others.

No, not all were laughing—not Sir Malud. When he grasped the significance of Blake's witticism he first turned very red and then went white, for the great Sir Malud liked not to be the butt of ridicule, which is ever the way of those most prone to turn ridicule upon others.

"Sirrah," he cried, "darest thou affront Malud? 'Od's blud, fellow! Low born varlet! Only thy blood canst atone this affront!"

"Hop to it, old thing!" replied Blake. "Name your poison!"

"I knowest not the meaning of thy silly words," cried Malud, "but I know that an' thou doest not meet me in fair tilt upon the morrow I shalt whip thee across the Valley of the Holy Sepulcher with a barrel starve."

"You're on!" snapped back Blake. "Tomorrow morning in the south ballium with——"

"Thou mayst choose the weapons, sirrah," said Malud.

"Don't call me sirrah, I don't like it," said Blake very quietly, and now he was not smiling. "I want to tell you something, Malud, that may be good for your soul. You are really the only man in Nimmr who didn't want to treat me well and give me a chance, a fair chance, to prove that I am all right."

"You think you are a great knight, but you are not. You have no intelligence, no heart, no chivalry. You are not what we would call in my country a good sport. You have a few horses and a few men-at-arms. That is all you have, for without them you would not have the favor of the Prince, and without his favor you would have no friends.

"You are not so good or great a man in any way as is Sir Richard, who combines all the qualities of chivalry that for centuries have glorified the order of knighthood; nor are you so good a man as I, who, with your own weapons, will best you on the morrow when, in the north ballium, I meet you on horseback with sword and buckler!"

The members of the party, upon seeing Malud's wrath, had gradually fallen away from Blake until, as he concluded his speech, he stood alone a few paces apart from Malud and those who surrounded him. Then it was that one stepped from among those at Malud's side and walked to Blake. It was Guinalda.

"Sir James." she said with a sweet smile, "thou spokest with thy mouth full!" She broke into a merry laugh. "Walk with me in the garden, sir knight," and taking his arm she guided him toward the south end of the eastern court.

"You're wonderful!" was all that Blake could find to say.

"Dost really think I be wonderful?" she demanded. " 'Tis hard to know if men speak the truth to such as I. The truth, as people see it, is spoke more oft to slaves than princes."

"I hope to prove it by my conduct," he said.

They had drawn a short distance away from the others now and the girl suddenly laid her hand impulsively upon his.

"I brought thee away, Sir James, that I might speak with thee alone," she said.

"I do not care what the reason was so long as you did it," he replied, smiling.

"Thou art a stranger among us, unaccustomed to our ways, unversed in knightly practice—so much so that there are many who doubt thy claims to knighthood. Yet thou art a brave man, or else a very simple one, or thou wouldst never have chosen to meet Sir Malud with sword and buckler, for he be skilled with these while thou art clumsy with them.

"Because I thinkest that thou goest to thy death tomorrow I have brought thee aside to speak with thee."

"What can be done about it now?" asked Blake.

"Thou art passing fair with thy lance," she said, "and it is still not too late to change thy selection of weapons. I beg thee to do so."

"You care?" he asked. There can be a world of meaning in two words.

The girl's eyes dropped for an instant and then flashed up to his and there was a touch of hauteur in them. "I am the daughter of the Prince of Nimmr," she said. "I care for the humblest of my father's subjects."

"I guess that will hold you for a while, Sir James," thought Blake, but to the girl he said nothing, only smiled.

Presently she stamped her foot. "Thou hast an impudent smile, sirrah!" she exclaimed angrily. "Meliketh it not. Then thou art too forward with the daughter of a prince."

"I merely asked you if you cared whether I was killed. Even a cat could ask that."

"And I replied. Why then didst thou smile?"

"Because your eyes had answered me before your lips had spoken and I knew that your eyes had told the truth."

Again she stamped her foot angrily. "Thou art indeed a forward boor," she exclaimed. "I shall not remain to be insulted further."

Her head held high she turned and walked haughtily away to rejoin the other party.

Blake stepped quickly after her. "Tomorrow," he whispered, "I meet Sir Malud with sword and buckler. With your favor upon my helm I could overthrow the best sword in Nimmr."

The Princess Guinalda did not deign to acknowledge that she had heard his words as she walked on to join the others clustered about Sir Malud.

"Tomorrow Thou Diest!"

THERE WAS a great celebration in the village of Batondo the chief the night that Ulala returned. A goat was killed and many chickens, and there were fruit and cassava bread and native beer in plenty for all. There was music, too, and dancing. With all of which it was morning before they sought their sleeping mats, with the result that it was after noon the following day before Fejjuan had an opportunity to speak of serious matters with Batando.

When finally he sought him out he found the old chief squatting in the shade before his hut, slightly the worse for the orgy of the preceding night.

"I have come to talk with you, Batando," he said, "of the desert people."

Batando grunted. His head ached.

"Yesterday you said that you would lead them to the entrance to the forbidden valley," said Fejjuan. "You mean, then, that you will not fight them?"

"We shall not have to fight them if we lead them to the entrance to the forbidden valley," replied Batando.

"You speak in riddles," said Fejjuan.

"Listen, Ulala," replied the old chief. "In childhood you were stolen from your people and taken from your country. Being young, there were many things you did not know and there are others that you have forgotten.

"It is not difficult to enter the forbidden valley, especially from the north. Every Galla knows how to find the northern pass through the mountains or the tunnel beyond the great cross that marks the southern entrance. There are only these two ways in—every Galla knows them; but every Galla also knows that there is no way out of the forbidden valley."

"What do you mean, Batando?" demanded Fejjuan. "If there are two ways in, there must be two ways out."

"No—there is no way out," insisted the chief. "As far back as goes the memory of man or the tales of our fathers and our fathers' fathers it is known that many men have entered the forbidden valley, and it is also known that no man has ever come out of it."

"And why have they not come out?"

Batando shook his head. "Who knows?" he asked. "We cannot even guess their fate."

"What sort of people inhabit the valley?" asked Fejjuan.

"Not even that is known. No man has seen them and returned to tell. Some say they are the spirits of the dead, others that the valley is peopled by leopards; but no one knows.

"Go therefore, Ulala, and tell the chief of the desert people that we will lead him to the entrance to the valley. If we do this we shall not have to fight him and his people, nor shall we ever again be bothered by them," and Batando laughed at his little joke.

"Will you send guides back with me to lead the Bedauwy to the valley?" asked Fejjuan.

"No," replied the chief. "Tell them we shall come in three days. In the meantime I shall gather together many warriors from other villages, for I do not trust the desert people. Thus we shall conduct them through our country. Explain this to their chief and also that in payment he must release to us all the Galla slaves he has with him—before he enters the valley."

"That Ibn Jad will not do," said Fejjuan.

"Perhaps, when he sees himself surrounded by Galla warriors, he will be glad to do even more," replied Batando.

And so Fejjuan, the Galla slave, returned to his masters and reported all that Batando had told him to report.

Ibn Jad at first refused to give up his slaves, but when Fejjuan had convinced him that under no other terms would Batando lead him to the entrance to the valley, and that his refusal to liberate the slaves would invite the hostile attentions of the Gallas, he finally consented; but in the back of his mind was the thought that before his promise was consummated he might find an opportunity to evade it.

Only one regret had Fejjuan in betraying the Beduins, and that was caused by his liking for Ateja, but being a fatalist he was consoled by the conviction that whatever was to be, would be, regardless of what he might do.

And as Ibn Jad waited and Batando gathered his black warriors from far and near, Tarzan of the Apes came to the water hole of the smooth, round rocks and took up the trail of the Beduins.

Since he had learned from Blake's blacks that the young American was missing and also that they had seen nothing of

Stimbol since the latter had separated from Blake and started for the coast, the ape-man was more convinced than ever that the white prisoner among the Arabs was Blake.

Still he felt no great concern for the man's safety, for if the Beduins had sufficient hopes of reward to spare his life at all he was in no great danger from them. Reasoning thus Tarzan made no pretense of speed as he followed the spoor of Ibn Jad and his people.

Two men sat upon rough benches at opposite sides of a rude table. Between them a cresset of oil with a cotton wick laying in it burned feebly, slightly illuminating the stone flagging of the floor and casting weird shadows of themselves upon the rough stone walls.

Through a narrow window, innocent of glass, the night air blew, driving the flame of the cresset now this way, now that. Upon the table, between the men, lay a square board blocked off into squares, and within some of these were several wooden pieces.

"It is your move, Richard," said one of the men. "You don't appear to be very keen about the game tonight. What's the matter?"

"I be thinking of the morrow, James, and my heart be heavy within me," replied the other.

"And why?" demanded Blake.

"Malud is not the best swordsman in Nimmr," replied Sir Richard," but——" he hesitated.

"I am the worst," Blake finished the sentence for him, laughingly.

Sir Richard looked up and smiled. "Thou wilt always joke, even in the face of death," he said. "Art all the men of this strange country thou tell'st of alike?"

"It is your move, Richard," said Blake.

"Hide not his sword from thine eyes with thy buckler, James," cautioned Richard. "Ever keep thine eyes upon his eyes until thou knowest whereat he striketh, then, with thy buckler ready, thou mayst intercept the blow, for he be over slow and always his eyes proclaim where his blade will fall. Full well I knoweth that for often have I exercised against him."

"And he hasn't killed you," Blake reminded him.

"Ah, we did but practice, but on the morrow it will be different, for Malud engages thee to the death, in mortal combat my friend, to wash away in blood the affront thou didst put upon him."

"He wants to kill me, just for that?" asked Blake. "I'll tell the world he's a touchy little rascal!"

"Were it only that, he might be satisfied merely to draw blood, but there is more that he hath against thee."

"More? What? I've scarcely spoken to him a dozen times," said Blake.

"He be jealous."

"Jealous? Of whom?"

"He would wed the Princess and he hath seen in what manner thou lookest at her," explained Richard.

"Poppycock!" cried Blake, but he flushed.

"Nay, he be not the only one who hath marked it," insisted Richard.

"You're crazy," snapped Blake.

"Often men look thus at the princess, for she be beautiful beyond compare, but——"

"Has he killed them all?" demanded the American.

"No, for the princess didst not look back at *them* in the same manner."

Blake leaned back upon his bench and laughed. "Now I know you're crazy," he cried, "all of you. I'll admit that I think the princess is a mighty sweet kid, but say young fellow, she can't see me a little bit."

"Enough of thy outlandish speech I grasp to gather thy meaning, James, but thou canst not confuse me upon the one subject nor deceive me upon the other. The eyes of the princess seldom leave thee whilst thou art at practice upon the lists and the look in thine when they rest upon her—hast ever seen a hound adoring his master?"

"Run along and sell your papers," admonished Blake.

"For this, Malud wouldst put thee out of the way and it is because I know this that I grieve, for I have learned to like thee over well, my friend."

Blake arose and came around the end of the table. "You're a good old scout, Richard," he said, placing a hand affectionately upon the other's shoulder, "but do not worry—I am not dead yet. I know I seem awkward with the sword, but I have learned much about its possibilities within the past few days and I think that Sir Malud has a surprise awaiting him."

"Thy courage and thy vast assurance should carry thee far, James, but they may not overcome a life-time of practice with the sword, and that is the advantage Malud hath over thee."

"Does Prince Gobred favor Malud's suit?" demanded Blake.

"Why not? Malud is a powerful knight, with a great castle

of his own and many horses and retainers. Besides a dozen knights he hath fully an hundred men-at-arms."

"There are several knights who have their own castles and following are there not?" asked Blake.

"Twenty, perchance," replied Richard.

"And they live close to Gobred's castle?"

"At the edge of the hills, within three leagues upon either hand of Gobred's castle," explained Richard.

"And no others live in all this great valley?" demanded Blake.

"You have heard mention made of Bohun?" asked Richard.

"Yes, often—why?"

"He calls himself king, but never will we refer to him as king. He and his followers dwell upon the opposite side of the valley. They number, perchance, as many as we and we be always at war against them."

"But I've been hearing quite a bit about a great tournament for which the knights are practicing now. I thought that Bohun and his knights were to take part in it."

"They be. Once each year, commencing upon the first Sunday of Lent and extending over a period of three days, there hath been from time immemorial a truce declared between the Fronters and the Backers, during which is held the Great Tourney, one year in the plain before the city of Nimmr and the next year in the plain before the City of the Sepulcher, as they call it."

"Fronters and Backers! What in heck do those mean?" demanded Blake.

"Thou art a knight of Nimmr and know not that?" exclaimed Richard.

"What I know about knighting would rattle around in a peanut shell," admitted Blake.

"Thou shouldst know and I shalt tell thee. Hark thee well, then," said Richard, "for I must need go back to the very beginning." He poured two goblets of wine from a flagon standing on the floor beside him, took a long drink and proceeded with his tale. "Richard I sailed from Sicily in the spring of 1191 with all his great following bound for Acre, where he was to meet the French king, Philip Augustus, and wrest the Holy Land from the power of the Saracen. But Richard tarried upon the way to conquer Cyprus and punish the vile despot who had placed an insult upon Berengaria, whom Richard was to wed.

"When the great company again set their sails for Acre there were many Cyprian maidens hidden away upon the ships by knights who had taken a fancy to their lovely faces, and it so befell that two of these ships, encountering a storm, were blown from their course and wrecked upon the Afric shore.

"One of these companies was commanded by a knight y-clept Bohun and the other by one Gobred and though they marched together they kept separate other than when attacked.

"Thus, searching for Jerusalem, they came upon this valley which the followers of Bohun declared was the Valley of the Holy Sepulcher and that the crusade was over. Their crosses, that they had worn upon their breasts as do all crusaders who have not reached their goal, they removed and placed upon their backs to signify that the crusade was over and that they were returning home.

"Gobred insisted that this was not the Valley of the Holy Sepulcher and that the crusade was not accomplished. He, therefore, and all his followers, retained their crosses upon their breasts and built a city and a strong castle to defend the entrance to the valley that Bohun and his followers might be prevented from returning to England until they had accomplished their mission.

"Bohun crossed the valley and built a city and a castle to prevent Gobred from pushing on in the direction in which the latter knew that the true Sepulcher lay, and for nearly seven and a half centuries the descendants of Bohun have prevented the descendants of Gobred from pushing on and rescuing the Holy Land from the Saracen, while the descendants of Gobred have prevented the descendants of Bohun from returning to England, to the dishonor of knighthood.

"Gobred took the title of prince and Bohun that of king and these titles have been handed down from father to son during the centuries, while the followers of Gobred still wear the cross upon their breasts and are called therefrom, the Fronters, and the followers of Bohun wear theirs upon their backs and are called Backers."

"And you would still push on and liberate the Holy Land?" asked Blake.

"Yes," replied Richard, "and the Backers would return to England; but long since have we realized the futility of either hope since we be surrounded by a vast army of Saracens and our numbers be too few to pit against them.

"Thinkest thou not that we are wise to remain here under such stress?" he demanded.

"Well, you'd certainly surprise 'em if you rode into Jerusalem, or London, either," admitted Blake. "On the whole, Richard, I'd remain right here, if I were you. You see, after seven hundred and thirty-five years most of the home folks may have forgotten you and even the Saracens might not know what it was all about if you came charging into Jerusalem."

"Mayhap you speak wisely, James," said Richard, "and then, too, we be content here, knowing no other country."

For a while both men were silent, in thought. Blake was the first to speak. "This big tourney interests me," he said. "You say it starts the first Sunday in Lent. That's not far away."

"No, not far. Why?"

"I was wondering if you thought I'd be in shape to have a part in it. I'm getting better and better with the lance every day."

Sir Richard looked sadly at him and shook his head. "Tomorrow thou wilt be dead," he said.

"Say! You're a cheerful party," exclaimed Blake.

"I am only truthful, good friend," replied Richard. "It grieveth my heart sorely that it should be true, but true it be—thou canst not prevail over Sir Malud on the morrow. Wouldst that I might take thy place in the lists against him, but that may not be. But I console myself with the thought that thou will comport thyself courageously and die as a good sir knight should, with no stain upon thy escutcheon. Greatly will it solace the Princess Guinalda to know that thou didst die thus."

"You think so?" ventured Blake.

"Verily."

"And if I don't die—will she be put out?"

"Put out! Put out of what?" demanded Richard.

"Will she be sore vexed, then," corrected Blake.

"I should not go so far as to say that," admitted Richard, "but natheless it appears certain that no lady would rejoice to see her promised husband overthrown and killed, and if thou art not slain it may only be because thou hast slain Malud."

"She is his affianced wife?" demanded Blake.

" 'Tis understood, that be all. As yet no formal marriage bans have been proclaimed."

"I'm going to turn in," snapped Blake. "If I've got to be killed tomorrow I ought to get a little sleep tonight."

As he stretched himself upon a rough wool blanket that was spread over a bed of rushes upon the stone floor in one corner of the room and drew another similar blanket over him, he felt less like sleep than he had ever felt before. The knowledge that on the morrow he was to meet a medieval knight in mortal combat naturally gave him considerable concern, but Blake was too self-reliant and too young to seriously harbor the belief that he would be the one to be killed. He knew it was possible but he did not intend to permit the thought to upset him. There was, however, another that did. It upset him very much and, too, it made him angry when he realized that he was concerned about it—about the proposed marriage of Sir Malud of West Castle and Guinalda, Princess of Nimmr.

Could it be that he had been ass enough, he soliloquized, to have fallen in love with this little medieval princess who probably looked upon him as dirt beneath her feet? And what was he going to do about Malud? Suppose he should get the better of the fellow on the morrow? Well, what about it? If he killed him that would make Guinalda unhappy. If he didn't kill him—what? Sir James did not know.

BN JAD waited three days in his menzil but no Galla guides arrived to lead him into the valley as Batando had promised, and so he sent Fejjuan once more to the chief to urge him to hasten, for always in the mind of Ibn Jad was the fear of Tarzan of the Apes and the thought that he might return to thwart and punish him.

He knew he was out of Tarzan's country now, but he also knew that where boundaries were so vague he could not definitely count upon this fact as an assurance of safety from reprisal. His one hope was that Tarzan was awaiting his return through Tarzan's country, and this Ibn Jad had definitely decided not to attempt. Instead he was planning upon moving directly west, passing north of the ape-man's stamping grounds, until he picked up the trail to the north down which he had travelled from the desert country.

In the mukaad of the sheik with Ibn Jad sat Tollog, his brother, and Fahd and Stimbol, besides some other 'Aarab. They were speaking of Batando's delay in sending guides and they were fearful of treachery, for it had long been apparent to them that the old chief was gathering a great army of warriors, and though Fejjuan assured them that they would not be used against the 'Aarab if Ibn Jad resorted to no treachery, yet they were all apprehensive of danger.

Ateja, employed with the duties of the hareem, did not sing nor smile as had been her wont, for her heart was heavy with mourning for her lover. She heard the talk in the mukaad but it did not interest her. Seldom did her eyes glance above the curtain that separated the women's quarters from the mukaad, and when they did the fires of hatred blazed within them as they crossed the countenance of Fahd.

She chanced to be thus glancing when she saw Fahd's eyes, which were directed outward across the menzil, go suddenly wide with astonishment.

"Billah, Ibn Jad!" cried the man. "Look!"

With the others Ateja glanced in the direction Fahd was

staring and with the others she voiced a little gasp of astonishment, though those of the men were rounded into oaths.

Walking straight across the menzil toward the sheik's beyt strode a bronzed giant armed with a spear, arrows and a knife. Upon his back was suspended an oval shield and across one shoulder and his breast was coiled a rope, hand plaited from long fibers.

"Tarzan of the Apes!" ejaculated Ibn Jad. "The curse of Ullah be upon him!"

"He must have brought his black warriors with him and left them hidden in the forest," whispered Tollog. "Not else would he dare enter the menzil of the Beduw."

Ibn Jad was heart sick and he was thinking fast when the ape-man halted directly in the outer opening of the mukaad. Tarzan let his eyes run quickly over the assemblage. They stopped upon Stimbol, finally.

"Where is Blake?" he demanded of the American.

"You ought to know," growled Stimbol.

"Have you seen him since you and he separated?"

"No."

"You are sure of that?" insisted the ape-man.

"Of course I am."

Tarzan turned to Ibn Jad. "You have lied to me. You are not here to trade but to find and sack a city; to take its treasure and steal its women."

"That is a lie!" cried Ibn Jad. "Whoever told thee that, lied."

"I do not think he lied," replied Tarzan. "He seemed an honest youth."

"Who was he?" demanded Ibn Jad.

"His name is Zeyd." Ateja heard and was suddenly galvanized to new interest. "He says all this and more, and I believe him."

"What else did he tell thee, Nasrany?"

"That another stole his musket and sought to slay thee, Ibn Jad, and then put the blame upon him.

"That is a lie, like all he hath told thee!" cried Fahd.

Ibn Jad sat in thought, his brows contracted in a dark scowl, but presently he looked up at Tarzan with a crooked smile. "Doubtless the poor youth thought that he spoke the truth," he said. "Just as he thought that he should slay his sheykh and for the same reason. Always hath his brain been sick, but never before did I think him dangerous.

"He hath deceived thee, Tarzan of the Apes, and that I can prove by all my people as well as by this Nasrany I have

befriended, for all will tell thee that I am seeking to obey thee
and leave thy country. Why else then should I have travelled
north back in the direction of my own beled?"

"If thou wished to obey me why didst thou hold me
prisoner and send thy brother to slay me in the night?" asked
Tarzan.

"Again thou wrongst Ibn Jad," said the sheik sadly. "My
brother came to cut thy bonds and set thee free, but thou set
upon him and then came el-fil and carried thee away."

"And what meant thy brother when he raised his knife and
cried: 'Die, Nasrany!'" demanded the ape-man. "Sayeth a
man thus who cometh to do a kindness?"

"I did but joke," mumbled Tollog.

"I am here again," said Tarzan, "but not to joke. My
Waziri are coming. Together we shall see you well on your
way toward the desert."

"It is what we wish," said the sheik quickly. "Ask this
other Nasrany if it be not true that we are lost and would be
but too glad to have thee lead us upon the right way. Here
we be beset by Galla warriors. Their chief hath been gathering
them for days and momentarily we fear that we shall be attacked. Is that not true, Nasrany?" he turned to Stimbol as he
spoke.

"Yes, it is true," said Stimbol.

"It is true that you are going to leave the country," said
Tarzan, "and I shall remain to see that you do so. T<morrow
you will start. In the meantime set aside a beyt for me—and
let there be no more treachery."

"Thou needst fear nothing," Ibn Jad assured him, then he
turned his face toward the women's quarters. "Hirfa! Ateja!"
he called. "Make ready the beyt of Zeyd for the sheykh of the
jungle."

To one side but at no great distance from the beyt of Ibn
Jad the two women raised the black tent for Tarzan, and when
the am'dan had been placed and straightened and the tunb
el-beyt made fast to the pegs that Ateja drove into the earth
Hirfa returned to her household duties, leaving her daughter
to stretch the side curtains.

The instant that Hirfa was out of ear shot Ateja ran to
Tarzan.

"Oh, Nasrany," she cried, "thou hast seen my Zeyd? He
is safe?"

"I left him in a village where the chief will care for him
until such time as thy people come upon thy return to the
desert country. He is quite safe and well."

"Tell me of him, oh, Nasrany, for my heart hungers for word of him," implored the girl. "How came you upon him? Where was he?"

"His mare had been dragged down by el-adrea who was about to devour your lover. I chanced to be there and slew el-adrea. Then I took Zeyd to the village of a chief who is my friend, for I knew that he could not survive the perils of the jungle should I leave him afoot and alone. It was my thought to send him from the country in safety, but he begged to remain until you returned that way. This I have permitted. In a few weeks you will see your lover."

Tears were falling from Ateja's long, black lashes—tears of joy—as she seized Tarzan's hand and kissed it. "My life is thine, Nasrany," she cried, "for that thou hast given me back my lover."

That night as the Galla slave, Fejjuan, walked through the menzil of his masters he saw Ibn Jad and Tollog sitting in the sheik's mukaad whispering together and Fejjuan, well aware of the inherent turpitude of this precious pair, wondered what might be the nature of their plotting.

Behind the curtain of the hareem Ateja lay huddled upon her sleeping mat, but she did not sleep. Instead she was listening to the whispered conversation of her father and her uncle.

"He must be put out of the way," Ibn Jad insisted.

"But his Waziri are coming," objected Tollog. "If they do not find him here what can we say? They will not believe us, whatever we say. They will set upon us. I have heard that they are terrible men."

"By Ullah!" cried Ibn Jad. "If he stays we are undone. Better risk something than to return empty handed to our own country after all that we have passed through."

"If thou thinkest that I shall again take this business upon myself thou art mistaken, brother," said Tollog. "Once was enough."

"No, not thee; but we must find a way. Is there none among us who might wish more than another to be rid of the Nasrany?" asked Ibn Jad, but to himself as though he were thinking aloud.

"The other Nasrany!" exclaimed Tollog. "He hateth him."

Ibn Jad clapped his hands together. "Thou hast it, brother!"

"But still shall we be held responsible," reminded Tollog.

"What matter if he be out of the way. We can be no worse off than we now are. Suppose Batando came tomorrow with the guides? Then indeed would the jungle sheykh know that we have lied to him, and it might go hard with us. No, we must be rid of him this very night."

"Yes, but how?" asked Tollog.

"Hold! I have a plan. Listen well, O brother!" and Ibn Jad rubbed his palms together and smiled, but he would not have smiled, perhaps had he known that Ateja listened, or had he seen the silent figure crouching in the dark just beyond the outer curtain of his beyt.

"Speak, Ibn Jad," urged Tollog, "tell me thy plan."

"Wellah, it is known by all that the Nasrany Stimbol hates the sheykh of the jungle. With loud tongue he hath proclaimed it many times before all when many were gathered in my mukaad."

"You would send Stimbol to slay Tarzan of the Apes?"

"Thou guessed aright," admitted Ibn Jad.

"But how wilt that relieve us of responsiblity? He wilt have been slain by thy order in thine own menzil," objected Tollog.

"Wait! I shall not command the one Nasrany to slay the other; I shall but suggest it, and when it is done I shall be filled with rage and horror that this murder hath been done in my menzil. And to prove my good faith I shall order that the murderer be put to death in punishment for his crime. Thus we shall be rid of two unbelieving dogs and at the same time be able to convince the Waziri that we were indeed the friends of their sheykh, for we shall mourn him with loud lamentations—when the Waziri shall have arrived."

"Allah be praised for such a brother!" exclaimed Tollog, enraptured.

"Go thou now, at once, and summon the Nasrany Stimbol," directed Ibn Jad. Send him to me alone, and after I have spoken with him and he hath departed upon his errand come thee back to my beyt."

Ateja trembled upon her sleeping mat, while the silent figure crouching outside the sheik's tent arose after Tollog had departed and disappeared in the darkness of the night.

Hastily summoned from the beyt of Fahd, Stimbol, cautioned to stealth by Tollog, moved silently through the darkness to the mukaad of the sheik where he found Ibn Jad awaiting him.

"Sit, Nasrany," invited the Beduin.

"What in hell do you want of me this time of night?" demanded Stimbol.

"I have been talking with Tarzan of the Apes," said Ibn Jad, "and because you are my friend and he is not I have

sent for you to tell you what he plans for you. He has interfered in all my designs and is driving me from the country,
but that is as nothing compared with what he intends for you."

"What in hell is he up to now?" demanded Stimbol. "He's
always butting into some one else's business."

"Thou dost not like him?" asked Ibn Jad.

"Why should I?" and Stimbol applied a vile epithet to
Tarzan.

"Thou wilt like him less when I tell thee," said Ibn Jad.

"Well, tell me."

"He says that thou hast slain thy companion, Blake," explained the sheik, "and for that Tarzan is going to kill thee
on the morrow."

"Eh? What? Kill me?" demanded Stimbol. "Why he can't
do it! What does he think he is—a Roman emperor?"

"Nevertheless he will do as he says," insisted Ibn Jad. "He
is all powerful here. No one questions the acts of this great
jungle sheykh. Tomorrow he will kill thee."

"But—you won't let him, Ibn Jad! Surely, you won't let
him?" Stimbol was already trembling with terror.

Ibn Jad elevated his palms. "What can I do?" he asked.

"You can—you can—why there must be something that
you can do," wailed the frightened man.

"There is naught that any can do—save yourself," whispered the sheik.

"What do you mean?"

"He lies asleep in yon beyt and—thou hast a sharp khusa."

"I have never killed a man," whispered Stimbol.

"Nor hast thou ever been killed," reminded the sheik;
"but tonight thou must kill or tomorrow thou wilt be killed."

"God!" gasped Stimbol.

"It is late," said Ibn Jad, "and I go to my sleeping mat. I
have warned thee—do what thou wilt in the matter," and he
arose as though to enter the women's quarters.

Trembling, Stimbol staggered out into the night. For a
moment he hesitated, then he crouched and crept silently
through the darkness toward the beyt that had been erected
for the ape-man.

But ahead of him ran Ateja to warn the man who had
saved her lover from the fangs of el-adrea. She was almost
at the beyt she had helped to erect for the ape-man when a
figure stepped from another tent and clapping a palm across
her mouth and an arm about her waist held her firmly.

"Where goest thou?" whispered a voice in her ear, a voice
that she recognized at once as belonging to her uncle; but

Tollog did not wait for a reply, he answered for her. "Thou goest to warn the Nasrany because he befriended thy lover! Get thee back to thy father's beyt. If he knew this he would slay thee. Go!" And he gave her a great shove in the direction from which she had come.

There was a nasty smile upon Tollog's lips as he thought how neatly he had foiled the girl, and he thanked Allah that chance had placed him in a position to intercept her before she had been able to ruin them all; and even as Tollog, the brother of the sheik, smiled in his beard a hand reached out of the darkness behind him and seized him by the throat—fingers grasped him and dragged him away.

Trembling, bathed in cold sweat, grasping in tightly clenched fingers the hilt of a keen knife, Wilbur Stimbol crept through the darkness toward the tent of his victim.

Stimbol had been an irritable man, a bully and a coward; but he was no criminal. Every fiber of his being revolted at the thing he contemplated. He did not want to kill, but he was a cornered human rat and he thought that death stared him in the face, leaving open only this one way of escape.

As he entered the beyt of the ape-man he steeled himself to accomplish that for which he had come, and he was indeed a very dangerous, a very formidable man, as he crept to the side of the figure lying in the darkness, wrapped in an old burnous.

14

Sword and Buckler

A S THE sun touched the turrets of the castle of the Prince of Nimmr a youth rolled from between his blankets, rubbed his eyes and stretched. Then he reached over and shook another youth of about his own age who slept beside him.

"Awaken, Edward! Awaken, thou sluggard!" he cried.

Edward rolled over on his back and essayed to say "Eh?" and to yawn at the same time.

"Up, lad!" urged Michel. "Forgottest thou that thy master fares forth to be slain this day?"

Edward sat up, now fully awake. His eyes flashed. " 'Tis a lie!" he cried, loyally. "He will cleave Sir Malud from poll to breast plate with a single blow. Livest no sir knight with such mighty thews as hast Sir James. Thou art disloyal, Michel, to Sir Richard's friend who hath been a good and kindly friend to us as well."

Michel patted the other lad upon the shoulder. "Nay, I did but jest, Edward," he said. "My hopes be all for Sir James, and yet——" he paused, "I fear——"

"Fear what?" demanded Edward.

"That Sir James be not well enough versed in the use of sword and buckler to overcome Sir Malud, for even were his strength the strength of ten men it shall avail him naught without the skill to use it."

"Thou shalt see!" maintained Edward, stoutly.

"I see that Sir James hath a loyal squire," said a voice behind them, and turning they saw Sir Richard standing in the doorway, "and may all his friends wish him well this day thus loyally!"

"I fell asleep last night praying to our Lord Jesus to guide his blade through Sir Malud's helm," said Edward.

"Good! Get thee up now and look to thy master's mail and to the trappings of his steed, that he may enter the lists bedight as befits a noble sir knight of Nimmr," instructed Richard, and left them.

It was eleven o'clock of this February morning. The sun shone down into the great north ballium of the castle of Nimmr, glinting from the polished mail of noble knights and from pike and battle-axe of men-at-arms, picking out the gay colors of the robes of the women gathered in the grandstand below the inner wall.

Upon a raised dais at the front and center of the grandstand sat Prince Gobred and his party, and upon either side of them and extending to the far ends of the stand were ranged the noble knights and ladies of Nimmr, while behind them sat men-at-arms who were off duty, then the freedmen and, last of all, the serfs, for under the beneficent rule of the house of Gobred these were accorded many privileges.

At either end of the lists was a tent, gay with pennons and the colors and devices of its owner; one with the green and gold of Sir Malud and the other with the blue and silver of Sir James.

Before each of these tilts stood two men-at-arms, resplendent in new apparel, the metal of their battle-axes gleaming brightly, and here a groom held a restive, richly caparisoned charger, while the squire of each of the contestants busied himself with last-minute preparations for the encounter.

A trumpeter, statuesque, the bell of his trumpet resting upon his hip, waited for the signal to sound the fanfare that would announce the entrance of his master into the lists.

A few yards to the rear a second charger champed upon his bit as he nuzzled the groom that held him in waiting for the knight who would accompany each of the contestants upon the field.

In the blue and silver tilt sat Blake and Sir Richard, the latter issuing instructions and advice, and of the two he was the more nervous. Blake's hauberk, gorget and bassinet were of heavy chain mail, the latter lined inside and covered outside, down to the gorget, with leopard skin, offering fair protection for his head from an ordinary, glancing blow; upon his breast was sewn a large, red cross and from one shoulder depended the streamers of a blue and silver rosette. Hanging from the pole of the tilt, upon a wooden peg, were Blake's sword and buckler.

The grandstand was filled. Prince Gobred glanced up at the sun and spoke to a knight at his side. The latter gave a brief command to a trumpeter stationed at the princely loge and presently, loud and clear, the notes of a trumpet rang in the ballium. Instantly the tilts at either end of the lists were galvanized to activity, while the grandstand seemed to spring to new life as necks were craned first toward the tent of Sir Malud and then toward that of Sir James.

Edward, flushed with excitement, ran into the tilt and seizing Blake's sword passed the girdle about his hips and buckled it in place at his left side, then, with the buckler, he followed his master out of the tilt.

As Blake prepared to mount Edward held his stirrup while the groom sought to quiet the nervous horse. The lad pressed Blake's leg after he had swung into the saddle (no light accomplishment, weighed down as he was by heavy chain mail) and looked up into his face.

"I have prayed for thee, Sir James," he said. "I know that thou wilt prevail."

Blake saw tears in the youth's eyes as he looked down at him and he caught a choking note in his voice. "You're a good boy, Eddie," he said. "I'll promise that you won't have to be ashamed of me."

"Ah, Sir James, how could I? Even in death thou wilt be a noble figure of a knight. An fairer one it hath never been given one to see, methinks," Edward assured him as he handed him his round buckler.

Sir Richard had by now mounted, and at a signal from him that they were ready there was a fanfare from the trumpet at Sir Malud's tilt and that noble sir knight rode forward, followed by a single knight.

Blake's trumpeter now announced his master's entry and the American rode out close along the front of the grandstand, followed by Sir Richard. There was a murmur of applause for each contestant, which increased as they advanced and met before Prince Gobred's loge.

Here the four knights reined in and faced the Prince and each raised the hilt of his sword to his lips and kissed it in salute. As Gobred cautioned them to fight honorably, as true knights, and reminded them of the rules governing the encounter Blake's eyes wandered to the face of Guinalda.

The little princess sat stiffly erect, looking straight before her. She seemed very white, Blake thought, and he wondered if she were ill.

How beautiful, thought Blake, and though she did not once appear to look at him he was not cast down, for neither did she look at Malud.

Again the trumpet sounded and the four knights rode slowly back to opposite ends of the lists and the principals waited for the final signal to engage. Blake disengaged his arm from the leather loop of his buckler and tossed the shield upon the ground.

Edward looked at him aghast. "My Lord knight!" he cried. "Art ill? Art fainting? Didst drop thy buckler?" and he snatched it up and held it aloft to Blake, though he knew full well that his eyes had not deceived him and that his master had cast aside his only protection.

To the horrified Edward there seemed but one explanation and that his loyalty would not permit him to entertain for an instant—that Blake was preparing to dismount and refuse to meet Sir Malud, giving the latter the victory by default and assuring himself of the contempt and ridicule of all Nimmr.

He ran to Richard who had not seen Blake's act. "Sir Richard! Sir Richard!" he cried in a hoarse whisper. "Some terrible affliction hath befallen Sir James!"

"Hey, what?" exclaimed Richard. "What meaneth thou lad?"

"He has cast aside his buckler," cried the youth. "He must be stricken sore ill, for it cannot be that otherwise he would refuse combat."

Richard spurred to Blake's side. "Hast gone mad, man?" he demanded. "Thou canst not refuse the encounter now unless thou wouldst bring dishonor upon thy friends!"

"Where did you get that line?" demanded Blake. "Who said I was going to quit?"

"But thy buckler?" cried Sir Richard.

The trumpet at the Prince's loge rang out peremptorily. Sir Malud spurred forward to a fanfare from his own trumpeter.

"Let her go!" cried Blake to his.

"Thy buckler!" screamed Sir Richard.

"The damned thing was in my way," shouted Blake as he spurred forward to meet the doughty Malud, Richard trailing behind him, as did Malud's second behind that knight.

There was a confident smile upon the lips of Sir Malud and he glanced often at the knights and ladies in the grandstand, but Blake rode with his eyes always upon his antagonist.

Both horses had broken immediately into a gallop, and as they neared one another Malud spurred forward at a run and Blake saw that the man's aim was doubtless to overthrow him at the first impact, or at least to so throw him out of balance as to make it easy for Malud to strike a good blow before he could recover himself.

Malud rode with his sword half raised at his right side,

while Blake's was at guard, a position unknown to the knights of Nimmr, who guarded solely with their bucklers.

The horsemen approached to engage upon each other's left, and as they were about to meet Sir Malud rose in his stirrups and swung his sword hand down, to gain momentum, described a circle with his blade and launched a terrific cut at Blake's head.

It was at that instant that some few in the grandstand realized that Blake bore no buckler.

"His buckler!" Sir James hath no buckler!" "He hath lost his buckler!" rose now from all parts of the stand; and from right beside him, where the two knights met before the log of Gobred, Blake heard a woman scream, but he could not look to see if it were Guinalda.

As they met Blake reined his horse suddenly toward Malud's, so that the two chargers' shoulders struck, and at the same time he cast all his weight in the same direction, whereas Malud, who was standing in his stirrups to deliver his blow, was almost in a state of equilibrium and having his buckler ready for defense was quite helpless insofar as maneuvering his mount was concerned.

Malud, overbalanced, lost the force and changed the direction of his blow, which fell, much to the knight's surprise, upon Blake's blade along which it spent its force and was deflected from its target.

Instantly, his horse well in hand by reason that his left arm was unencumbered by a buckler, Blake reined in and simultaneously cut to the left and rear, his point opening the mail on Malud's left shoulder and biting into the flesh before the latter's horse had carried him out of reach.

A loud shout of approbation arose from the stands for the thing had been neatly done and then Malud's second spurred to the Prince's loge and entered a protest.

"Sir James hath no buckler!" he cried. " 'Tis no fair combat!"

" 'Tis fairer for thy knight than for Sir James," said Gobred.

"We would not take that advantage of him," parried Malud's second, Sir Jarred.

"What sayest thou?" demanded Gobred of Sir Richard who had quickly ridden to Jarred's side. "Is Sir James without a buckler through some accident that befell before he entered the lists?"

"Nay, he cast it aside," replied Richard, "and averred that the 'damned thing' did annoy him; but if Sir Jarred feeleth that, because of this, they be not fairly matched we are willing that Sir Malud, also, should cast aside his buckler."

Gobred smiled. "That be fair," he said.

The two men, concerned with their encounter and not with the argument of their seconds, had engaged once more. Blood was showing upon Malud's shoulder and trickling down his back, staining his skirts and the housing of his charger.

The stand was in an uproar, for many were still shouting aloud about the buckler and others were screaming with delight over the neat manner in which Sir James had drawn his first blood. Wagers were being freely made, and though Sir Malud still ruled favorite in the betting, the odds against Blake were not so great, and while men had no money to wager they had jewels and arms and horses. One enthusiastic adherent of Sir Malud bet three chargers against one that his champion would be victorious and the words were scarce out of his mouth ere he had a dozen takers, whereas before the opening passage at arms offers as high as ten to one had found no takers.

Now the smile was gone from Malud's lips and he glanced no more at the grandstand. There was rage in his eyes as he spurred again toward Blake, who he thought had profited by a lucky accident.

Unhampered by a buckler Blake took full advantage of the nimbleness of the wiry horse he rode and which he had ridden daily since his arrival in Nimmr, so that man and beast were well accustomed to one another.

Again Sir Malud saw his blade glance harmlessly from the sword of his antagonist and then, to his vast surprise, the point of Sir James' blade leaped quickly beneath his buckler and entered his side. It was not a deep wound, but it was painful and again it brought blood.

Angrily Malud struck again, but Blake had reined his charger quickly to the rear and before Malud could gather his reins Blake had struck him again, this time a heavy blow upon the helm.

Half stunned and wholly infuriated Malud wheeled and charged at full tilt, once again determined to ride his adversary down. They met with a crash directly in front of Gobred's loge, there was a quick play of swords that baffled the eyesight of the onlookers and then, to the astonishment of all, most particularly Malud, that noble sir knight's sword flew from his grasp and hurtled to the field, leaving him entirely to the mercy of his foe.

Malud reined in and sat erect, waiting. He knew and

Blake knew that under the rules that governed their encounter Blake was warranted in running him through unless Malud sued for mercy, and no one, Blake least of all, expected this of so proud and haughty a knight.

Sir Malud sat proudly on his charger waiting for Blake to advance and kill him. Utter silence had fallen upon the stands, so that the champing of Malud's horse upon its bit was plainly audible. Blake turned to Sir Jarred.

"Summon a squire, sir knight," he said, "to return Sir Malud's sword to him."

Again the stands rocked to the applause, but Blake turned his back upon them and rode to Richard's side to wait until his adversary was again armed.

"Well, old top," he inquired of Sir Richard, "just how much a dozen am I offered for bucklers now?"

Richard laughed. "Thou hast been passing fortunate, James," he replied; "but methinks a good swordsman would long since have cut thee through."

"I know Malud would have if I had packed that chopping bowl along on the party," Blake assured him, though it is doubtful if Sir Richard understood what he was talking about, as was so often the case when Blake discoursed that Richard had long since ceased to even speculate as to the meaning of much that his friend said.

But now Sir Malud was rearmed and riding toward Blake. He stopped his horse before the American and bowed low. "I do my devoirs to a noble and generous knight," he said, graciously.

Blake bowed. "Are you ready sir?" he asked.

Malud nodded.

"On guard, then!" snapped the American.

For a moment the two jockeyed for position. Blake feinted and Malud raised his buckler before his face to catch the blow, but as it did not fall he lowered his shield, just as Blake had known that he would, and as he did so the edge of the American's weapon fell heavily upon the crown of his bassinet.

Malud's arm dropped at his side, he slumped in his saddle and then toppled forward and rolled to the ground. Agile, even in his heavy armor, Blake dismounted and walked to where his foe lay stretched upon his back almost in front of Gobred's loge. He placed a foot upon Malud's breast and pressed the point of his sword against his throat.

The crowd leaned forward to see the coup-de-grace administered, but Blake did not drive his point home. He looked up at Prince Gobred and addressed him.

"Here is a brave knight," he said, "with whom I have no real quarrel. I spare him to your service, Prince, and to those who love him," and his eyes went straight to the eyes of the Princess Guinalda. Then he turned and walked back along the front of the grandstand to his own tilt, while Richard rode behind him, and the knights and the ladies, the men-at-arms, the freedmen and the serfs stood upon their seats and shouted their applause.

Edward was beside himself with joy, as was Michel. The former knelt and embraced Blake's legs, he kissed his hand, and wept, so great were his happiness and his excitement.

"I knew it! I knew it!" he cried. "Didst I not tell thee, Michel, that my own sir knight would overthrow Sir Malud?"

The men-at-arms, the trumpeter and the grooms at Blake's tilt wore grins that stretched from ear to ear. Whereas a few minutes before they had felt ashamed to have been detailed to the losing side, now they were most proud and looked upon Blake as the greatest hero of Nimmr. Great would be their boasting among their fellows as they gathered with their flagons of ale about the rough deal table in their dining hall.

Edward removed Blake's armor and Michel got Richard out of his amidst much babbling upon the part of the youths who could not contain themselves, so doubly great was their joy because so unexpected.

Blake went directly to his quarters and Richard accompanied him, and when the two men were alone Richard placed a hand upon Blake's shoulder.

"Thou hast done a noble and chivalrous thing, my friend," he said, "but I know not that it be a wise one."

"And why?" demanded Blake. "You didn't think I could stick the poor mutt when he was lying there defenseless?"

Richard shook his head. " 'Tis but what he would have done for thee had thy positions been reversed," said he.

"Well, I couldn't do it. We're not taught to believe that it is exactly ethical to hit a fellow when he's down, where I come from," explained Blake.

"Had your quarrel been no deeper than appeared upon the surface thou might well have been thus magnanimous; but Malud be jealous of thee and that jealousy will be by no means lessened by what hath transpired this day. Thou might have been rid of a powerful and dangerous enemy had thou given him the coup-de-grace, as was thy right; but now thou hast raised up a greater enemy since to his jealousy is added hatred and envy against thee for thy prowess over him. Thou

didst make him appear like a monkey, James, and that Sir
Malud wilt never forgive, and I know the man."

The knights and ladies attached to the castle of Gobred
ate together at a great table in the huge hall of the castle.
Three hundred people could be accommodated at the single
board and it took quite a company of serving men to fill their
needs. Whole pigs, roasted, were carried in upon great trench-
ers and there were legs of mutton and sides of venison and
bowls of vegetables, with wine and ale, and at the end im-
mense puddings.

There was much laughter and loud talking, and it all presented a wild and fascinating picture to Sir James Blake as he
sat at the lower end of the table far below the salt that night,
in his accustomed place as one of the latest neophytes in the
noble ranks of the knighthood of Nimmr.

The encounter between himself and Malud was the subject
of the moment and many were the compliments bestowed
upon him and many the questions as to where and how he
had acquired his strange technique of swordsmanship. Although they had seen him accomplish it, yet they still appeared
to believe it inconceivable that a man might prevail without a
buckler over one who carried this essential article of defense.

Prince Gobred and his family sat, with the higher nobles
of Nimmr, at a table slightly raised above the rest of the
board and running across its upper end, the whole forming a
huge T. When he wished to speak to anyone farther down the
table he resorted to the simple expedient of raising his
voice, so that if several were so inclined at the same time the
room became a bedlam of uproar and confusion.

And as Blake sat at the farthest end of the table it was
necessary for one at Gobred's end to scream to attract attention, though when it was discovered that it was the prince
who was speaking the rest of the company usually lapsed into
silence out of respect for him, unless they were too far gone
in drink.

Shortly after the feasters were seated Gobred had arisen
and lifted his goblet high in air, and silence had fallen upon
the whole company as knights and ladies rose and faced their
prince.

"Hal to our King!" cried Gobred. "Hal to our liege lord,
Richard of England!"

And in a great chorus rose the answering "Hal!" as the
company drank the health of Richard Coeur de Lion seven
hundred and twenty-eight years after his death!

Then they drank the health of Gobred and of the Princess

Brynilda, his wife, and of the Princess Guinalda, and each time a voice boomed from just below the dais of the prince: "Here I be looking at thee!" as Sir Richard with a proud smile displayed his newly acquired knowledge.

Again Prince Gobred arose. "Hal!" he cried, "to that worthy sir knight who hath most nobly and chivalrously acquitted himself in the lists this day! Hal to Sir James, Knight Templar and, now, Knight of Nimmr!"

Not even the name of Richard I of England had aroused the enthusiasm that followed the drinking to Sir James. The length of the long hall Blake's eyes travelled straight to where Guinalda stood. He saw her drink to him and he saw that her eyes were regarding him, but the distance was too great and the light of the pitch torches and the oil cressets too dim for him to see whether her glance carried a message of friendship or dislike.

When the noise had partially subsided and the drinkers had retaken their seats Blake arose.

"Prince Gobred," he called the length of the room, "knights and ladies of Nimmr, I give you another toast! To Sir Malud!"

For a moment there was silence, the silence of surprise, and then the company arose and drank the health of the absent Sir Malud.

"Thou art a strange sir knight, with strange words upon thy lips and strange ways, Sir James," shouted Gobred, "but though thou callest a hal 'a toast' and thy friends be 'old top' and 'kid,' yet withal it seemeth that we understand thee and we would know more about thy country and the ways of the noble knights that do abide there.

"Tell us, are they all thus chivalrous and magnanimous to their fallen foes?"

"If they're not they get the raspberry," explained Blake.

" 'Get the raspberry'!" repeated Gobred. " 'Tis some form of punishment, methinks."

"You said it, Prince!"

"Of a surety I said it, Sir James!" snapped Gobred with asperity.

"I mean, Prince, that you hit the nail on the head—you guessed it the first time. You see the raspberry is about the only form of punishment that the Knights of the Squared Circle, or the Knights of the Diamond can understand."

" 'Knights of the Squared Circle'! 'Knights of the Diamond'! Those be knightly orders of which I wot not. Be they doughty knights?"

"Some of them are dotty, but a lot of them are regulars.

Take Sir Dempsey, for instance, a knight of the Squared Circle. He showed 'em all he was a regular knight in defeat, which is much more difficult than being a regular knight in victory."

"Be there other orders of knighthood these days?" demanded Gobred.

"We're lousy with them!"

"What?" cried Gobred.

"We're all knights these days," explained Blake.

"All knights! Be there no serfs nor yeomen? 'Tis incredible!"

"Well, there are some yeomen in the navy, I think; but all the rest of us, pretty much, are knights. You see things have changed a lot since the days of Richard. The people have sort of overthrown the old order of things. They poked a lot of ridicule at knights and wanted to get rid of knighthood, and as soon as they had they all wanted to be knights themselves; so we have Knights Templar now and Knights of Pythias and Knights of Columbus and Knights of Labor and a lot more I can't recall."

"Methinks it must be a fine and noble world," cried Gobred, "for what with so many noble sir knights it would seemeth that they must often contend, one against another—is that not true?"

"Well, they do scrap some," Blake admitted.

15

The Lonely Grave

WITHIN the dark interior of the beyt Stimbol could
see nothing. Just before him he heard a man breathing heavily as might one in a troubled sleep. The
would-be murderer paused to steady his nerves. Then, on
hands and knees, he crept forward inch by inch.

Presently one of his hands touched the prostrate figure of
the sleeper. Lightly, cautiously, Stimbol groped until he had
definitely discovered the position in which his victim lay. In
one hand, ready, he grasped the keen knife. He scarce
dared breathe for fear he might awaken the ape-man. He
prayed that Tarzan was a sound sleeper, and he prayed that
the first blow of his weapon would reach that savage heart.

Now he was ready! He had located the exact spot where he
must strike! He raised his knife and struck. His victim shuddered spasmodically. Again and again with savage maniacal
force and speed the knife was plunged into the soft flesh. Stimbol felt the warm blood spurt out upon his hand and wrist.

At length, satisfied that his mission had been accomplished,
he scurried from the beyt. Now he was trembling so that he
could scarcely stand—terrified, revolted by the horrid crime he
had committed.

Wild-eyed, haggard, he stumbled to the mukaad of Ibn
Jad's beyt and there he collapsed. The sheik stepped from the
women's quarters and looked down upon the trembling figure
that the dim light of a paper lantern revealed.

"What doest thou here, Nasrany?" he demanded.

"I have done it, Ibn Jad!" muttered Stimbol.

"Done what?" cried the sheik.

"Slain Tarzan of the Apes."

"Ai! Ai!" screamed Ibn Jad. "Tollog! Where art thou?
Hirfa! Ateja! Come! Didst hear what the Nasrany sayeth?"

Hirfa and Ateja rushed into the mukaad.

"Didst hear him?" repeated Ibn Jad. "He hath slain my
good friend the great sheykh of the Jungle, Motlog! Fahd!
Haste!" His voice had been rising until now he was screaming

at the top of his lungs and 'Aarab were streaming toward his beyt from all directions.

Stimbol, stunned by what he had done, dumb from surprise and terror at the unexpected attitude of Ibn Jad, crouched speechless in the center of the mukaad.

"Seize him!" cried the sheik to the first man that arrived. "He hath slain Tarzan of the Apes, our great friend, who was to preserve us and lead us from this land of dangers. Now all will be our enemies. The friends of Tarzan will fall upon us and slay us. Allah, bear witness that I be free from guilt in this matter and let Thy wrath and the wrath of the friends of Tarzan fall upon this guilty man!"

By this time the entire population of the menzil was gathered in front of the sheik's beyt, and if they were surprised by his protestations of sudden affection for Tarzan they gave no evidence of it.

"Take him away!" commanded Ibn Jad. "In the morning we shall gather and decide what we must do."

They dragged the terrified Stimbol to Fahd's beyt, where they bound him hand and foot and left him for Fahd to guard. When they had gone the Beduin leaned low over Stimbol, and whispered in his ear.

"Didst really slay the jungle sheykh?" he demanded.

"Ibn Jad forced me to do so and now he turns against me," whispered Stimbol.

"And tomorrow he will have you killed so that he may tell the friends of Tarzan that he hath punished the slayer of Tarzan," said Fahd.

"Save me, Fahd!" begged Stimbol. "Save me and I will give you twenty million francs—I swear it! Once I am safe in the nearest European colony I will get the money for you. Think of it, Fahd—twenty million francs!"

"I am thinking of it, Nasrany," replied the Beduin, "and I think that thou liest. There be not that much money in the world!"

"I swear that I have ten times that amount. If I have lied to you you may kill me. Save me! Save me!"

"Twenty million francs!" murmured Fahd. "Perchance he does not lie! Listen, Nasrany. I do not know that I can save thee, but I shall try, and if I succeed and thou forgettest the twenty million francs I shall kill thee if I have to follow thee across the world—dost understand?"

Ibn Jad called two ignorant slaves to him and commanded them to go to the beyt that had been Zeyd's and carry Tarzan's body to the edge of the menzil where they were to dig a grave and bury it.

With paper lanterns they went to the beyt of death and wrapping the dead man in the old burnous that already covered him they carried him across the menzil and laid him down while they dug a shallow grave; and so, beneath a forest giant in the land that he loved the grave of Tarzan of the Apes was made.

Roughly the slaves rolled the corpse into the hole they had made, shovelled the dirt upon it and left it in its lonely, unmarked tomb.

Early the next morning Ibn Jad called about him the elders of the tribe, and when they were gathered it was noted that Tollog was missing, and though a search was made he could not be found. Fahd suggested that he had gone forth early to hunt.

Ibn Jad explained to them that if they were to escape the wrath of the friends of Tarzan they must take immediate steps to disprove their responsibility for the slaying of the ape-man and that they might only do this and express their good faith by punishing the murderer.

It was not difficult to persuade them to take the life of a Christian and there was only one that demurred. This was Fahd.

"There are two reasons, Ibn Jad, why we should not take the life of this Nasrany," he said.

"By Ullah, there never be any reason why a true believer should not take the life of a Nasrany!" cried one of the old men.

"Listen," admonished Fahd, "to what I have in mind and then I am sure that you will agree that I am right."

"Speak, Fahd," said Ibn Jad.

"This Nasrany is a rich and powerful man in his own beled. If it be possible to spare his life he will command a great ransom—dead he is worth nothing to us. If by chance, the friends of Tarzan do not learn of his death before we are safely out of this accursed land it will have profited us naught to have killed Stimbol and, billah, if we kill him now they may not believe us when we say that he slew Tarzan and we took his life in punishment.

"But if we keep him alive until we are met with the friends of Tarzan, should it so befall that they overtake us, then we may say that we did hold him prisoner that Tarzan's own people might mete out their vengeance to him, which would suit them better."

"Thy words are not without wisdom," admitted Ibn Jad, "but suppose the Nasrany spoke lies concerning us and said that it was we who slew Tarzan? Wouldst they not believe him above us?"

"That be easily prevented," said the old man who had spoken before. "Let us cut his tongue out forthwith that he may not bear false witness against us."

"Wellah, thou hast it!" exclaimed Ibn Jad.

"Billah, nay!" cried Fahd. "The better we treat him the larger will be the reward that he will pay us."

"We can wait until the last moment," said Ibn Jad, "and we see that we are to lose him and our reward, then may we cut out his tongue."

Thus the fate of Wilbur Stimbol was left to the gods, and Ibn Jad, temporarily freed from the menace of Tarzan, turned his attention once more to his plans for entering the valley. With a strong party he went in person and sought a palaver with the Galla chief.

As he approached the village of Batando he passed through the camps of thousands of Galla warriors and realized fully what he had previously sensed but vaguely—that his position was most precarious and that with the best grace possible he must agree to whatever terms the old chief might propose.

Batando received him graciously enough, though with all the majesty of a powerful monarch, and assured him that on the following day he would escort him to the entrance to the valley, but that first he must deliver to Batando all the Galla slaves that were with his party.

"But that will leave us without carriers or servants and will greatly weaken the strength of my party," cried Ibn Jad.

Batando but shrugged his black shoulders.

"Let them remain with us until we have returned from the valley," implored the sheik.

"No Galla man may accompany you," said Batando with finality.

Early the next morning the tent of Ibn Jad was struck in signal that all were to prepare for the rahla, and entirely surrounded by Galla warriors they started toward the rugged mountains where lay the entrance to the valley of Ibn Jad's dreams.

Fejjuan and the other Galla slaves that the 'Aarab had brought with them from beled el-Guad marched with their own people, happy in their new-found freedom. Stimbol, friendless, fearful, utterly cowed, trudged wearily along under guard of two young Beduins, his mind constantly reverting to the horror of the murdered man lying in his lonely grave behind them.

Winding steadily upward along what at times appeared to be an ancient trail and again no trail at all, the 'Aarab and their escort climbed higher and higher into the rugged mountains that rim the Valley of the Sepulcher upon the north. At the close of the second day, after they had made camp beside a rocky mountain brook, Batando came to Ibn Jad and pointed to the entrance to a rocky side ravine that branched from the main canyon directly opposite the camp.

"There," he said, "lies the trail into the valley. Here we leave you and return to our villages. Upon the morrow we go."

When the sun rose the following morning Ibn Jad discovered that the Gallas had departed during the night, but he did not know it was because of the terror they felt for the inhabitants of the mysterious valley from which no Galla ever had returned.

That day Ibn Jad spent in making a secure camp in which to leave the women and children until the warriors had returned from their adventure in the valley or had discovered that they might safely fetch their women, and the next morning, leaving a few old men and boys to protect the camp, he set forth with those who were accounted the fighting men among them, and presently the watchers in the camp saw the last of them disappear in the rocky ravine that lay opposite the menzil.

16

The Great Tourney

K ING BOHUN with many knights and squires and serving men had ridden down from his castle above the City of the Sepulcher two days ago to take his way across the valley to the field before the city of Nimmr for the Great Tourney that is held once each year, commencing upon the first Sunday in Lent.

Gay pennons fluttered from a thousand lance tips and gay with color were the housings of the richly caparisoned chargers that proudly bore the Knights of the Sepulcher upon whose backs red crosses were emblazoned to denote that they had completed the pilgrimage to the Holy Land and were returning to home and England.

Their bassinets, unlike those of the Knights of Nimmr, were covered with bullock hide, and the devices upon their bucklers differed, and their colors. But for these and the crosses upon their backs they might have been Gobred's own good knights and true.

Sturdy sumpter beasts, almost as richly trapped as the knight's steeds, bore the marquees and tilts that were to house the knights during the tourney, as well as their personal belongings, their extra arms and their provisions for the three days of the tourney; for custom, over seven centuries old, forbade the Knights of Nimmr and the Knights of the Sepulcher breaking bread together.

The Great Tourney was merely a truce during which they carried on their ancient warfare under special rules which transformed it into a gorgeous pageant and an exhibition of martial prowess which noncombatants might witness in comfort and with impunity. It did not permit friendly intercourse between the two factions as this was not compatible with the seriousness of the event, in which knights of both sides often were killed, or the spirit in which the grand prize was awarded.

This prize as much as any other factor had kept open the breach of seven and a half centuries' duration that separated the Fronters from the Backers, for it consisted of five maidens whom the winners took back with them to their own city and who were never again seen by their friends or relatives.

Though the sorrow was mitigated by the honorable treatment that custom and the laws of knighthood decreed should be accorded these unfortunate maidens, it was still bitter because attached to it was the sting of defeat.

Following the tournament the maidens became the especial charges of Gobred or Bohun, dependent of course upon whether the honors of the tourney had fallen to the Fronters or the Backers, and in due course were given in honorable marriage to knights of the victorious party.

The genesis of the custom, which was now fully seven centuries old, doubtless lay in the wise desire of some ancient Gobred or Bohun to maintain the stock of both factions strong and virile by the regular infusion of new blood, as well, perhaps, as to prevent the inhabitants of the two cities from drifting too far apart in manners, customs and speech.

Many a happy wife of Nimmr had been born in the City of the Sepulcher and seldom was it that the girls themselves repined for long. It was considered an honor to be chosen and there were always many more who volunteered than the requisite number of five that anually made the sacrifice.

The five who constituted the prize offered by the City of the Sepulcher this year rode on white palfreys and were attended by a guard of honor in silver mail. The girls, selected for their beauty to thus honor the city of their birth, were gorgeously attired and weighed down with ornaments of gold and silver and precious stones.

Upon the plain before the city of Nimmr preparations for the tourney had been in progress for many days. The lists were being dragged and rolled with heavy wooden rollers, the ancient stands of stone from which the spectators viewed the spectacle were undergoing their annual repairs and cleansing, a frame superstructure was being raised to support the canopies that would shade the choice seats reserved for the nobility, and staffs for a thousand pennons had been set around the outer margin of the lists—these and a hundred other things were occupying a company of workmen; and in the walled city and in the castle that stood above it the hammers of armorers and smiths rang far into the night forging iron shoes and mail and lance tips.

Blake had been assured that he was to have a part in the Great Tourney and was as keen for it as he had been for the big game of the season during his football days at college. He had been entered in two sword contests—one in which

five Knights of Nimmr met five Knights of the Sepulcher and
another in which he was pitted against a single antagonist, but
his only contest with the lance was to be in the grand finale
when a hundred Fronters faced a hundred Backers, since,
whereas, before his encounter with Malud he had been considered hopeless with sword and buckler now Prince Gobred
looked to him to win many points with these, his lance work
being held but mediocre.

King Bohun and his followers were camped in a grove of
oaks about a mile north of the lists, nor did the laws governing
the Great Tourney permit them to come nearer until the
hour appointed for their entrance upon the first day of the
spectacle.

Blake, in preparing for the tourney, had followed the custom
adopted by many of the knights of wearing distinctive armor
and trapping his charger similarly. His chain mail was all of
solid black, relieved only by the leopard skin of his bassinet
and the blue and silver pennon upon his lance. The housings
of his mount were of black, edged with silver and blue, and
there were, of course, the prescribed red crosses upon his
breast and upon his horse housings.

As he came from his quarters upon the opening morning
of the tourney, followed by Edward bearing his lance and
buckler, he appeared a somber figure among the resplendently
caparisoned knights and the gorgeously dressed women that
were gathered in the great court awaiting the word to mount
their horses which were being held in the north ballium by
the grooms.

That his black mail was distinctive was evidenced by the
attention he immediately attracted, and that he had quickly
become popular among the knights and ladies of Nimmr was
equally apparent by the manner in which they clustered
about him, but opinion was divided in the matter of his
costume, some holding that it was too dismal and depressing.

Guinalda was there but she remained seated upon a bench
where she was conversing with one of the maidens that had
been chosen as Nimmr's prize. Blake quickly disengaged himself from those who had crowded about him and crossed the
court to where Guinalda sat. At his approach the princess
looked up and inclined her head slightly in recognition of his
bow and then she resumed her conversation with the maiden.

The rebuff was too obvious to permit of misunderstanding,
but Blake was not satisfied to accept it and go his way without
an explanation. He could scarce believe, however, that the
princess was still vexed merely because he had intimated that

he had believed that she took a greater interest in him than she had admitted. There must be some other reason.

He did not turn and walk away, then, although she continued to ignore him, but stood quietly before her waiting patiently until she should again notice him.

Presently he noted that she was becoming nervous as was also the maiden with whom she spoke. There were lapses in their conversation; one of Guinalda's feet was tapping the flagging irritably; a slow flush was creeping upward into her cheeks. The maiden fidgeted, she plucked at the ends of the wimple that lay about her shoulders, she smoothed the rich cyclas of her mantle and finally she arose and bowing before the princess asked if she might go and bid farewell to her mother.

Guinalda bade her begone and then, alone with Blake and no longer able to ignore him, nor caring to, she turned angrily upon him.

"I was right!" she snapped. "Thou art a forward boor. Why standeth thou thus staring at me when I have made it plain that I wouldst not be annoyed by thee? Go!"

"Because——" Blake hesitated, "because I love you."

"Sirrah!" cried Guinalda, springing to her feet. "How darest thou!"

"I would dare anything for you, my princess," replied Blake, "because I love you."

Guinalda looked straight at him for a moment in silence, then her short upper lip curved in a contemptuous sneer.

"Thou liest!" she said. "I have heard what thou hast said concerning me!" and without waiting for a reply she brushed past him and walked away.

Blake hurried after her. "What have I said about you?" he demanded. "I have said nothing that I would not repeat before all Nimmr. Not even have I presumed to tell my best friend, Sir Richard, that I love you. No other ears than yours have heard that."

"I have heard differently," said Guinalda, haughtily, "and I care not to discuss the matter further."

"But——" commenced Blake, but at that instant a trumpet sounded from the north gate leading into the ballium. It was the signal for the knights to mount. Guinalda's page came running to her to summon her to her father's side. Sir Richard appeared and seized Blake by the arm.

"Come, James!" he cried. "We should have been mounted before now for we ride in the forerank of the knights to-day." And so Blake was dragged away from the princess before he could obtain an explanation of her, to him, inexplicable attitude.

The north ballium presented a scene of color and activity, crowded as it was with knights and ladies, pages, squires, grooms, men-at-arms and horses, nor would it accommodate them all, so that the overflow stretched into the east and south balliums and even through the great east gate out upon the road that leads down into the valley.

For half an hour something very like chaos reigned about the castle of the Prince of Nimmr, but eventually perspiring marshals and shouting heralds whipped the cortege into shape as it took its slow and imposing way down the winding mountain road toward the lists.

First rode the marshals and heralds and behind them a score of trumpeters; then came Prince Gobred, riding alone, and following was a great company of knights, their colored pennons streaming in the wind. They rode just before the ladies and behind the ladies was another company of knights, while in the rear marched company after company of men-at-arms, some armed with cross bows, others with pikes and still others again with battle-axes of huge proportions.

Perhaps a hundred knights and men-at-arms all told were left behind to guard the castle and the entrance to the Valley of the Sepulcher, but these would be relieved to witness the second and third days' exercises.

As the Knights of Nimmr wound down to the lists, the Knights of the Sepulcher moved out from their camp among the oaks, and the marshals of the two parties timed their approach so that both entered the lists at the same time.

The ladies of Nimmr dropped out of the procession and took their places in the stand; the five maidens of Nimmr and the five from the City of the Sepulcher were escorted to a dais at one end of the lists, after which the knights lined up in solid ranks, the Knights of Nimmr upon the south side of the lists, the Knights of the Sepulcher upon the north.

Gobred and Bohun rode forward and met in the center of the field, where, in measured and imposing tones, Bohun delivered the ancient challenge prescribed by custom and the laws of the Great Tourney and handed Gobred the gage, the acceptance of which constituted an acceptance of the challenge and marked the official opening of the tourney.

As Gobred and Bohun reined about and faced their own knights these rode out of the lists, those who were not to take part in the encounters of the day seeking places in the stands after turning their chargers over to grooms, while those who were to participate formed again to ride once around the lists, for the double purpose of indicating to their opponents and the spectators the entrants for that day and of viewing the prizes offered by their opponents.

In addition to the maidens there were many minor prizes consisting of jeweled ornaments, suits of mail, lances, swords, bucklers, splendid steeds and the many articles that were valued by knights or that might find favor in the eyes of their ladies.

The Knights of the Sepulcher paraded first, with Bohun at their head, and it was noticeable that the eyes of the king were often upon the women in the stands as he rode past. Bohun was a young man, having but just ascended the throne following the recent death of his father. He was arrogant and tyrannical and it had been common knowledge in Nimmr that for years he had been at the head of a faction that was strong for war with Nimmr, that the city might be reduced and the entire Valley of the Sepulcher brought under the rule of the Bohuns.

His charger prancing, his colors flying, his great company of knights at his back, King Bohun rode along the stands reserved for the people of Nimmr, and when he came to the central loge in which sat Prince Gobred with the Princess Brynilda and Princess Guinalda, his eyes fell upon the face of the daughter of Gobred.

Bohun reined in his charger and stared straight into the face of Guinalda. Gobred flushed angrily, for Bohun's act was a breach of courtesy, and half rose from his seat, but at that moment Bohun, bowing low across his mount's withers, moved on, followed by his knights.

That day the honors went to the Knights of the Sepulcher, for they scored two hundred and twenty seven points against one hundred and six that the Knights of Nimmr were able to procure.

Upon the second day the tourney opened with the riding past of the entrants who, ordinarily, were conducted by a herald, but to the surprise of all, Bohun again led his knights past the stands and again he paused and looked full at the Princess Guinalda.

This day the Knights of Nimmr fared a little better, being for the day but seven points behind their opponents, though the score for the two days stood two hundred and sixty nine to three hundred and ninety seven in favor of the Knights of the Sepulcher.

So the third day opened with the knights from the north

boasting what seemed an insuperable lead of one hundred and twenty eight points and the Knights of Nimmr spurred to greater action by the knowledge that to win the tourney they must score two hundred and thirty two of the remaining three hundred and thirty four points.

Once again, contrary to age old custom, Bohun led his entrants about the lists as they paraded before the opening encounter, and once again he drew rein before the loge of Gobred and his eye rested upon the beautiful face of Guinalda for an instant before he addressed her sire.

"Prince Gobred of Nimmr," he said in his haughty and arrogant voice, "as ye well know my valiant sir knights have bested thine by more than six score points and the Great Tourney be as good as ours already. Yet we would make thee a proposition."

"Speak Bohun! The Great Tourney is yet far from won, but an' ye have any proposition that an honorable prince may consider thou hast my assurance that 'twill be given consideration."

"Thy five maidens are as good as ours," said Bohun, "but give me thy daughter to be queen of the Valley of the Sepulcher and I will grant thee the tourney."

Gobred went white with anger, but when he replied his voice was low and even for he was master of his own emotions, as befitted a princely man.

"Sir Bohun," he said, refusing to accord to his enemy the title of king, "thy words are an offense in the ears of honorable men, implying as they do that the daughter of a Gobred be for sale and that the honor of the knighthood of Nimmr may be bartered for.

"Get thee hence to thine own side of the lists before I set serfs upon ye to drive ye there with staves."

"So that be thine answer, eh?" shouted Bohun. "Then know ye that I shall take the five maidens by the rules of the Great Tourney and thy daughter by force of arms!" With this threat delivered he wheeled his steed and spurred away.

Word of Bohun's proposition and his rebuff spread like wild fire throughout the ranks of the Knights of Nimmr so that those who were to contend this last day of the tourney were keyed to the highest pitch of derring do in the defence of the honor of Nimmr and the protection of the Princess Guinalda.

The great lead attained by the Knights of the Sepulcher during the first two days was but an added incentive to greater effort, provoking them, as a spur, to the utmost limits of daring and exertion. There was no need that their marshals should exhort them. The youth and chivalry of Nimmr had heard the challenge and would answer it in the lists!

Blake's sword and buckler encounter with a Knight of the Sepulcher was scheduled for the first event of the day. When the lists were cleared he rode in to a fanfare of trumpets, moving parallel with the south stands while his adversary rode along the front of the north stands, the latter halting before the loge of Bohun as Blake drew rein in front of that of Gobred, where he raised the hilt of his sword to his lips to the Prince, though his eyes were upon Guinalda.

"Conduct thyself as a true knight this day to the glory and honor of Nimmr," charged Gobred, "and may the blessings of Our Lord Jesus be upon thee and thy sword, our well beloved Sir James!"

"To the glory and honor of Nimmr I pledge my sword and my life!" should have been Blake's reply according to the usages of the Great Tourney.

"To the glory and honor of Nimmr and to the protection of my Princess I pledge my sword and my life!" is what he said, and it was evident from the expression on Gobred's face that he was not displeased, while the look of haughty disdain which had been upon Guinalda's face softened.

Slowly she arose and tearing a ribbon from her gown stepped to the front of the loge. "Receive this favor from thy lady, sir knight," she said, "bearing it with honor and to victory in thy encounter."

Blake reined closed to the rail of the loge and bent low while Guinalda pinned the ribbon upon his shoulder. His face was close to hers; he sensed the intoxicating perfume of her hair; he felt her warm breath upon his cheek.

"I love you," he whispered, so low that no other ears than hers could hear.

"Thou art a boor," she replied in a voice as low as his. "It be for the sake of the five maidens that I encourage ye with this favor."

Blake looked straight into her eyes. "I love you, Guinalda," he said, "and—you love me!"

Before she could reply he had wheeled away, the trumpets had sounded, and he was cantering slowly toward the end of the field where the tilts of the Knights of Nimmr stood.

Edward, very much excited, was there and Sir Richard and Michel, with a marshal, heralds, trumpeters, men-at-arms— a martial company to urge him on with encouragement and advice.

Blake cast aside his buckler, nor was there any to reprove him now. Instead they smiled proudly and knowingly, for had they not seen him best Sir Malud without other defense than his horsemanship and his sword?

The trumpets blared again. Blake turned and put spurs to his charger. Straight down the center of the lists he rode. From the opposite end came a Knight of the Sepulcher to meet him!

"Sir James! Sir James!" cried the spectators in the stands upon the south side, while the north stands answered with the name of their champion.

"Who is the black knight?" asked many a man in the north stands of his neighbor.

"He hath no buckler!" cried some. "He be mad!" "Sir Guy wilt cleave him open at the first pass!" "Sir Guy! Sir Guy!"

17

"The Saracens!"

JUST as the second day of the Great Tourney had opened in the Valley of the Sepulcher upon the plains below the city of Nimmr, a band of swart men in soiled thobs and carrying long matchlocks topped the summit of the pass upon the north side of the valley and looked down upon the City of the Sepulcher and the castle of King Bohun.

They had followed upward along what may once have been a trail, but for so long a time had it been unused, or so infrequently had it been used that it was scarce distinguishable from the surrounding brush; but below them now Ibn Jad saw at a short distance a better marked road and, beyond, what appeared to him a fortress. Beyond that again he glimpsed the battlements of Bohun's castle.

What he saw in the foreground was the barbican guarding the approach to the castle and the city, both of which were situated in much the same relative position as were the barbican and castle upon the south side of the valley where Prince Gobred guarded the city of Nimmr and the valley beyond it against the daily expected assault of the Saracens.

Seeking cover, Ibn Jad and his Beduins crept down toward the barbican where an old knight and a few men-at-arms kept perfunctory ward. Hiding in the mountain brush the 'Aarab saw two strangely apparelled blacks hunting just outside the great gateway. They were armed with cross bows and arrows and their prey was rabbits. For years they had seen no stranger come down this ancient road, and for years they had hunted between the gate and the summit of the mountains, though farther than this they were not permitted to wander. Nor had they any great desire to do so, for, though they were descendants of Gallas who lived just beyond this mountain top, they thought that they were Englishmen and that a horde of Saracens awaited to annihilate them should they venture too far afield.

Today they hunted as they had often hunted when they chanced to be placed in the guard at the outer barbican. They moved silently forward, warily awaiting the break of a rabbit. They did not see the dark-faced men in the brush.

Ibn Jad saw that the great gateway was open and that the gate that closed it raised and lowered vertically. It was raised now. Great was the laxity of the old knight and the men-at-arms, but King Bohun was away and there was none to reprove them.

Ibn Jad motioned those nearest him to follow and crept slowly closer to the gateway.

What of the old knight and the other watchers? The former was partaking of a late breakfast just within one of the great towers of the barbican and the latter were taking advantage of the laxity of his discipline to catch a few more winks of sleep as they stretched beneath the shade of some trees within the ballium.

Ibn Jad won to within a few yards of the gateway and waited for the others to reach his side. When they were all there he whispered to them and then trotted on silent sandals toward the gate, his matchlock ready in his hands. Behind him came his fellows. They were all within the ballium before the men-at-arms were aware that there was an enemy this side of Palestine.

With cross bow and battle-axe the men-at-arms sprang to defend the gate. Their cries of "The Saracens! The Saracens!" brought the old sir knight and the hunters running toward the ballium.

Below, at the castle of King Bohun, the men at the gates and the other retainers who had been left while Bohun sallied forth to the Great Tourney heard strange noises from the direction of the outer barbican. The shouts of men floated down to them and strange, sharp sounds that were like thunder and yet unlike it. Such sounds they had never heard before, nor any of their forbears. They rallied at the outer castle gate and the knights with them consulted as to what was best to be done.

Being brave knights there seemed but one thing open for them. If those at the far outer barbican had been attacked they must hasten to their defense. Summoning all but four of the knights and men-at-arms at his disposal the marshal of the castle mounted and rode forth toward the outer gate.

Half way there they were espied by Ibn Jad and his men who, having overcome the poorly armed soldiers at the gate, were advancing down the road toward the castle. At sight of these reinforcements Ibn Jad hastened to secrete his followers and himself in the bushes that lined the roadway. So it fell that the marshal rode by them and did not see them and, when they had passed, Ibn Jad and his followers came out of the bushes and continued down the winding mountain road toward the castle of King Bohun.

The men at the castle gate, now fully upon the alert, stood ready with the portcullis raised as the marshal instructed them, so that in the event that those who had ridden out should be hard pressed upon their return by an enemy at their rear they could still find sanctuary within the ballium. The plan was, in such event, to lower the portcullis behind the men of the Sepulcher and in the faces of the pursuing Saracens, for that an enemy must be such was a forgone conclusion—had not they and their ancestors waited for near seven and a half centuries now for this momentarily expected assault? They wondered if it really had come at last.

While they discussed the question Ibn Jad watched them from a concealing clump of bushes a few yards away.

The wily Beduin knew the purpose of that portcullis and he was trying to plan best how he might enter the enclosure beyond before it could be dropped before his face. At last he found a plan and smiled. He beckoned three men to come close and into their ears he whispered that which he had in mind.

There were four men-at-arms ready to drop the portcullis at the psychological moment and all four of them stood in plain sight of Ibn Jad and the three that were beside him. Carefully, cautiously, noiselessly the four 'Aarab raised their ancient matchlocks and took careful aim.

"Now!" whispered Ibn Jad and four matchlocks belched forth flame and black powder and slugs of lead.

The four men-at-arms dropped to the stone flagging and Ibn Jad and all his followers raced forward and stood within the ballium of the castle of King Bohun. Before them, across the ballium, was another gate and a broad moat, but the drawbridge was lowered, the portcullis raised and the gateway unguarded.

The marshal and his followers had ridden unhindered into the ballium of the outer barbican and there they had found all its defenders lying in their own blood, even to the little squire of the old knight who should have watched the gate and did not.

One of the men-at-arms still lived and in his dying breath

he gasped the terrible truth. The Saracens had come at last!

"Where are they?" demanded the marshal.

"Didst thou not see them, sir?" asked the dying man. "They marched down the road toward the castle."

"Impossible!" cried the marshal. "We didst but ride along that very road and saw no one."

"They marched down toward the castle," gasped the man.

The marshal knit his brows. "Were there many?" he demanded.

"There are few," replied the man-at-arms. "It was but the advance guard of the armies of the sultan."

Just then the volley that laid low the four warders at the castle gate crashed upon the ears of the marshal and his men.

" 'Ods blud!" he cried.

"They must have hid themselves in the bush as we passed," exclaimed a knight at the marshal's side, "for of a surety they be there and we be here and there be but one road between.'"

"There be but four men at the castle gate," said the marshal, "and I did bid them keep the 'cullis up til we returned. God pity me! I have given over the Sepulcher to the Saracens. Slay, me, Sir Morley!"

"Nay, man! We need every lance and sword and cross bow that we may command. This be no time to think of taking thy life when thou canst give it to Our Lord Jesus in defense of His Sepulcher against the infidels!"

"Thou art right, Morley," cried the marshal. "Remain you here, then, with six men and hold this gate. I shall return with the others and give battle at the castle!"

But when the marshal came again to the castle gate he found the portcullis down and a dark-faced, bearded Saracen glaring at him through the iron bars. The marshal at once ordered the cross bowmen to shoot the fellow down, but as they raised their weapons to their shoulder there was a loud explosion that almost deafened them and flame leaped from a strange thing that the Saracen held against his shoulder and pointed at them. One of the cross bowmen screamed and lunged forward upon his face and the others turned and fled.

They were brave men in the face of dangers that were natural and to be expected, but in the presence of the supernatural, the weird, the uncanny, they reacted as most men do, and what could have been more weird than death leaping in flame and with a great noise through space to strike their fellow down?

But Sir Bulland, the marshal, was a knight of the Sepulcher.

He might wish to run away fully as much as the simple and lowly men-at-arms, but there was something that held him there that was more potent than fear of death. It is called Honor.

Sir Bulland could not run away and so he sat there on his great horse and challenged the Saracens to mortal combat; challenged them to send their doughtiest sir knight to meet him and thus decide who should hold the gate.

But the 'Aarab already held it. Futhermore they did not understand him. In addition to all this they were without honor as Sir Bulland knew it, and perhaps as any one other than a Beduin knows it, and would but have laughed at his silly suggestion.

One thing they did know—two things they knew—that he was a Nasrany and that he was unarmed. They did not count his great lance and his sword as weapons, for he could not reach them with either. So one of them took careful aim and shot Sir Bulland through his chain mail where it covered his noble and chivalrous heart.

Ibn Had had the run of the castle of King Bohun and he was sure that he had discovered the fabled City of Nimmr that the sahar had told him of. He herded together the women and children and the few men that remained and held them under guard. For a while he was minded to slay them, since they were but Nasrany, but he was so pleased at having found and taken the treasure city that he let them live—for the time at least.

At his command his followers ransacked the castle in search of the treasure. Nor were they disappointed, for the riches of Bohun were great. There was gold in the hills of the Valley of the Sepulcher and there were precious stones to be found there, also. For seven and a half centuries the slaves of the Sepulcher and of Nimmr had been washing gold from the creek beds and salvaging precious stones from the same source. The real value of such was not to the men of the Sepulcher and Nimmr what it would be to men of the outer world. They but esteemed these things as trinkets, yet they liked them and saved them and even bartered for them on occasion, but they did not place them in vaults under lock and key. Why should they in a land where such things were not stolen? Their women and their horses they guarded, but not their gold or their jewels.

And so Ibn Jad gathered a great sack full of treasure, enough to satisfy the wildest imaginings of his cupidity. He gathered all that he could find in the castle of King Bohun, more than he had hoped to find in this fabled city; and then a strange thing happened. Having more wealth than he possibly could use he wanted more. No, not so strange after all, for Ibn Jad was human.

He spent the night with his followers in the castle of King Bohun and during the night he planned, for he had seen a wide valley stretching far away to other mountains and at the base of those mountains he had seen that which appeared to be a city. "Perhaps," thought Ibn Jad, "it is a richer city than this. I shall start on the morrow to see."

18

The Black Knight

OWN the field thundered the two chargers. Silence fell upon the stands. They were almost met when Sir Guy realized that his adversary bore no shield. But what of that? He had been sent to the lists by his own people—the responsibility was theirs, the advantage Sir Guy's. Had they sent him in without a sword Sir Guy might still have slain him without besmirching his knightly honor, for such were the laws of the Great Tourney.

Yet his discovery had its effect upon the Knight of the Sepulcher as just for an instant it had distracted his attention from the thought that should have been uppermost in his mind—gaining the primary advantage by the skill of his opening attack.

He saw his antagonist's horse swing out just before they met. He stood in his stirrups, as had Sir Malud, to deliver a terrific cut; then Blake threw his horse straight into the shoulder of Sir Guy's. The latter's sword fell and with a loud, clanging noise slipped harmlessly from the blade of the Knight of Nimmr. Guy had raised his buckler to protect his own head and neck and could not see Sir James. Guy's horse stumbled and nearly fell. As it recovered itself Blake's blade slipped beneath the buckler of the Knight of the Sepulcher and its point pierced the gorget of his adversary and passed through his throat.

With a cry that ended in a blood choked gurgle Sir Guy of the Sepulcher toppled backward upon his horse's rump and rolled upon the ground while the south stands went mad with joy.

The laws of the Great Tourney account the knight who is unhorsed as slain, so the coup-de-grace is never given and no knight is killed unnecessarily. The victor rides to the tilt of the vanquished, wheels about and gallops to his own tilt, the full length of the lists, where he waits until a herald of the opposing side fetches the prize to him.

And so it was that as Blake swung from his saddle, sword in hand, and approached the fallen Sir Guy, a gasp arose from the south stands and a roar of angry protest from the north.

Marshals and heralds galloped madly from the tilt of the fallen Backer and, seeing this, Sir Richard, fearing that Blake would be set upon and slain, led a similar party from his end of the field.

Blake approached the fallen knight, who lay upon his back, feebly struggling to arise, and when the spectators looked to see him run Sir Guy through with his sword they saw him instead toss the weapon to the ground and kneel beside the wounded man.

With an arm beneath Sir Guy's shoulders he raised him and held him against his knee while he tore off his helm and gorget, and when the marshals and the heralds and the others drew rein beside him Blake was trying to staunch the flow of blood.

"Quick!" he cried to them, "a chirurgeon! His jugular is not touched, but this flow of blood must be stopped."

Several of the knights dismounted and gathered about, and among them was Sir Richard. A herald of Sir Guy's faction kneeled and took the youth from Blake's arms.

"Come!" said Richard. "Leave the sir knight to his own friends."

Blake arose. He saw how peculiar were the expressions upon the faces of the knights about him, but as he drew away one of them spoke. An older man, who was one of Bohun's marshals.

"Thou art a generous and chivalrous knight," he said to Blake, "and a courageous one too who would thus set at naught the laws of the Great Tourney and the customs of centuries."

Blake faced him squarely. "I do not give a damn for your laws or your customs," he said. "Where I come from a decent man wouldn't let a yellow dog bleed to death without trying to save him, much less a brave and gallant boy like this, and because he fell by my hand, by the customs of my country I should be compelled to aid him."

"Yes," explained Sir Richard, "as otherwise he would be punished with a raspberry."

The winning of the first event of the day was but a forerunner of a series of successes on the part of the Knights of

Nimmr until, at the opening of the last event, the score showed four hundred fifty two points for them against four hundred forty eight for their opponents. A margin of four points, however, was as nothing at this stage of the tourney, as the final event held one hundred points which Fate might allot almost entirely to one side.

This was the most spectacular event of the whole tourney and one which the spectators always looked forward to with the greatest anticipation. Two hundred knights were engaged in it, one hundred Knights of Nimmr against one hundred Knights of the Sepulcher. They formed at opposite ends of the lists and as the trumpets sounded the signal they charged with lances, and thus they fought until all of one side had been unhorsed or had retired from the field because of wounds. Broken lances could be replaced as a polo player may ride out and obtain a fresh mallet when he breaks his. Otherwise there were few rules to govern this concluding number of the Great Tourney, which more nearly approximated a battle scene than any other event of the three days of conflict.

Blake had won his fifteen points for the Knights of Nimmr in the opening event of the day and again with four other comrades, pitted against five mounted swordsmen from the north, he had helped to add still further points to the growing score of the Fronters.

He was entered in the last event largely because the marshals appreciated the value of his horsemanship and felt that it would more than compensate for his inexperience with the lance.

The two hundred mailed knights had paraded for the final event and were forming line at opposite ends of the lists, one hundred Knights of the Sepulcher at one end and one hundred Knights of Nimmr at the other. Their chargers, especially selected for this encounter, were powerful and fleet, chosen for their courage as were the youths who bestrode them.

The knights, with few exceptions, were youths in their twenties, for to youth went the laurels of this great sport of the Middle Ages as they still do in the sports of today. Here and there was a man of middle age, a hardened veteran whose heart and hand had withstood the march of years and whose presence exerted a steadying influence upon the young knights the while it spurred them to their utmost efforts, for these were champions whose deeds were sung by minstrels in the great halls of the castles of Nimmr.

In proud array, with upright lances and fluttering pennons, the sunlight glinting from burnished mail and bit and boss and shining brightly upon the gorgeous housings of their mounts, the two hundred presented a proud and noble spectacle as they awaited the final summons of the trumpet.

Rearing and plunging, eager to be off, many a war horse broke the line as will a thoroughbred at the barrier, while at one side and opposite the center of the lists a herald waited for the moment that both lines should be formed before he gave the signal that would send these iron men hurtling into combat.

Blake found himself well toward the center of the line of Nimmr's knights, beneath him a great black that fretted to be off, before him the flower of the knighthood of the Sepulcher. In his right hand he grasped a heavy, iron-shod lance, the butt of which rested in a boot at his stirrup, and upon his left arm he bore a great shield, nor had he any wish to discard it in the face of all those sturdy, iron-tipped lances.

As he looked down the long length of the lists upon the hundred knights that would presently be racing toward him in solid array with lance points projecting far ahead of their horses, Blake felt that his shield was entirely inadequate and he experienced a certain nervousness that reminded him of similar moments of tense waiting for the referee's whistle during his football days—those seemingly long gone days of another life that he sensed now as a remote and different incarnation.

As last came the signal! He saw the herald raise his sword on high. With the two hundred he gathered his restive charger and couched his lance. The sword fell! From the four corners of the lists trumpets blared; from two hundred throats rose the cri de guerre; four hundred spurs transmitted the awaited signal from man to horse.

The thundering lines bore down the field while a score of heralds raced along the flanks and rear to catch any infraction of the sole regulation that bore upon the final tumultuous collision. Each knight must engage the foe upon his bridle hand, for to couch his lance upon the one to his right was an unknightly act, since thus a single knight might have two lances set upon him at once, against which there could be no defence.

From above the rim of his shield Blake saw the solid front of lances, iron-shod chargers and great shields almost upon him. The speed, the weight, the momentum seemed irresistible and, metaphorically, with deep respect Blake took his hat off to the knights of old.

Now the two lines were about to meet! The spectators sat

in spellbound silence; the riders, grim-jawed, with tight set lips, were voiceless now.

Blake, his lance across his horse's withers, picked the knight racing toward him upon his left hand; for an instant he caught the other's eyes and then each crouched behind his shield as the two lines came together with a deafening crash.

Blake's shield smashed back against his face and body with such terrific force that he was almost carried from his saddle. He felt his own lance strike and splinter and then, half stunned, he was through the iron line, his charger, frantic and uncontrolled, running wildly toward the tilts of Bohun's knights.

With an effort Blake pulled himself together, gathered his reins and finally managed to get his horse under control, and it was not until he had reined him about that he got his first glimpse of the result of the opening encounter. A half dozen chargers were scrambling to their feet and nearly a score more were galloping, riderless, about the lists. A full twenty-five knights lay upon the field and twice that many squires and serving men were running in on foot to succor their masters.

Already several of the knights had again set their lances against an enemy and Blake saw one of the Knights of the Sepulcher bearing down upon him, but he raised his broken spear shaft above his head to indicate that he was momentarily hors de combat and galloped swiftly back to his own end of the lists where Edward was awaiting him with a fresh weapon.

"Thou didst nobly well, beloved master," cried Edward.

"Did I get my man?" asked Blake.

"That thou didst, sir," Edward assured him, beaming with pride and pleasure, "and all be thou breakest thy lance upon his shield thou didst e'en so unhorse him."

Armed anew Blake turned back toward the center of the lists where many individual encounters were taking place. Already several more knights were down and the victors looking for new conquests in which the stands were assisting with hoarse cries and advice, and as Blake rode back into the lists he was espied by many in the north stands occupied by the knights and followers of the Sepulcher.

"The black knight!" they cried. "Here! Here! Sir Wildred! Here is the black knight that overthrew Sir Guy. Have at him, Sir Wildred!"

Sir Wildred, a hundred yards away, couched his lance. "Have at thee, Sir Black Knight!" he shouted.

"You're on!" Blake shouted back, putting spurs to the great black.

Sir Wildred was a large man and he bestrode a raw-boned

roan with the speed of a deer and the heart of a lion. The pair would have been a match for the best of Nimmr's knighthood.

Perhaps it was as well for Blake's peace of mind that Wildred appeared to him like any other knight and that he did not know that he was the most sung of all the heroes of the Sepulcher.

As a matter of fact, any knight looked formidable to Blake, who was still at a loss to understand how he had unhorsed his man in the first encounter of this event.

"The bird must have lost both stirrups," is what he had mentally assured himself when Edward had announced his victory.

But he couched his lance like a good sir knight and true and bore down upon the redoubtable Sir Wildred. The Knight of the Sepulcher was charging diagonally across the field from the south stands. Beyond him Blake caught a glimpse of a slim, girlish figure standing in the central loge. He could not see her eyes, but he knew that they were upon him.

"For my Princess!" he whispered as Sir Wildred loomed large before him.

Lance smote on shield as the two knights crashed together with terrific force and Blake felt himself lifted clear of his saddle and hurled heavily to the ground. He was neither stunned nor badly hurt and as he sat up a sudden grin wreathed his face, for there, scarce a lance length from him, sat Sir Wildred. But Sir Wildred did not smile.

" 'Sdeath!" he cried. "Thou laughest at me, sir-rah?"

"If I look as funny as you do," Blake assured him, "you've got a laugh coming too."

Sir Wildred knit his brows. "Ods blud!" he exclaimed. "An thou beest a knight of Nimmr I be a Saracen! Who beest thou? Thy speech savoreth not of the Valley."

Blake had arisen. "Hurt much?" he asked stepping forward. "Here, I'll give you a hand up."

"Thou art, of a certainty, a strange sir knight," said Wildred. "I recall now that thou didst offer succor to Sir Guy when thou hadst fairly vanquished him."

"Well, what's wrong with that?" asked Blake. "I haven't anything against you. We've had a bully good scrap and are out of it. Why should we sit here and make faces at one another?"

Sir Wildred shook his head. "Thou art beyond my comprehension," he admitted.

By this time their squires and a couple of serving men had

arrived, but neither of the fallen knights was so badly injured that he could not walk without assistance. As they started for their respective tilts Blake turned and smiled at Wildred.

"So long, old man!" he cried cheerily. "Hope we meet again some day."

Still shaking his head Sir Wildred limped away, followed by the two who had come to assist him.

At his tilt Blake learned that the outcome of the Great Tourney still hung in the balance and it was another half hour before the last of the Knights of Nimmr went down in defeat, leaving two Knights of the Sepulcher victorious upon the field. But this was not enough to overcome the lead of four points that the Fronters had held at the opening of the last event and a moment later the heralds announced that the Knights of Nimmr had won the Great Tourney by the close margin of two points.

Amidst the shouting of the occupants of the stands at the south the Knights of Nimmr who had taken part in the tourney and had won points for the Fronters formed to ride upon the lists and claim the grand prize. Not all were there, as some had been killed or wounded in encounters that had followed their victories, though the toll on both sides had been much smaller than Blake had imagined that it would be. Five men were dead and perhaps twenty too badly injured to ride, the casualties being about equally divided.

As the Knights of Nimmr rode down the field to claim the five maidens from the City of the Sepulcher, Bohun gathered all his knights at his side of the lists as though preparing to ride back to his camp. At the same time a Knight of the Sepulcher, wearing the leopard skin bassinet of Nimmr, entered the stands upon the south side of the field and made his way toward the loge of Prince Gobred.

Bohun watched. The Knights of Nimmr were at the far end of the field engrossed in the ritualistic rites that the laws of the Great Tourney prescribed for the reception of the five maidens.

Close beside Bohun two young knights sat their chargers, their eyes upon their king, and one of them held the bridle of a riderless horse.

Suddenly Bohun raised his hand and spurred across the field followed by his knights. They moved a little toward the end of the field where the Knights of Nimmr were congregated so that the bulk of them were between this end of the field and Gobred's loge.

The young knight who had sat close beside Bohun, and his

companion leading the riderless horse, spurred at a run straight
for the stands of Nimmr and the loge of the Prince. As they
drew in abreast of it a knight leaped into the loge from the
rear, swept Guinalda into his arms, tossed her quickly to the
young knight waiting to receive her, sprang to the edge of the
rail and leaped into the saddle of the spare horse being held in
readiness for him; then they both wheeled and spurred away
before the surprised Gobred or those about him could raise a
hand to stay them. Behind them swept Bohun and the Knights
of the Sepulcher, out toward the camp among the oaks.

Instantly all was pandemonium. A trumpeter in Gobred's
loge sounded the alarm; the prince ran from the stands to the
spot where his horse was being held by a groom; the Knights
of Nimmr, ignorant of what had occurred, not knowing where
to rally or against whom, milled about the lists for a few moments.

Then Gobred came, spurring swiftly before them. "Bohun
has stolen the Princess Guinalda!" he cried. "Knights of
Nimmr—" but before he could say more, or issue orders to
his followers, a black knight on a black charger spurred
roughly through the ranks of surrounding men and was away
after the retreating Knights of the Sepulcher.

19

Lord Tarzan

THERE was a nasty smile upon Tollog's lips as he thought how neatly he had foiled Ateja, who would have warned the Nasrany of the plot to slay him, and he thanked Allah that chance had placed him in a position to intercept her before she had been able to ruin them all. Even as Tollog, the brother of the sheik, smiled in his beard a hand reached out of the darkness behind him and seized him by the throat —fingers grasped him and he was dragged away.

Into the beyt that had been Zeyd's and which had been set up for the Nasrany, Tollog was dragged. He struggled and tried to scream for help, but he was powerless in the grip of steel that held him and choked him.

Inside the beyt a voice whispered in his ear. "Cry out, Tollog," it said, "and I shall have to kill you." Then the grasp upon his throat relaxed, but Tollog did not call for help, for he had recognized the voice that spoke and he knew that it had made no idle threat.

He lay still while the bonds were drawn tight about his wrists and ankles and a gag fastened securely in his mouth. He felt the folds of his burnous drawn across his face and then—silence.

He heard Stimbol creep into the beyt, but he thought that it was still he who had bound him. And thus died Tollog, the brother of Ibn Jad, died as he had planned that Tarzan of the Apes should die.

And, knowing that he would die thus, there was a smile upon the lips of the ape-man as he swung through the forest toward the southeast.

Tarzan's quest was not for Beduins but for Blake. Having assured himself that the white man in the menzil of Ibn Jad was Stimbol and that none knew the whereabouts of the other American, he was hastening back to the locality where Blake's boys had told him their bwana had disappeared, in the hope of picking up his trail and, if unable to assist him, at least to learn what fate had overtaken him.

Tarzan moved swiftly and his uncanny senses of sight and smell aided him greatly in wresting its secrets from the jungle, yet it was three days before he found the spot where Ara the lightning had struck down Blake's gun bearer.

Here he discovered Blake's faint spoor leading toward the north. Tarzan shook his head, for he knew that there was a stretch of uninhabited forest laying between this place and the first Galla villages. Also he knew that if Blake survived hunger and the menace of wild beasts he might only live to fall victim to a Galla spear.

For two days Tarzan followed a spoor that no other human eye might have discerned. On the afternoon of the second day he came upon a great stone cross built directly in the center of an ancient trail. Tarzan saw the cross from the concealment of bushes for he moved as beasts of prey moved, taking advantage of every cover, suspicious of every strange object, always ready for flight or battle as occasion might demand.

So it was that he did not walk blindly into the clutches of the two men-at-arms that guarded the outer way to the City of Nimmr. To his keen ears was borne the sound of their voices long before he saw them.

Even as Sheeta or Numa approach their prey, so Tarzan of the Apes crept through the brush until he lay within a few yards of the men-at-arms. To his vast astonishment he heard them conversing in a quaint form of English that, while understandable to him, seemed yet a foreign tongue. He marvelled at their antiquated costumes and obsolete weapons, and in them he saw an explanation of Blake's disappearance and a suggestion of his fate.

For a time Tarzan lay watching the two with steady, unblinking eyes—it might have been Numa himself, weighing the chances of a sudden charge. He saw that each was armed with a sturdy pike and a sword. They could speak English, after a fashion, therefore, he argued, they might be able to give him word of Blake. But would they receive him in a friendly spirit or would they attempt to set upon and slay him?

He determined that he could never ascertain what their attitude would be by lying hidden among the brush, and so he gathered himself, as Numa does when he is about to spring.

The two blacks were idly gossiping, their minds as far from thoughts of danger as it were possible they could be, when suddenly without warning Tarzan launched himself full upon the back of the nearer, hurling him to the ground. Before the other could gather his wits the ape-man had dragged his victim into the concealment of the bush from which he had sprung, while the fellow's companion turned and fled in the direction of the tunnel.

The man in Tarzan's grasp fought and struggled to be free but the ape-man held him as easily as he might have held a child.

"Lie still," he advised, "I shall not harm you."

"Ods blud!" cried the black. "What manner of creature be thou?"

"One who will not harm you if you will tell him the truth," replied Tarzan.

"What wouldst thou know?" demanded the black.

"A white man came this way many weeks ago. Where is he?"

"Thou speakest of Sir James?" asked the soldier.

"Sir James!" mused Tarzan and then he recollected that Blake's first name was James. "His name was James," he replied, "James Blake."

"Verily, 'tis the same," said the soldier.

"You have seen him? Where is he now?"

"He be defending the honor of Our Lord Jesus and the Knights of Nimmr in the Great Tourney in the lists upon the plain below the city, and have ye come to wreak dispite upon our good Sir James thou wilt find many doughty knights and men-at-arms who will take up the gage in his behalf."

"I am his friend," said Tarzan.

"Then why didst thou leap upon me thus, if thou art a friend to Sir James?" demanded the man.

"I did not know how you had received him or how you would receive me."

"A friend of Sir James will be received well in Nimmr," said the man.

Tarzan took the man's sword from him and permitted him to rise—his pike he had dropped before being dragged among the bushes.

"Go before me and lead me to your master," commanded the ape-man, "and remember that your life will be the forfeit that you must pay for treachery."

"Do not make me leave the road unguarded against the Saracens," begged the man. "Soon my companion will return with others and then I shall beg them to take thee where thou wilt."

"Very well," agreed the ape-man. They had not waited long before he heard the sound of hastening footsteps and a strange jingling and clanking that might have been caused by the shaking of many chains and the striking against them of objects of metal.

Shortly afterward he was surprised to see a white man clothed in chain mail and carrying a sword and buckler descending the trail at a trot, a dozen pike-men at his back.

"Tell them to halt!" commanded Tarzan, placing the point of the man's sword in the small of his back. "Tell them I would talk with them before they approach too closely."

"Stop, I pray thee!" cried the fellow. "This be a friend of Sir James, but he wilt run me through with my own sword an' ye press him too close. Parley with him, most noble sir knight, for I wouldst live at least to know the result of the Great Tourney."

The knight halted a few paces from Tarzan and looked him up and down from feet to head. "Thou art truly a friend to Sir James?" he demanded.

Tarzan nodded. "I have been seeking him for days."

"And some mishap befell thee and thou lost thy apparel."

The ape-man smiled. "I go thus, in the jungle," he said.

"Art thou a sir knight and from the same country as Sir James?"

"I am an Englishman," replied Tarzan of the Apes.

"An Englishman! Thrice welcome then to Nimmr! I be Sir Bertram and a good friend to Sir James."

"And I am called Tarzan," said the ape-man.

"And thy rank?" inquired Sir Bertram.

Tarzan was mystified by the strange manners and garb of his seemingly friendly inquisitor, but he sensed that whatever the man might be he took himself quite seriously and would be more impressed if he knew that Tarzan was a man of position, and so he answered him truthfully, in his quiet way.

"A Viscount," he said.

"A peer of the realm!" exclaimed Sir Bertram. "Prince Gobred wilt be o'er pleased to greet thee, Lord Tarzan. Come thou with me and I wilt furnish thee with apparel that befits thee."

At the outer barbican Bertram took Tarzan into the quarters reserved for the knight commanding the warders and kept him there while he sent his squire to the castle to fetch raiment and a horse, and while they waited Bertram told Tarzan all that had befallen Blake since his arrival in Nimmr and, too, much of the strange history of this unknown British colony.

When the squire returned with the clothing it was found that it fitted the ape-man well, for Bertram was a large man, and presently Tarzan of the Apes was garbed as a Knight of Nimmr and was riding down toward the castle with Sir Bertram. Here the knight announced him at the gate as the Lord Viscount Tarzan. Once within he introduced him to another knight whom he persuaded to relieve him at the gate while he conducted Tarzan to the lists that he might be presented to Gobred and witness the final scenes of the tourney, were it not concluded before they arrived.

And so it was that Tarzan of the Apes, clad in chain mail, and armed with lance and sword, rode down into the Valley of the Sepulcher just as Bohun put his foul scheme into execution and carried off the Princess Guinalda.

Long before they reached the lists Bertram was aware that something was amiss, for they could see the dust clouds racing rapidly north away from the lists as though one body of knights pursued another. He put spurs to his mount and Tarzan followed suit, and so they came at a stiff run to the lists and there they found all pandemonium.

The women were mounting preparatory to riding back to Nimmr under escort of a few knights that Gobred had sent back to guard them. The men-at-arms were forming themselves into companies, but all was being done in a confused manner since every now and then a great part of the company would rush to the highest part of the stands and peer off toward the north after the clouds of dust that revealed nothing to them.

Sir Bertram accosted one of his fellows. "What hath befallen?" he demanded.

"Bohun hath seized the Princess Guinalda and carried her away," came the astounding reply.

"Zounds!" cried Bertram, reining about. "Wilt ride with me in the service of our princess, Lord Tarzan?"

For answer Tarzan spurred his horse alongside of Bertram's and stirrup to stirrup the two set out across the plain, while far ahead of them Blake drew gradually closer and closer to the fleeing Knights of the Sepulcher. So thick was the cloud of dust they threw up that they were hid from their pursuer even as he was hid from them and so were unaware that Blake was near them.

The American carried no lance nor shield, but his sword clattered and clashed at his side and at his right hip swung his forty-five. Whenever he had been armed, since he entered

Nimmr, he had carried this weapon of another world and another age. To their queries he had answered that it was but a lucky talisman that he carried, but in his heart was the thought that some day it might stand him in better stead than these simple knights and ladies could dream.

He drew that he would never use it except in battle, or as a last resort against overwhelming odds or unfair tactics, but he was glad that he carried it today as it might mean the difference between liberty and captivity for the woman he loved.

Slowly he drew closer to the rearmost Knights of the Sepulcher. Their mounts bred and trained to the utmost endurance and to carry the great weight of man and mail kept to a brisk canter even after the first long spurt of speed that had carried them away from the lists of Nimmr.

The dust rolled up in clouds from iron-shod feet. Through it Blake groped, catching vague glimpses of mounted men just ahead. The black, powerful, fleet, courageous, showed no sign of fatigue. The rider carried his sword in his hand, ready. He was no longer a black knight, but a gray. Bassinet, hauberk, all the rich caparisons of his horse, the horse itself, were gray with dust.

Blake glimpsed a knight toward whom he was slowly drawing closer. This knight was gray! Like a flash Blake realized the value of the camouflage that chance had laid upon him. He might ride among them and they would not suspect that he was not of them!

Instantly he sheathed his sword and pressed forward, but he edged off a little from the knight before he passed him. Urging the black ever a little faster Blake crept up through the ranks of Bohun's knights. Somewhere a knight was carrying double and this knight he sought.

The nearer the head of the column he forged the greater became the danger of discovery, for now the dust was less thick and men could see farther, but yet his own armor, his face, the leopard skin of his bassinet were coated thick with gray and though knights peered intently at him as he passed none recognized him.

Once one hailed him. "Is't thou, Percival?" he demanded.

"Nay," replied Blake and spurred on a trifle faster.

Now, dimly, just ahead, he saw several knights bunched close and once he thought he glimpsed the fluttering garments of a woman in their midst. Pressing on, he drew close behind these and there, surrounded by knights, he saw a woman held before one of the riders.

Drawing his sword he spurred straight between two knights

who rode close behind he who carried Guinalda, and as Blake passed he cut to the right and left and the two knights rolled from their saddles.

At a touch of the spurs the black leaped abreast the young knight that was bearing off the princess. So quickly was the thing accomplished that the knights who rode scarce an arm's length from him had not the time to realize what was occurring and prevent it.

Blake slipped his left arm about the girl and at the same time thrust to the left above his left forearm, driving his blade far into the body of the youthful knight. Then he spurred forward carrying Guinalda from the dead arms as the knight pitched headlong from his saddle.

Blake's sword was wrenched from his grasp, so far had he driven it into the body of the man who dared commit this wrong against the woman Blake loved.

Cries of rage arose about him as knights spurred in pursuit and the black ran free with no guiding hand upon the reins. A huge fellow loomed just at Blake's rear and another was closing in from the other side. The first man swung his sword as he stood in his stirrups and the second was already reaching for Blake with his point.

Strange oaths were on their lips and their countenances were contorted by rage as they strove to have the life of the rash man who had almost thwarted them in their design, but that he could succeed they had not the remotest belief, for he was one against a thousand.

Then something happened the like of which had never been known to them or their progenitors. A blue barreled forty-five flashed from the holster at Blake's hip, there was a loud report and the knight upon Blake's right rear lunged head foremost to the ground. Blake turned in his saddle and shot the knight upon his other side between the eyes.

Terrified, the horses of other knights close by, who might have menaced him, bolted, as did the great black that Blake bestrode; but while the American was trying to replace his weapon in its holster and gather the reins in his right hand he leaned to the left and thus forced the horse slowly around toward the direction he wished him to go, Blake's plan being to cut across the front of the Knights of the Sepulcher and then turn southward toward Nimmr.

He was sure that Gobred and his followers must be close in pursuit, and that it would be but a matter of minutes before he would have Guinalda safe behind a thousand or more knights, any one of whom would lay down his life for her.

But the Knights of the Sepulcher had spread out over a greater front than Blake had anticipated, and now he saw them coming rapidly upon his left and was forced to swerve in a more northerly direction.

Closer and closer they came and once more the American found it necessary to drop his reins and draw his forty-five. One shot sent the horses of the menacing knights rearing and plunging away from the terrifying sound, and it sent the black into a new paroxysm of terror that almost resulted in Blake and the girl being unhorsed.

When the man finally brought the animal again under control the dust cloud that marked the position of the Knights of the Sepulcher was far behind, and close upon Blake's left was a great forest, whose dark depths offered concealment for the moment at least.

Reining quickly within Sir James drew up and gently lowered Guinalda to the ground. Then he dismounted and tied the black to a tree, for Blake was spent after what he had been through this day since his first entry upon the lists, and the black was spent as well.

He slipped the housing and the heavy saddle from the horse's back and took the great bit from his mouth, replacing a portion of the housing to serve as a cooler until the horse should be less heated, nor once did he glance at the princess until he had finished caring for his horse.

Then he turned and faced her. She was standing leaning against a tree, looking at him.

"Thou art brave, sir knight," she said softly, and then added, arrogantly, "but still a boor."

Blake smiled, wanly. He was very tired and had no wish to argue.

"I'm sorry to ask you to do it," he said, ignoring what she had said to him, "but Sir Galahad here will have to be kept moving about a bit until he cools off and I'm too fagged to do it."

The Princess Guinalda looked at him in wide-eyed amazement. "Ye—ye," she stammered, "ye mean that I should lead the beast? I, a princess!"

"I can't do it, Guinalda," replied Blake. "I tell you I'm just about all in, lugging all these skid chains about since sunrise. I guess you'll have to do it."

"Have to! Durst thou command, knave?"

"Snap out if it girl!" advised Blake curtly. "I'm responsible for your safety and it may all depend on this horse. Get busy, and do as I tell you! Lead him back and forth slowly."

There were tears of rage in the eyes of the Princess Guinalda as she prepared to make an angry retort, but there was something in Blake's eyes that silenced her. She looked at him for a long moment and then turned and walked to the black. Untying the rope that tethered him to the tree she led him slowly to and fro, while Blake sat with his back against a great tree and watched out across the plain for the first sign of pursuit.

But there was no pursuit, for the knights of Nimmr had taken the Knights of the Sepulcher and the two forces were engaging in a running fight that was leading them farther and farther away toward the City of the Sepulcher upon the north side of the valley.

Guinalda led the black for half an hour. She led him in silence and in silence Blake sat gazing out across the valley. Presently he turned toward the girl and rose to his feet.

"That'll be good," he said, approaching her. "Thank you. I'll rub him a bit now. I was too exhausted to do it before."

Without a word she turned the black over to him and with dry leaves he rubbed the animal from muzzle to dock. When he had finished he threw the housing over him again and came and sat down beside the girl.

He let his eyes wander to her profile—to her straight nose, her short upper lip, her haughty chin. "She is beautiful," thought Blake, "but selfish, arrogant and cruel." But when she turned her eyes toward him, even though they passed over him as though he had not been there, they seemed to belie all the other evidence against her.

He noticed that her eyes were never quiet. Her glances roved from place to place, but most often into the depths of the wood and upward among the branches of the trees. Once she started and turned suddenly to gaze intently into the forest.

"What is it?" asked Blake.

"Methought something moved within the wood," she said. "Let us be gone."

"It is almost dusk," he replied. "When it is dark we can ride to Nimmr in safety. Some of Bohun's knights may still be searching for you."

"What!" she exclaimed. "Remain here until dark? Knowest thou not where we be?"

"Why, what's wrong with this place?" demanded the man.

She leaned toward him, her eyes wide with terror. "It be the Wood of the Leopards!" she whispered.

"Yes?" he queried casually.

"Here lair the great leopards of Nimmr," she continued, "and after night falls only a camp with many guards and beast fires be safe from them. And even so not always then, for they have been known to leap upon a warder and, dragging him into the wood, devour him within hearing of the camp.

"But," suddenly her eyes responded to a new thought, "I hadst forgot the strange, roaring weapon with which thou slew the knights of Bohun! Of a surety with that thou couldst slay all the leopards of the wood!"

Blake hesitated to undeceive her and add to her alarm. "Perhaps," he said, "it will be as well to start now, for we have a long ride and it will soon be dark."

As he spoke he started toward Sir Galahad. He had almost reached the horse when the animal suddenly raised its head and with up pricked ears and dilated nostrils looked into the gathering shadows of the wood. For an instant Sir Galahad trembled like a leaf and then, with a wild snort, he lay back with all his weight upon the tether, and as it parted with a snap he wheeled and raced out upon the plain.

Blake drew his gun and peered into the wood, but he saw nothing nor could his atrophied sense of smell catch the scent that had come so clearly to the nostrils of Sir Galahad.

Eyes that he could not see were watching him, but they were not the eyes of Sheeta the leopard.

20

"I Love You!"

LORD TARZAN rode with Sir Bertram in the wake of the Knights of Nimmr, nor did they overtake them until after Blake had borne Guinalda out of the battle which had followed immediately the hosts of Gobred had overhauled the Knights of the Sepulcher.

As the two approached, Tarzan saw opposing knights paired off in mortal combat. He saw a Knight of Nimmr go down before an adversary's lance and then the victor espied Tarzan.

"Have at you, sir knight!" cried he of the Sepulcher, and couched his lance and put spurs to his charger.

This was a new experience for the ape-man, a new adventure, a new thrill. He knew as much about jousting as he did about ping-pong, but from childhood he had wielded a spear, and so he smiled as the knight charged upon him.

Lord Tarzan waited, and the Knight of the Sepulcher was disconcerted to see his adversary awaiting him, motionless, his spear not even couched to receive him.

Lord Bertram had reined in his horse to watch the combat and observe how this English peer accounted for himself in battle and he too was perplexed. Was the man mad, or was he fearful of the issue?

As his antagonist approached him, Tarzan rose in his stirrups and carried his lance hand above and behind his head, and when the tip of the other's lance was yet five paces from him the ape-man launched the heavy weapon as he had so often launched his hunting spear and his war spear in the chase and in battle.

It was not Viscount Greystoke who faced the Knight of the Sepulcher; it was not the king of the great apes. It was the chief of the Waziri, and no other arm in the world could cast a war spear as could his.

Forward his spear hand shot, straight as an arrow sped the great lance. It struck the shield of the Knight of the Sepulcher just above the boss and, splitting the heavy wood, drove into the heart of Tarzan's fore, and at the same instant the ape-

158

man reined his horse aside as that of his fallen antagonist thundered past.

Sir Bertram shook his head and spurred to meet an antagonist that had just challenged him. He was not sure that the act of Lord Tarzan had been entirely ethical, but he had to admit that it had been magnificent.

The fortunes of the battle carried Tarzan toward the west. His lance gone, he fought with his sword. Luck and his great strength and wondrous agility carried him through two encounters. By this time the battle had drawn off toward the northeast.

Tarzan had accounted for his second man since he had lost his lance and a Knight of the Sepulcher had slain a Knight of Nimmr. Now these two remained alone upon the field, nor did the other lose a moment in shouting his challenge to the ape-man.

Never in his life had Tarzan seen such fierce, bold men, such gluttons for battle. That they gloried in conflict and in death with a fierce lust that surpassed the maddest fanaticism he had ever witnessed filled Tarzan's breast with admiration. What men! What warriors!

Now the last knight was upon him. Their swords clashed on ready buckler. They wheeled and turned and struck again. They passed and spurred once more to close quarters. Each rose in his stirrups to deliver a terrified cut, each sought to cleave the other's skull.

The blade of the Knight of the Sepulcher glanced from Tarzan's buckler and bit into the skull of the ape-man's charger, but Tarzan's edge smote true.

As his horse went down Tarzan leaped free, his antagonist falling dead at his feet, while the riderless horse of the slain knight galloped swiftly off in the direction in which lay the City of the Sepulcher.

Tarzan looked about him. He was alone upon the field. Far to the north and east he saw the dust of battle. The City of Nimmr lay across the plain toward the south. When the battle was over it was there that Blake would ride and it was Blake whom Tarzan wanted to find. The sun was sinking behind the western hills as Tarzan turned toward Nimmr.

The chain mail that he wore was heavy, hot and uncomfortable, and Tarzan had not gone far before he discarded it. He had his knife and his rope. These he always kept with him, but he left the sword with the armor and with a sigh of relief continued on his way.

Ibn Jad, as he had come across the valley from the City of the Sepulcher toward the city that he had seen upon the opposite side, had been perturbed by the great clouds of dust that had been raised by the Knights of the Sepulcher and the pursuing Nimmrians.

Seeing a forest close upon his right hand he had thought it wiser to seek its concealing shadows until he could learn more concerning that which caused so great a dust cloud, which he saw was rapidly approaching.

Within the forest it was cool and here Ibn Jad and his followers rested.

"Let us remain here," suggested Abd el-Aziz, "until evening, when we may approach the city under cover of darkness."

Ibn Jad approved the plan and so they camped just within the forest and waited. They watched the dust cloud pass and continue on toward the City of the Sepulcher.

"Billah, it is well we did escape that village before yon host returned," said Ibn Jad.

They saw a horseman enter the forest, or pass to the south of it—they could not know which—but they were not interested in single horsemen, or in any horseman, so they did not investigate. He seemed to be either carrying another person upon his horse with him, or some great bundle. At a distance they could not see which.

"Perhaps," said Abd el-Aziz, "we shall find greater treasure in the city to the south."

"And perhaps the beautiful woman of whom the sahar spoke," added Ibn Jad, "for she was not within the city we left this morning."

"There were some there that were beautiful," said Fahd.

"The one I seek is more beautiful than an houri," said Ibn Jad.

When they took up their march again just before dark they moved cautiously just within the edge of the forest. They had covered a mile, perhaps, when those in the lead heard voices ahead. Ibn Jad sent one to investigate.

The man was soon back. His eyes were bright with excitement. "Ibn Jad," he whispered, "thou needst seek no farther—the houri is just ahead!"

Following the suggestion of the scout Ibn Jad, followed by his companions, went deeper into the woods and approached Blake and Guinalda from the west. When Sir Galahad broke loose and Blake drew his forty-five Ibn Jad knew that they could remain in concealment no longer. He called Fahd to him.

"Many of the Nasranys speak the language thou didst learn among the soldiers of the North," he said. "Speak thou therefore to this one in the same tongue, telling him we are friends and that we are lost."

When Fahd saw the Princess Guinalda his eyes narrowed and he trembled almost as might a man with ague. Never in his life had Fahd seen so beautiful a woman, never had he dreamed that an houri might be so lovely.

"Do not fire upon us," he called to Blake from the concealment of some bushes. "We are friends. We are lost."

"Who are you?" demanded Blake, surprised to hear French spoken in the Valley of the Sepulcher.

"We be poor men from the desert country," replied Fahd. "We are lost. Help us to find our way and the blessings of Allah shall be upon thee."

"Come out and let me see you," said Blake. "If you are friendly you need not fear me. I've had all the trouble I'm looking for."

Fahd and Ibn Jad stepped out into view and at sight of them Guinalda voiced a little scream and seized Blake's arm. "The Saracens!" she gasped.

"I guess they're Saracens all right," said Blake, "but you needn't worry—they won't hurt you."

"Not harm a crusader?" she demanded incredulously.

"These fellows never heard of a crusader."

"Melikes not the way they look at me," whispered Guinalda.

"Well, neither do I, but perhaps they mean no harm."

With many smiles the Arabs gathered around the two and through Fahd Ibn Jad repeated his protestations of friendship and his delight at meeting one who could direct him from the valley. He asked many questions about the City of Nimmr; and all the while his followers pressed closer to Blake.

Of a sudden the smiles vanished from their faces as, at a signal from their sheik, four stalwart Beduins leaped upon the American and bore him to the ground, snatching his gun from him, while simultaneously two others seized the Princess Guinalda.

In a moment Blake was securely bound and the 'Aarab were debating what disposition to make of him. Several wanted to slit his throat, but Ibn Jad counseled against it since they were in a valley filled with the man's friends and should the fortunes of war decide to throw some of the Beduins into the hands of the enemy such would fare better if they spared this one's life.

Blake threatened, promised, begged that they give Guinalda

her liberty, but Fahd only laughed at him and spit upon him. For a time it seemed almost certain that they were going to kill Blake, as one of the Beduins stood over him with a keen khusa in his hand, awaiting the word from Ibn Jad.

It was then that Guinalda tore free from those who held her and threw herself upon Blake to shield his body from the blade with her own.

"Thou shalt not slay him!" she cried. "Take my life an' thou must have Christian blood, but spare him."

"They cannot understand you, Guinalda," said Blake. "Perhaps they will not kill me, but that does not matter. You must escape them."

"Oh, they must not kill thee—they shall not! Canst ever forgive me the cruel words I spoke? I did not mean them. My pride was hurt that thou shouldst say of me what Malud told me thou didst say and so I spoke to hurt thee and not from my heart. Canst forgive me?"

"Forgive you? God love you, I could forgive you murder! But what did Malud tell you I had said?"

"Oh, mind not now. I care not what thou said. I tell thee I forgive it! Say to me again thy words that thou didst speak when I pinned my favor upon thy hauberk and I can forgive thee anything."

"What did Malud say?" insisted Blake.

"That thou hadst bragged that thou wouldst win me and then cast my love aside," she whispered.

"The cur! You must know that he lied, Guinalda."

"Say what I have asked and I shall know he lied," she insisted.

"I love you! I love you, Guinalda!" cried Blake.

The Arabs laid heavy hands upon the girl and dragged her to her feet. Ibn Jad and the others still argued about the disposition to be made of Blake.

"By Ullah!" exclaimed the sheik, at last, "we shall leave the Nasrany where he lies and if he dies none can say that the Beduw did slay him.

"Abd el-Aziz," he continued, "let thou take men and continue across the valley to that other city. Come, I shall accompany you a way and we will talk out of hearing of this Nasrany who, perchance, understandeth more of our tongue than he would have us guess."

As they moved away toward the south Guinalda tried to free herself again from the grasp of her captors, but they dragged her with them. Until the last Blake saw her struggling and saw her dear face turned toward him, and as they passed out of sight among the trees she called back through the falling night three words that meant more to him than all the languages of all the world combined: "I love you!"

At a distance from Blake the 'Aarab halted. "I leave thee here, Abd el-Aziz," said Ibn Jad. "Go thou and see if the city appears to be a rich place, and if it be too strongly guarded make no attempt to loot it, but return to the menzil that will be just beyond the northern summit where it now is, or, if we move it, we shall make our trail plain that you may follow us.

"I shall hasten from the valley with this rich treasure that we now have, not the least of which is the woman. Billah! in the north she will fetch the ransom of a dozen sheykh.

"Go, Abd el-Aziz, and may Allah be with thee!"

Ibn Jad turned directly north. His belief that the great body of horsemen he had glimpsed amid the distant dust were returning to the city he had sacked argued against his attempting to leave the valley by the same route that he had entered it, and so he had determined to attempt to scale the steep mountains at a point west of the City of the Sepulcher, avoiding the castle and its defenders entirely.

Blake heard the retreating footsteps of the Beduins die away in the distance. He struggled with his bonds, but the camel leather held securely. Then he lay quiet. How silent, how lonely the great, black wood—the Wood of the Leopards! Blake listened. Momentarily he expected to hear the fall of padded feet, the sound of a great, furred body approaching through the underbrush. The slow minutes dragged. An hour had passed.

The moon rose—a great, swollen, red moon that floated silently up from behind distant mountains. This moon was looking down upon Guinalda as it was on him. He whispered a message to it—a message for his princess. It was the first time that Blake ever had been in love and he almost forgot his bonds and the leopards in recalling those three words that Guinalda had called back at the instant of their separation.

What was that? Blake strained his eyes into the darkness of the shadowy wood. Something was moving! Yes, it was the sound of stealthy, padded feet—the scraping of a furred body against leaves and twigs. The leopard of the wood was coming!

Hark! There must be another in a nearby tree, for he was sure that he could see a shadowy form almost above him.

The moonlight, shining from the low moon near the eastern horizon, crept beneath the trees and lighted the ground upon which Blake lay and beyond him for a dozen yards and more.

Presently into this moonlit space stepped a great leopard.

Blake saw the blazing eyes, felt them burning into him like fire. He could not tear his own from the great snarling figure, where they were held in awful fascination.

The carnivore crouched and crept closer. Inch by inch it crept upon him as though with the studied cruelty of premeditated torture. He saw the sinuous tail lashing from side to side. He saw the great fangs bared. He saw the beast flatten against the ground, its muscles tensed. It was about to spring! Helpless, horrified, Blake could not take his eyes from the hideous, snarling face.

He saw it leap suddenly with the lightness and agility of a house cat, and at the same instant he saw something flash through the air. The leopard stopped in mid-leap and was hauled upward into a tree that overhung the spot.

He saw the shadowy form that he had seen before, but now he saw that it was a man and that he was hauling the leopard upward by a rope that had been cast about its neck at the instant that it had risen to leap upon him.

Screaming, pawing with raking talons, Sheeta the leopard was dragged upward. A mighty hand reached out and grasped the great cat by the scruff of the neck and another hand drove a knife blade into the savage heart.

When Sheeta ceased to struggle, and hung quiet, the hand released its grasp and the dead body of the carnivore thudded to the ground beside Blake. Then the god-like figure of an almost naked white man dropped lightly to the leafy mold.

Blake voiced an exclamation of surprised delight. "Tarzan of the Apes!" he cried.

"Blake?" demanded the ape-man, and then: "At last! And I didn't find you much too soon, either."

"I'll tell the world you didn't!" exclaimed Blake.

Tarzan cut the bonds that held the American.

"You've been looking for me?" asked Blake.

"Ever since I learned that you had become separated from your safari."

"By George, that was white of you!"

"Who left you trussed up here?"

"A bunch of Arabs."

Something like a growl escaped the lips of the ape-man. "That villainous old Ibn Jad here?" he demanded incredulously.

"They took a girl who was with me," said Blake. "I do not need to ask you to help me rescue her, I know."

"Which way did they go?" asked Tarzan.

"There." Blake pointed toward the south.

"When?"

"About an hour ago."

"You'd better shed that armor," advised Tarzan, "it makes walking a punishment—I just tried it."

With the ape-man's help Blake got out of his coat of mail and then the two set out upon the plain trail of the Arabs. At the point where Ibn Jad had turned back toward the north they were at a loss to know which of the two spoors to follow, for here the footprints of Guinalda, that the ape-man had been able to pick up from time to time since they left the spot where the girl had been seized, disappeared entirely.

They wondered what had become of them. They could not know that here, when she found that Ibn Jad was going to turn back with her away from Nimmr, she had refused to walk farther. It had been all right as long as they were approaching Nimmr, but she refused absolutely to be a party to her own abduction when it led away from home.

What breeze there was was blowing from the east, nullifying the value of Tarzan's sense of smell so that even the great ape-man could not know in what direction or with which party Guinalda had been carried off.

"The most reasonable assumption," said Tarzan, "is that your princess is with the party that has gone north, for I know that Ibn Jad's menzil must lay in that direction. He did not enter the valley from the south. That I know because I just came in that way myself and Sir Bertram assured me that there are only two entrances—the one through which I came and a pass above the City of the Sepulcher.

"Ibn Jad would want to get the girl out of the valley and into his camp as soon as possible whether he is going to hold her for ransom or take her north to sell her. The party that went south toward Nimmr may have been sent to treat with her people for a ransom; but the chances are that she is not with that party.

"However, it is at best but a matter of conjecture. We must ascertain definitely, and I suggest that you follow the northern spoor, which is, I am certain, the one that will lead to the girl, while I overtake the party to the south.

"I can travel faster than you and if I am right and the girl is with the northern party I'll turn back and overtake you without much loss of time. If you catch up with the other band and find the girl is not with them, you can turn back and join me; but if she is with them you'd better not risk trying to recover her until you have help, for you are unarmed and those Beduins would think no more of cutting your throat than they would of drinking a cup of coffee.

"Now, good-bye and good luck!" And Tarzan of the Apes was off at a trot upon the trail of the party that had gone in the direction of Nimmr, while Blake turned northward to face a dismal journey through the black depths of the Wood of the Leopards.

21

"For Every Jewel a Drop of Blood!"

A LL night Ibn Jad and his party marched northward. Though they were hampered by the refusal of Guinalda to walk, yet they made rapid progress for they were spurred on by their great desire to escape from the valley with their booty before they should be discovered and set upon by the great host of fighting men they were now convinced were quartered in the castle and city they had been fortunate enough to find almost deserted.

Avarice gave them strength and endurance far beyond that which they normally displayed, with the result that dawn found them at the foot of the ragged mountains that Ibn Jad had determined to scale rather than attempt an assault upon the castle which guarded the easy way from the valley.

It was a jaded party that won eventually to the pass just above the outer barbican that guarded the road to the City of the Sepulcher, nor were they discovered by the warders there until the last man of them was safely on the trail leading to the low saddle at the summit of the mountains, beyond which lay the menzil of the Beduins.

The defenders of the barbican made a sortie against them and approached their rear so closely that the knight who commanded saw Guinalda and recognized her, but a volley from the matchlocks of the desert people sent the crudely armed soldiers of Bohun back in retreat, though the brave knight couched his lance and charged again until his hosse was brought down by a bullet and he lay pinned beneath it.

It was afternoon before Ibn Jad with his fagged company staggered into the menzil. Though they dropped in their tracks from sheer exhaustion, he allowed them but an hour of sleep before he gave the signal for the rahla, for the sheik of the fendy el-Guad was filled with an ever increasing fear that the treasure and the woman would be taken away from him before he could reach the sandy wastes of his own barren beled.

The heavy weight of the treasure had been divided into several bundles and these were distributed among his least mistrusted followers, while the custody of the girl captive was placed in the hands of Fahd, whose evil eyes filled the princess with fear and loathing.

Stimbol, who had secretly scoffed at the stories of treasure and the mad tales of a beautiful woman that the 'Aarab expected to find in some fabulous, hidden city, was dumbfounded when he viewed the spoils of the Beduin, and at first was inclined to attribute them to the hallucinations of his fever-racked brain.

Weak, Stimbol staggered feebly along the trail, keeping as close to Fahd as he could, for he knew that of all the company this unscrupulous scoundrel would be most likely to assist him, for to Fahd a live Stimbol meant great wealth; nor was Fahd unmindful of the fact. And now there was another purpose in the evil mind of the Beduin who had conceived for the white girl an infatuation that was driving him to the verge of madness.

With the wealth that Stimbol had promised him Fahd realized that he could afford to possess this lovely houri whom otherwise a poor Beduwy must sell for the great price that she would bring, and so there revolved in the mind of Fahd many schemes whereby he might hope to gain sole possession of both Guinalda and Stimbol; but always there loomed in the path of every plan that he considered the dour figure of his greedy sheykh.

At the foot of the Mountains of the Sepulcher Ibn Jad turned toward the east, thus to avoid passing again through the country of Batando. Beyond the eastern end of the range he would turn south again and later strike west just above the northern limits of the territory that was nominally Tarzan's, for though he knew that the Lord of the Jungle was dead he yet feared the vengeance of his people.

It was late before Ibn Jad made camp. The preparations for the evening meal were hurried. The light from the cooking fire and the paper lanterns in the beyt of the sheik was dim and flickering, yet not so dim but that Ateja saw Fahd drop something into the bowl of food that she had prepared for Ibn Jad and which stood upon the ground between him and his would-be assassin.

As the shiek reached for the receptacle Ateja stepped from the women's quarters and struck it from his hand, but before she could explain her act or charge Fahd with his villainy the culprit, realizing that his perfidy had been discovered, leaped to his feet and seizing his matchlock sprang into the women's quarters where Guinalda had been left under the watchful care of Hirfa and Ateja.

Seizing the girl by the wrist and dragging her after him Fahd broke through the curtains at the rear of the beyt and ran in the direction of his own tent. By this time the mukaad of Ibn Jad was in an uproar. The sheik was demanding an explanation from Ateja and still unaware that Fahd had escaped through the rear of the beyt no one had followed him into the women's quarters.

"He placed *simm* in thy food!" cried Ateja. "I saw him and the proof of it be that he fled when he knew that I had seen."

"Billah," exclaimed Ibn Jad. "The son of a jackal would poison me? Seize him and fetch him to me!"

"He hath fled through the beyt!" cried Hirfa, "and taken the Nasrawia with him."

The Beduins sprang to their feet and took after Fahd, but at his own beyt he stopped them with a bullet and they retreated. In his tent he seized Stimbol who was lying upon a filthy sleeping mat and dragged him to his feet.

"Hasten!" he hissed in the American's ear. "Ibn Jad has ordered that thou be slain! Quick! follow me and I will save thee."

Again Fahd had recourse to the rear curtains of a beyt and as his fellows approached the front in anger but with caution, Fahd, dragging Guinalda and followed by Stimbol, sneaked through the darkness of the menzil and turned toward the west.

It was dusk when James Blake, following the plain trail of Ibn Jad, finally clambered over the last escarpment and stood upon the trail that led through the pass toward the outer world beyond the valley of the Sepulcher.

A hundred yards to his right loomed the gray towers of the barbican, to his left was the trail that led in the direction of his heart's desire, and all about him, concealed in the bushes, were the men-at-arms of King Bohun of the Sepulcher; but this he did not guess, for how could he know that for hours the eyes of the warders had been watching his slow ascent toward the pass trail?

Spent by the long climb following hours of gruelling exertion without food or rest, unarmed, Blake was helpless to resist or to attempt escape when a dozen armed men stepped from the surrounding bushes and encircled him in a band of steel. And so Sir James of Nimmr was seized and haled before King Bohun, and when he was questioned and Bohun found that he was the same black knight that had thwarted his plan to abduct the Princess Guinalda he could scarce contain himself.

Assuring Blake only of the fact that he would be put to death as soon as Bohun could determine upon a fate commensurate with the heinousness of the crime, the king ordered him to be placed in chains, and the American was led away by guards to a black hole beneath the castle, where by the light of flares a smith forged a heavy iron band about one ankle and he was chained to a damp stone wall.

In the light of the flare Blake saw two emaciated, naked creatures similarly chained, and in a far corner glimpsed a skeleton among the bones of which rusted a length of chain and a great anklet. Then silently the guards and the smith departed, taking the flares with them, and James Blake was left in darkness and despair.

Upon the plain, below the City of Nimmr, Tarzan had overtaken the party of Beduins led by Abd el-Aziz, and after assuring himself that the girl was not with them he had turned without revealing himself to them and hurried northward to take up the trail of the other party.

Requiring food and rest he lay up in the Wood of the Leopards during the heat of the day after stalking Horta the boar and making a quick kill. His belly filled, the ape-man found a high flung tree crotch where there was little likelihood of the heavy leopards of Nimmr disturbing his slumbers, and here he slept until the sun was sinking behind the western menzil where Ibn Jad's people had camped during his incursion of the Valley of the Sepulcher.

Some time since, he had lost the spoor of Blake, but that of the girl frequently recurred, and as her rescue now took precedence over other considerations he followed doggedly along the trail of Ibn Jad. For a time he was mystified by the fact that Guinalda's spoor, well marked by the imprints of the tiny sandals of medieval design, did not appear among the footprints of those who left the Beduin menzil.

He lost some time searching about in an effort to discover a clew to the riddle and presently he hit upon the truth, which lay in the fact that Guinalda's light sandals having been badly worn by her journey and far too tight for comfortable walking she had been given a pair belonging to Ateja, and thus it became difficult to differentiate between the spoor of the two girls, who were of equal weight and of a similarity of carriage that rendered their footprints practically identical.

Tarzan therefore contented himself with following the spoor

of the party, and so it was that he passed their first night's camp, where Fahd had stolen Guinalda from the Sheik, without discovering that three of its members had there turned to the west, while the main body of the 'Aarab marched toward the east.

And as Tarzan followed the spoor of Ibn Jad a hundred stalwart Waziri moved northward from the water hole of the smooth, round rocks upon the old trail of the Beduins. With them was Zeyd, who had begged so hard to accompany them when they passed the village where he had been waiting that at last the sub-chief had consented.

When Tarzan overtook the 'Aarab they had already turned south around the eastern end of the Mountains of the Sepulcher. He saw the bags they carried and the evident concern with which Ibn Jad watched and guarded them, and he shrewdly guessed that the wily old thief had indeed found the treasure he had sought; but he saw no evidence of the presence of the Princess, and Stimbol, too, was missing.

Tarzan was furious. He was furious at the thieving Beduins for daring to invade his country and he was furious at himself because he felt that in some way he had been tricked.

Tarzan had his own methods of inflicting punishment upon his enemies and he had, as well, his own grim and grisly sense of humor. When men were doing wrong it pleased him to take advantage of whatever might cause them the greatest suffering and in this he was utterly ruthless with his enemies.

He was confident that the 'Aarab thought him dead and it did not suit his whim to reveal their error to them at this time, but it did accord with his fancy to let them commence to feel the weight of his displeasure and taste the first fruits of their villainy.

Moving silently through the trees Tarzan paralleled the course of the 'Aarab. They were often plainly visible to him; but none saw Tarzan, nor dreamed that savage eyes were watching their every move.

Five men carried the treasure, though its weight was not so great but that one powerful man might have borne it for a short distance. Tarzan watched these men most often, these and the Sheik Ibn Jad.

The trail was wide and the sheik walked beside one of those who bore the treasure. It was very quiet in the jungle. Even the 'Aarab, garrulous among themselves, were quiet, for they were very tired and the day was hot and they were unused to the burdens they were forced to carry since Batando had robbed them of their slaves.

Of a sudden, without warning and with only the swish of its flight through the air to announce it, an arrow passed through the neck of the Beduin who walked beside Ibn Jad.

With a scream the man lunged forward upon his face and the 'Aarab, warned by their sheik, cocked their muskets and prepared to receive an attack, but look where they would they saw no sign of an enemy. They waited, listening, but there was no sound other than the droning of insects and the occasional raucous cry of a bird; but when they moved on again, leaving their fellow dead upon the trail, a hollow voice called to them from a distance.

"For every jewel a drop of blood!" it wailed dismally, for its author knew well the intensely superstitious nature of the desert dwellers and how best to affright them.

It was a shaken column that continued on its way, nor was there any mention of making camp until almost sunset, so anxious were they all to leave behind this gloomy wood and the horrid afrit that inhabited it; but the forest persisted and at length it became necessary to make camp.

Here the camp fires and food relieved the tension upon their overwrought nerves, and their spirits had revived to such an extent that there were again singing and laughter in the menzil of Ibn Jad.

The old sheik himself sat in his mukaad surrounded by the five bags of treasure, one of which he had opened and beneath the light of a lantern was fondling the contents. About him were his cronies, sipping their coffee.

Suddenly something fell heavily upon the ground before the beyt and rolled into the mukaad among them. It was the severed head of a man! Glaring up at them were the dead eyes of their fellow, whose corpse they had left lying in the trail earlier in the day.

Horror struck, spellbound, they sat staring at the gruesome thing when, from out of the dark forest, came the hollow voice again: *"For every jewel a drop of blood!"*

Ibn Jad shook as a man with ague. The men of the camp gathered close together in front of the beyt of the sheik. Each grasped a musket in one hand and searched for his hijab with the other, for each carried several of these amulets, and that in demand this night was the one written against the jin, for certainly none but a jin could have done this thing.

Hirfa stood half within the mukaad staring at the dead face of her fellow while Ateja crouched upon a sleeping mat in the quarters of the women. She did not see the back curtain rise, nor the figure that crept within. It was dark in the quarters of the hareem since little light filtered in from the lanterns in the mukaad.

Ateja felt a hand clapped across her mouth at the same instant that another grasped her by the shoulder. A voice whispered in her ear. "Make no sound! I shall not hurt thee. I am a friend to Zeyd. Tell me the truth and no harm will befall you or him. Where is the woman Ibn Jad brought from the valley?"

He who held her placed his ear close to her lips and removed his hand from them. Ateja trembled like a leaf. She had never seen a jin. She could not see the creature that leaned close to her, but she knew that it was one of those fearsome creatures of the night.

"Answer!" whispered the voice in her ear. "If thou wouldst save Zeyd, speak and speak the truth!"

"Fahd took the woman from our menzil last night," she gasped. "I do not know where they went."

As it came, in silence the presence left the side of the terrified girl. When Hirfa sought her a moment later she found her in a swoon.

BLAKE squatted upon the stone floor in the utter darkness of his dungeon. After his jailers had left he had spoken to his fellow prisoners, but only one had replied and his jibbering tones assured the American that the poor wretch had been reduced to stark insanity by the horrors of imprisonment in this foul hole.

The young man, accustomed to freedom, light, activity, already felt the hideousness of his position and wondered how long it would be before he, too, jibbered incoherently at the end of a rusting chain, how long before he, too, was but mildewed bones upon a clammy floor.

In utter darkness and in utter silence there is no time, for there is no means by which one may compute the passage of time. How long Blake crouched in the stifling air of his dank dungeon he could not know. He slept once, but whether he had dozed for an instant or slept the clock around he could not even hazard a guess. And of what moment was it? A second a day, a year meant nothing here. There were only two things that could mean anything to Jim Blake now—freedom or death. He knew that it would not be long before he would welcome the latter.

A sound disturbed the silence of the buried vault. Footsteps were approaching. Blake listened as they came nearer. Presently he discerned a flickering light that grew in intensity until a pine torch illuminated the interior of his prison. At first it blinded his eyes so that he could not see who came, bearing the light, but whoever it was crossed and stopped before him.

Blake looked up, his eyes more accustomed to the unwonted brilliance, and saw two knights standing before him.

"It be he," said one.

"Dost thou not know us, Sir Black Knight?" demanded the other.

Blake looked at them closely. A slow smile lighted his face, as he saw a great bandage wrapped about the neck of the younger man.

"I suppose," he said, "here is where I get mine."

"Get thine! What meanest thou?" demanded the older man.

"Well, you two certainly haven't come to pin any medals on me, Sir Wildred," said Blake, with a wry smile.

"Thou speakest in riddles," said Wildred. "We have come to free thee that the young king may not bring disgrace upon the Knights of the Sepulcher by carrying out his wicked will with thee. Sir Guy and I heard that he would burn thee at the stake, and we said to one another that while blood flowed in our bodies we would not let so valorous a knight be thus shamelessly wronged by any tyrant."

As he spoke Wildred stooped and with a great rasp commenced filing upon the iron rivets that held the hinged anklet in place.

"You are going to help me to escape!" exclaimed Blake. "But suppose you are discovered—will not the king punish you?"

"We shall not be discovered," said Wildred, "though I would take that chance for so noble a knight as thee. Sir Guy be upon the outer barbican this night and 'twill be no trick to get thee that far. He can pass thee through and thou canst make thy way down the mountain side and cross to Nimmr. We cannot get thee through the city gates for these be held by two of Bohun's basest creatures, but perchance upon the morrow Sir Guy or I may find the way to ride out upon the plain with a led horse, and that we shall if so it hap that it be possible."

"Tell us a thing that hath filled us with questioning," said Sir Guy.

"I don't follow you," said Blake.

"Thou didst, and mighty prettily too, take the Princess Guinalda from under the very nose of Bohun," continued Guy, "and yet later she was seen in the clutches of the Saracens. How came this to pass?"

"She was seen?" demanded Blake. "Where?"

"Beyond the outer barbican she was and the Saracens carried her away through the pass that leadeth no man knoweth where," said Wildred.

Blake told them of all that had transpired since he had taken Guinalda from Bohun, and by the time he had finished the rivets had been cut and he stood again a free man.

Wildred smuggled him through secret passages to his own quarters and there gave him food and new clothing and a suit of armor, for now that they knew he was riding out over the pass into the strange country they had decided that he could

only be permitted to do so properly armored, armed an
mounted.

It was midnight when Wildred smuggled Blake through th
castle gate and rode with him toward the outer barbican. Her
Sir Guy met them and a few minutes later Blake bid thes
chivalrous enemies good-bye and, mounted on a powerfu
charger, his own colors flying from his lance tip, rode beneat'
the portcullis and out upon the starlit road that led to th
summit of the Mountains of the Sepulcher.

Toyat, the king ape, picked a succulent beetle from the de
caying bark of a fallen tree. About him were the great, savag
people of his tribe. It was afternoon and the apes loafed in th
shade of great trees beside a little natural clearing in the jungle
They were content and at peace with all the world.

Coming toward them were three people, but the wind ble
from the apes toward the people and so neither Toyat nor an
of his fellows caught the scent spoor of the Tarmangani. Th
jungle trail was soft with damp mold, for it had rained th
night before, and the feet of the three gave forth no soun
that the apes heard. Then, too, the three were moving cau
tiously for they had not eaten for two days and they wer
hunting for food.

There was a gray old man, emaciated by fever, totterin
along with the aid of a broken tree branch; there was
wicked-eyed Beduin carrying a long musket; and the thir
was a girl whose strange garments of splendid stuffs were tor
and soiled. Her face was streaked with dirt and was draw
and thin, yet still it was a face of almost heavenly beauty. Sh
walked with an effort, and though she sometimes stumble
from weariness never did she lose a certain regalness of car
riage, nor lower the haughty elevation of her well moulde
chin.

The Beduin was in the lead. It was he who first sighted
young ape playing at the edge of the clearing, farthest fror
the great bulls of the tribe of Toyat. Here was food! Th
Beduin raised his ancient weapon and took aim. He presse
the trigger and the ensuing roar mingled with the scream c
pain and terror that burst from the wounded balu.

Instantly the great bulls leaped to action. Would they fle
the feared and hated thunder stick of the Tarmangani, c
would they avenge the hurting of the balu? Who might know
Today they might do the one, tomorrow, under identical cir
cumstances, the other. Today they chose vengeance.

Led by Toyat, growling hideously, the bulls lumbered forward to investigate. It was this sight that met the horrified gaze of the three as they followed up Fahd's shot to learn if at last they were to eat or if they must plod on hopelessly, weakened by the hunger gnawing at their vitals.

Fahd and Stimbol turned and bolted back down the trail, the Arab, in his cowardly haste, pushing Guinalda to one side and hurling her to the ground. The leading bull, seeing the girl, leaped upon her and was about to sink his teeth into her neck when Toyat seized him and dragged him from her, for Toyat had recognized her for what she was. The king ape had once seen another Tarmangani she and had decided that he would like to have one as a wife.

The other ape, a huge bull, seeing that Toyat wanted the prey and angered by the bullying manner of the king, immediately decided to contest Toyat's right to what he had first claimed. Baring his fangs he advanced menacingly toward Toyat who had dragged the girl back into the clearing.

Toyat snarled back at him. "Go away," said Toyat. "This is Toyat's she."

"It is Go-yad's," replied the other, advancing.

Toyat turned back. "I kill!" he screamed.

Go-yad came on and suddenly Toyat seized Guinalda in his hairy arms and fled into the jungle. Behind him, bellowing and screaming, pursued Go-yad.

The Princess Guinalda, wide-eyed with horror, fought to free herself from the hideous, hairy creature that was bearing her off. She had never seen nor even heard of such a thing as a great ape, and she thought them now some hideous, low inhabitant of that outer world that she had always been taught consisted of encircling armies of Saracens and beyond and at a great distance a wonderful country known as England. What else was there she had not even tried to guess, but evidently it was a horrid place peopled by hideous creatures, including dragons.

Toyat had run no great distance when he realized that he could not escape while burdened with the she, and as he had no mind to give her up he turned suddenly and faced the roaring Go-yad. Go-yad did not stop. He came on frothing at the mouth, bristling, snarling—a picture of bestial savagery, power and frenzied rage.

Toyat, relinquishing his hold upon the girl, advanced to meet the charge of his rebellious subject, while Guinalda, weakened by unaccustomed exertion and lace of nourishment, appalled by the hideous circumstances of her plight, sank panting to the ground.

Toyat and Go-yad, immersed in the prospect of battle, were oblivious to all else. Could Guinalda have taken advantage of this temporary forgetfulness of her she might have escaped; but she was too stunned, too exhausted to take advantage of her opportunity. Spellbound, fascinated by the horror of it, she watched these terrifying, primordial man-beasts preparing to do battle for possession of her.

Nor was Guinalda the sole witness of these savage preliminaries. From the concealment of a low bush behind which he lay another watched the scene with steady, interested eyes. Absorbed by their own passion neither Toyat nor Go-yad noted the occasional movement of the outer leaves of the bush behind which this other watcher lay, a movement imparted by the body of the watcher with each breath and with each slightest change of position.

Perhaps the watcher discovered no sporting interest in the impending duel, for just as the two apes were about to engage he arose and stepped into the open—a great black-maned lion, whose yellow coat gleamed golden in the sunlight.

Toyat saw him first and with a growl of rage turned and fled, leaving his adversary and their prize to whatever fate Providence might hold in store for them.

Go-yad, thinking his rival had abandoned the field through fear of him, beat loudly upon his breast and roared forth the victory cry of the bull ape, then, swaggering as became a victor and a champion, he turned to claim the prize.

Between himself and the girl he saw the lion standing, gazing with serious mien straight into his eyes. Go-yad halted. Who would not have? The lion was within springing distance but he was not crouched. Go-yad backed away, snarling, and when the lion made no move to follow, the great ape suddenly turned and lumbered off into the jungle, casting many a backward glance in the direction of the great cat until intervening foliage shut him from his view.

Then the lion turned toward the girl. Poor little Princess! Hopeless, resigned, she lay upon the ground staring, wide-eyed, at this new engine of torture and destruction. The king of beasts surveyed her for a moment and then walked toward her. Guinalda clasped her hands and prayed—not for life, for hope of that she had long since resigned, but for death, speedy and painless.

The tawny beast came close. Guinalda closed her eyes to shut out the fearsome sight. She felt hot breath upon her cheek, its fetid odor assailed her nostrils. The lion sniffed about her. God! why did he not end it? Tortured nerves could endure no more and Guinalda swooned. Merciful surcease of her suffering.

NERVE shaken, the remnants of Ibn Jad's company turned toward the west and hastened by forced marches to escape the hideous forest of the jin. Abd el-Aziz and those who had accompanied him from the Wood of the Leopards toward Nimmr had not rejoined them. Nor ever would they, for upon the plain below the treasure city of the Beduins' dreaming the knights of Gobred had discovered them and, despite the thundering havoc of the ancient matchlocks, the iron Knights of Nimmr had couched their spears against the Saracens and once again the victorious cri de guerre of the Crusaders had rung out after seven centuries of silence to announce a new engagement in the hoary war for the possession of the Holy Land—the war that is without end.

From the north a mailed knight rode down through the forest of Galla land. A blue and silver pennon fluttered from his lance. The housings of his great charger were rich with gold and silver from the treasure vaults of Wildred of the Sepulcher. Wide-eyed Galla warriors viewed this solitary anachronism from afar, and fled.

Tarzan of the Apes, ranging westward, came upon the spoor of Fahd and Stimbol and Guinalda and followed it toward the south.

Northward marched a hundred ebon giants, veterans of a hundred battles—the famed Waziri—and with them came Zeyd, the lover of Ateja. One day they came upon a fresh spoor crossing their line of march diagonally toward the southwest. It was the spoor of Arab sandals, those of two men and a woman, and when the Waziri pointed them out to Zeyd the young Beduin swore that he recognized those of the woman as belonging to Ateja, for who knew better the shape and size of her little foot, or the style of the sandals she fabricated? He begged the Waziri to turn aside for a time and aid him in finding his sweetheart, and while the sub-chief was debating the question in his mind the sound of something hurrying through the jungle attracted the attention of every ear.

While they listened a man staggered into view. It was Fahd. Zeyd recognized him instantly and as immediately became doubly positive that the footprints of the woman had been made by Ateja.

Zeyd approached Fahd menacingly. "Where is Ateja?" he demanded.

"How should I know? I have not seen her for days," replied Fahd, truthfully enough.

"Thou liest!" cried Zeyd, and pointed at the ground. "Here are her own footprints beside thine!"

A cunning expression came into the eyes of Fahd. Here he saw an opportunity to cause suffering to the man he hated. He shrugged his shoulders.

"Wellah, if you know, you know," he said.

"Where is she?" demanded Zeyd.

"She is dead. I would have spared you," answered Fahd.

"Dead?" The suffering in that single word should have melted a heart of stone—but not Fahd's.

"I stole her from her father's beyt," continued Fahd, wishing to inflict as much torture as possible upon his rival. "For days and nights she was mine; then a huge ape stole her from me. By now she must be dead."

But Fahd had gone to far. He had encompassed his own undoing. With a scream of rage Zeyd leaped upon him with drawn khusa, and before the Waziri could interfere or Fahd defend himself the keen blade had drunk thrice in the heart of the lying Beduin.

With bent head and dull eyes Zeyd marched on northward with the Waziri, as, a mile behind them, a wasted old man, burning with fever, stumbled in the trail and fell. Twice he tried to regain his feet, only to sink weakly back to earth. A filthy, ragged bundle of old bones, he lay—sometimes raving in delirium, sometimes so still that he seemed dead.

Down from the north came Tarzan of the Apes upon the spoor of Guinalda and the two who had accompanied her. Knowing well the windings of the trail he took short cuts, swinging through the branches of the trees, and so it happened that he missed the Waziri at the point where their trail had encountered that of Fahd, where Zeyd had slain his rival, and presently his nostrils picked up the scent of the Mangani in the distance.

Toward the great apes he made his way swiftly for he

feared that harm might befall the girl should she, by any mis-
chance, fall into the hands of the anthropoids. He arrived
in the clearing where they lazed, a short time after the return of Toyat and Go-yad, who, by now, had abandoned their
quarrel, since the prize had been taken by one stronger than
either of them.

The preliminaries of meeting over and the apes having
recognized and acknowledged Tarzan, he demanded if any
had seen the Tarmangani she who had recently passed through
the jungle.

M'walat pointed at Toyat and Tarzan turned toward the
king.

"You have seen the she?" demanded Tarzan, fearful, for he
did not like the manner of the king ape.

Toyat jerked a thumb toward the south. "Numa," he said
and went on hunting for food, but Tarzan knew what the ape
meant as surely as though he had spoken a hundred words of
explanation.

"Where?" asked Tarzan.

Toyat pointed straight to where he had abandoned Guinalda
to the lion, and the ape-man, moving straight through the
jungle along the line indicated by the king ape, went sadly to
investigate, although he already guessed what he would find.
At least he could drive Numa from his kill and give decent
burial to the unfortunate girl.

Slowly consciousness returned to Guinalda. She did not open
her eyes, but lay very quiet wondering if this was death. She
felt no pain.

Presently a sickly sweet and pungent odor assailed her
nostrils and something moved very close to her, so close that
she felt it against her body, pressing gently, and where it
pressed she felt heat as from another body.

Fearfully she opened her eyes and the horror of her predicament again swept over her for she saw that the lion had
lain down almost against her. His back was toward her, his
noble head was lifted, his black mane almost brushed her face.
He was looking off, intently, toward the north.

Guinalda lay very quiet. Presently she felt, rather than
heard, a low rumbling growl that seemed to have its origin
deep in the cavernous chest of the carnivore.

Something was coming! Even Guinalda sensed that, but it
could not be succor, for what could succor her from this hideous beast?

There was a rustling among the branches of the trees a hundred feet away and suddenly the giant figure of a demigod dropped to the ground. The lion rose and faced the man. The two stood thus, eying one another for a brief moment. Then the man spoke.

"Jad-bal-ja!" he exclaimed, and then: "Come to heel!"

The great, golden lion whined and strode across the open space, stopping before the man. Guinalda saw the beast look up into the face of the demigod and saw the latter stroke the tawny head affectionately, but meanwhile the eyes of the man, or god, or whatever he was, were upon Guinalda and she saw the sudden relief that came to them as Tarzan realized that the girl was unharmed.

Leaving the lion the ape-man crossed to where the princess lay and knelt beside her.

"You are the Princess Guinalda?" he asked.

The girl nodded, wondering how he knew her. As yet she was too stunned to command her own voice.

"Are you hurt?" he asked.

She shook her head.

"Do not be afraid," he assured her in a gentle voice. "I am your friend. You are safe now."

There was something in the way he said it that filled Guinalda with such a sense of safety as all the mailed knights of her father's realm had scarce imparted.

"I am not afraid—any more," she said simply.

"Where are your companions?" he asked.

She told him all that had happened.

"You are well rid of them," said the ape-man, "and we shall not attempt to find them. The jungle will account for them in its own way and in its own good time."

"Who art thou?" asked the girl.

"I am Tarzan."

"How didst thou know my name?" she queried.

"I am a friend of one whom you know as Sir James," he explained. "He and I were searching for you."

"Thou art his friend?" she cried. "Oh, sweet sir, then thou art mine as well!"

The ape-man smiled. "Always!" he said.

"Why did the lion not kill thee, Sir Tarzan?" she demanded, thinking him a simple knight, for in her land there were only these beside the members of her princely house and the pseudo king of the City of the Sepulcher. For in the original company that had been wrecked upon the coast of Africa at the time of

the Third Crusade there were only knights, except one bastard
son of Henry II, who had been the original Prince Gobred.
Never having been in contact with an English king since they
parted from Richard at Cyprus no Gobred had assumed the
right to issue patents of nobility to his followers, solely the
prerogative of the king.

"Why did the lion not kill me?" repeated Tarzan. "Because
he is Jad-bal-ja, the Golden Lion, which I raised from cub-
hood. All his life he has known me only as friend and master.
He would not harm me and it was because of his lifelong
association with human beings that he did not harm you;
though I was fearful when I saw him beside you that he had,
for a lion is always a lion!"

"Thou dwellest nearby?" asked the girl.

"Far away," said Tarzan, "But there must be some of my
people nearby, else Jad-bal-ja would not be here. I sent for
my warriors and doubtless he has accompanied them."

Finding that the girl was hungry Tarzan bade the Golden
Lion remain and guard her while he went in search of food.

"Do not fear him," he told her, "and remember that you
could not have a protector more competent than he to dis-
courage the approach of enemies."

"And well mayst I believe it," admitted Guinalda.

Tarzan returned with food and then, as the day was not
done, he started back toward Nimmr with the rescued girl,
carrying her, as she was now too weak to walk; and beside
them strode the great, black-maned lion of gold.

During that journey Tarzan learned much of Nimmr and
also discovered that Blake's love for his princess was apparently fully reciprocated by the girl, for she seemed never so
content as when talking about her Sir James and asking questions concerning his far country and his past life, of which,
unfortunately, Tarzan could tell her nothing.

Upon the second day the three came to the great cross and
here Tarzan hailed the warders and bade them come and
take their princess.

She urged the ape-man to accompany her to the castle and
receive the thanks of her father and mother, but he told her
that he must leave at once to search for Blake, and at that
she ceased her urging.

"An' thou findst him," she said, "tell him that the gates of
Nimmr be always open to him and that the Princess Guinalda
awaits his return."

Down from the Cross went Tarzan and Jad-bal-ja and before she turned back to enter the tunnel that led to her father's

castle the Princess Guinalda stood watching them until a turn in the trail hid them from her view.

"May Our Lord Jesus bless thee, sweet sir knight," she murmured, "and watch o'er thee and fetch thee back once more with my beloved!"

Where Trails Met

DOWN through the forest rode Blake searching for some clew to the whereabouts of the Arabs, ranging this way and that, following trails and abandoning them.

Late one day he came suddenly in to a large clearing where once a native village had stood. The jungle had not yet reclaimed it and as he entered it he saw a leopard crouching upon the far side, and before the leopard lay the body of a human being. At first Blake thought the poor creature dead, but presently he saw it attempt to rise and crawl away.

The great cat growled and advanced toward it. Blake shouted and spurred forward, but Sheeta paid no attention to him, evidently having no mind to give up its prey; but as Blake came nearer the cat turned to face him with an angry growl.

The American wondered if his horse would dare the close proximity of the beast of prey, but he need not have feared. Nor would he had he been more fully acquainted with the customs of the Valley of the Sepulcher, where one of the greatest sports of the knights of the two enemy cities is hunting the giant cats with lance alone when they venture from the sanctuary of the Wood of the Leopards.

The charger that Blake bestrode had faced many a savage cat, and larger, too, by far than this one, and so he fell into his charging stride with no show of fear or nervousness and the two thundered down upon Sheeta while the creature that was to have been its prey looked on with wide, astounded eyes.

Within the length of its spring Sheeta rose swiftly to meet the horse and man. He leaped and as he leaped he struck full on the metal tip of the great lance, and the wooden shaft passed through him so far that it was with difficulty that the man forced the carcass from it. When he had done so he turned and rode to the side of the creature lying helpless on the ground.

"My God!" he cried as his eyes rested on the face below him. "Stimbol!"

"Blake!"

The younger man dismounted.

"I'm dying, Blake," whispered Stimbol. "Before I go I want to tell you that I'm sorry. I acted like a cad. I guess I've got what was coming to me."

"Never mind that, Stimbol," said Blake. "You're not dead yet. The first thing is to get you where there are food and water." He stooped and lifted the emaciated form and placed the man in his saddle. "I passed a small native village a few miles back. They all ran when they saw me, but we'll try there for food."

"What are you doing here?" asked Stimbol. "And in the name of King Arthur, where did you get the outfit?"

"I'll tell you about it when we get to the village," said Blake. "It's a long story. I'm looking for a girl that was stolen by the Arabs a few days ago."

"God!" ejaculated Stimbol.

"You know something about her?" demanded Blake.

"I was with the man that stole her," said Stimbol, "or at least who stole her from the other Arabs."

"Where is she?"

"She's dead, Blake!"

"Dead?"

"A bunch of those big anthropoid apes got her. The poor child must have been killed immediately."

Blake was silent for a long time, walking with bowed head as, weighted down by heavy armor, he led the horse along the trail.

"Did the Arabs harm her?" he asked presently.

"No," said Stimbol. "The sheik stole her either for ransom or to sell her in the north, but Fahd stole her for himself. He took me along because I had promised him a lot of money if he'd save me, and I kept him from harming the girl by telling him that he'd never get a cent from me if he did. I felt sorry for the poor child and I made up my mind that I was going to save her if I could."

When Blake and Stimbol approached the village the blacks fled, leaving the white men in full possession of the place. It did not take Blake long to find food for them both.

Making Stimbol as comfortable as possible, Blake found fodder for his horse and presently returned to the old man. He was engaged in narrating his experiences when he was suddenly aware of the approach of many people. He could hear voices and the pad of naked feet. Evidently the villagers were returning.

Blake prepared to meet them with friendly overtures, but

the first glimpse he had of the approaching party gave him a distinct shock, for these were not the frightened villagers he had seen scurrying into the jungle a short time before.

With white plumes waving about their heads a company of stalwart warriors came swinging down the trail. Great oval shields were upon their backs, long war spears in their hands.

"Well," said Blake, "I guess we're in for it. The villagers have sent for their big brothers."

The warriors entered the village and when they saw Blake the halted in evident wonder. One of their number approached him and to Blake's surprise addressed him in fairly good English.

"We are the Waziri of Tarzan," he said. "We search for our chief and master. Have you seen him, Bwana?"

The Waziri! Blake could have hugged them. He had been at his wits end to know what he was to do with Stimbol. Alone he never could have brought the man to civilization, but now he knew that his worries were over.

Had it not been for the grief of Blake and Zeyd, it had been a merry party that made free with the cassava and beer of the villagers that night, for the Waziri were not worrying about their chief.

"Tarzan cannot die," said the sub-chief to Blake, when the latter asked if the other felt any fear as to the safety of his master, and the simple conviction of the quiet words almost succeeded in convincing Blake of their truth.

Along the trail plodded the weary 'Äarab of the Beny Salem fendy, el-Guad. Tired men staggered beneath the weight of half-loads. The women carried even more. Ibn Jad watched the treasure with greedy eyes. An arrow came from no where and pierced the heart of a treasure bearer close before Ibn Jad. A hollow voice sounded from the jungle: *"For every jewel a drop of blood!"*

Terrified, the Beduins hastened on. Who would be next? They wanted to cast aside the treasure, but Ibn Jad, greedy, would not let them. Behind them they caught a glimpse of a great lion. He terrified them because he did not come nearer or go away—he just stalked silently along behind. There were no stragglers.

An hour passed. The lion paced just within sight of the tail end of the column. Never had the head of one of Ibn Jad's columns been so much in demand. Everyone wished to go in the lead.

A scream burst from another treasure carrier. An arrow had passed through his lungs. *"For every jewel a drop of blood!"*

The men threw down the treasure. "We will not carry the accursed thing more!" they cried, and again the voice spoke.

"Take up the treasure, Ibn Jad!" it said. *"Take up the treasure! It is thou who murdered to acquire it. Pick it up, thief and murderer, and carry it thyself!"*

Together the 'Aarab made the treasure into one load and lifted it to Ibn Jad's back. The old sheik staggered beneath the weight.

"I cannot carry it!" he cried aloud. "I am old and I am not strong."

"Thou canst carry it, or—die!" boomed the hollow voice, while the lion stood in the trail behind them, his eyes glaring fixedly at them.

Ibn Jad staggered on beneath the great load. He could not now travel as fast as the others and so he was left behind with only the lion as company; but only for a short time. Ateja saw his predicament and came back to his side, bearing a musket in her hands.

"Fear not," she said, "I am not the son thou didst crave, but yet I shall protect thee even as a son!"

It was almost dusk when the leaders of the Beduin company stumbled upon a village. They were in it and surrounded by a hundred warriors before they realized that they were in the midst of the one tribe of all others they most feared and dreaded—the Waziri of Tarzan.

The sub-chief disarmed them at once.

"Where is Ibn Jad?" demanded Zeyd.

"He cometh!" said one.

They looked back along the trail and presently Zeyd saw two figures approaching. One was a man bent beneath a great load and the other was that of a young girl. What he did not see was the figure of a great lion in the shadows behind them.

Zeyd held his breath because, for an instant, his heart had stopped beating.

"Ateja!" he cried and ran forward to meet her and clasp her in his arms.

Ibn Jad staggered into the village. He took one look at the stern visages of the dread Waziri and sank weakly to the ground, the treasure almost burying him as it fell upon his head and shoulders.

Hirfa voiced a sudden scream as she pointed back along the trail, and as every eye turned in that direction, a great golden lion stepped into the circle of the firelight in the village, and at its side strode Tarzan, Lord of the Jungle.

As Tarzan entered the village Blake came forward and grasped his hand.

"We were too late!" said the American sadly.

"What do you mean?" asked the ape-man.

"The Princess Guinalda is dead!"

"Nonsense!" exclaimed Tarzan. "I left her this morning at the entrance to the City of Nimmr."

A dozen times Tarzan was forced to assure Blake that he was not playing a cruel joke upon him. A dozen times Tarzan had to repeat Guinalda's message: "An' thou findst him tell him that the gates of Nimmr be always open to him and that the Princess Guinalda awaits his return!"

Later in the evening Stimbol, through Blake, begged Tarzan to come to the hut in which he lay.

"Thank God!" exclaimed the old man fervently. "I thought that I had killed you. It has preyed on my mind and now I know that it was not you I believe that I can recover."

"You will be taken care of properly, Stimbol," said the ape-man, "and as soon as you are well enough you will be taken to the coast," then he walked away. He would do his duty by the man who had disobeyed him and tried to kill him, but he would not feign a friendship he did not feel.

The following morning they prepared to leave the village. Ibn Jad and his Arabs, with the exception of Zeyd and Ateja, who had asked to come and serve Tarzan in his home, were being sent to the nearest Galla village under escort of a dozen Waziri. Here they would be turned over to the Galla and doubtless sold into slavery in Abyssinia.

Stimbol was borne in a litter by four stout Waziri as the party prepared to take up its march toward the south and the country of Tarzan. Four others carried the treasure of the City of the Sepulcher.

Blake, dressed again in his iron mail, bestrode his great charger as the column started out of the village and down the trail into the south. Tarzan and the Golden Lion stood beside him. Blake reached down and extended his hand to the ape-man.

"Good-bye, sir!" he said.

"Good-bye?" demanded Tarzan. "Aren't you coming home with us?"

Blake shook his head.

"No," he said, "I'm going back into the middle ages with the woman I love!"

Tarzan and Jad-bal-ja stood in the trail watching as Sir James rode out toward the City of Nimmr, the blue and silver of his pennon fluttering bravely from the iron tip of his great lance.

570-208-9900

The Tarzan Novels
of Edgar Rice Burroughs

* TARZAN OF THE APES
* THE RETURN OF TARZAN
* THE BEASTS OF TARZAN
* THE SON OF TARZAN
* TARZAN AND THE JEWELS OF OPAR
* JUNGLE TALES OF TARZAN
* TARZAN THE UNTAMED
* TARZAN THE TERRIBLE
* TARZAN AND THE GOLDEN LION
* TARZAN AND THE ANT MEN
* TARZAN, LORD OF THE JUNGLE
* TARZAN AND THE LOST EMPIRE
** TARZAN AT THE EARTH'S CORE
** TARZAN THE INVINCIBLE
** TARZAN TRIUMPHANT
** TARZAN AND THE CITY OF GOLD
** TARZAN AND THE LION MAN
** TARZAN AND THE LEOPARD MEN
** TARZAN'S QUEST
** TARZAN AND THE FORBIDDEN CITY
** TARZAN THE MAGNIFICENT
** TARZAN AND "THE FOREIGN LEGION"
** TARZAN AND THE MADMAN
** TARZAN AND THE CASTAWAYS

*Available now from Ballantine Books
**To be available in 1973 from Ballantine Books

The authorized Ballantine Editions of Tarzan
are complete and unabridged.

To order by mail, send 95¢ per book plus
10¢ for handling to Dept. CS, Ballantine
Books, 36 West 20th Street, New York, N.Y.
10003